Tales of the Were ~ Grizzly Cove

Black Magic Bear

BIANCA D'ARC

This book is a work of fiction. The names, characters, places, and incidents are products of the writer's imagination or have been used fictitiously and are not to be construed as real. Any resemblance to persons, living or dead, actual events, locale or organizations is entirely coincidental.

No part of this book may be used or reproduced in any manner whatsoever without written permission, except in the case of brief quotations embodied in critical articles and reviews.

On a mission, Jack finds a lot more than he bargains for, including witchcraft, black magic, a spooky fey garden, and a woman who just might be his mate.

And then, there was one…

Jack is happy to see his two older brothers mated and settled in Grizzly Cove, but he's definitely the odd man out—the lone bachelor of their tight-knit family. He takes a job and a mission to track down the problems at a paper plant in Pennsylvania. There's magic afoot there, and Jack's special sensitivity to the dark arts will help him crack the case where others have failed.

She's a practical girl…

Kiki is trying to adjust to her new job, but when she stumbles on something that sets her senses tingling in warning, she doesn't know where to turn…or, who to trust. Her down-home upbringing in the traditions of the farm folk of the area, she knows simple ways to protect herself from evil, but will it be enough?

Together, can they shine a light against the darkness?

The new guy from corporate is altogether too handsome for Kiki's peace of mind, and he actually seems interested in her. Dare she trust him? Jack isn't sure about anyone at the plant, but something about Kiki makes him want to believe in her innocence. When her life is put in mortal peril, they will have to work together to end the evil threat and save not only their own lives, but that of nearly every person who works in the plant. Can they do it? Or, will the darkness win and douse their light forevermore?

DEDICATION

To my family, for sticking by me through all the ups and downs of this crazy artistic career.

And to those readers who have become dear friends over the years. Particularly, Peggy McChesney, who has offered opinions when they were most needed. Her insights have always been incredibly helpful.

I'd also like to thank Staci Thacker for lending her nickname to the heroine in this book. Thanks for reading and thanks for supporting my work!

PROLOGUE

"Here's another one." Sheriff Brody flipped through some reports as he wrapped up his weekly presentation to the Town Council of Grizzly Cove. "A request that we keep our eyes peeled and information sources tapped in the disappearance of a seven-year-old bear shifter girl in Pennsylvania." Brody shook his head. "Not sure why they'd think we'd have any better luck than anyone else in finding her, but there it is. Somehow, Grizzly Cove has become the epicenter for all things bear related."

"Personally, I don't mind that in the least," John Marshall said. He was the Alpha of the town, the strategic thinker all the others followed by choice. "I like the idea of knowing what's going on in the wider world of bear shifters, and I'd like them to think that they could come to us if they need help."

"Are you changing our mission, John?" Brody asked, while the rest of the Town Council looked on with interest.

They were all old friends and comrades from the days they'd spent in a very unique Special Forces unit, fighting evil in every corner of the world. They had each decided to follow John's lead when he'd laid out the plans for this new town and retirement from active duty.

"The town mission remains, as it has been, to build a place

for us to settle and find mates, and welcome Others who need a sanctuary from the evil that stalks us." John shook his head. "I didn't anticipate the full furor of what's come at us here, and I sure didn't realize we'd be stirring up things in the ocean, but we've adapted and overcome. We'll continue to do the same. The thing is, I've come to conclusion that the time for us to keep acting without regard to other bear shifters is at an end. The enemy could pick the rest of our kind off easily, one by one, if we stick to that path."

"Like the little girl." Brody nodded at the paper in front of him. "She was abducted from the playground at her school during recess."

"It's a sad state of affairs when cubs aren't safe in their schoolyards," John said, shaking his head. "I think, more and more, we're all going to have to help keep track of each other. I've spoken to the Lords about this, and I'm going to give them another call once we finish here. I want to propose that we volunteer to be the clearing house for bear shifter issues. We all know Rocky Garibaldi has been doing the job for years, but he's got a family now, which is rightly, his first priority. Plus, incidents have escalated beyond what he can handle on his own. We have the manpower, the technology, and the experience to keep track of any problems our fellow bear shifters might encounter. We also have skilled personnel we can deploy to help solve those problems, if necessary, and a pretty broad network that seems to grow every day. So, what do you guys think?"

"Would it be just for grizzly and brown bears?" Sven, the town's doctor and resident polar bear, wanted to know.

"You know I'm more than willing to help polar bears and even pandas if they want it, but aside from our one and only token town koala—who is, by definition, a marsupial and not a bear—I think we'll limit it to actual bears. Brown, black, white, or any combination is okay with me."

There were nods of agreement all around when Zak, a black bear and owner of the town's premier restaurant, spoke up. "What about the other species that have joined us here in recent months?"

"I can't speak for the mer, but if they want to do the same for their people, I don't see a problem with it. They, as you know, have stockpiled a lot of money and power in the human world, but they lack any real military skills or contacts on land. I anticipate they may reach out to us for help if a situation arises—which is already happening on a small scale as Trevor and his mate, Beth, try to sort out the mess her stepfather left behind with SeaLife Enterprises." John mentioned the giant conglomerate that had been turned to evil by Beth's late stepfather, which was now in the process of cleaning house. "I also know that a few of our comrades are already working for SeaLife, troubleshooting problems around the country. I think we can do the same on a bigger scale, if needed. As a group, we have more military and ex-military connections we can call on, if the mer want to foot the bill. Especially if we need to hire mercenaries."

The former Special Forces soldiers all around the large table nodded their agreement. John was glad to see they were all taking this as seriously as he was. They'd had a good time in the idle after they'd all retired and moved to Grizzly Cove to build the town, but evil had caught up with them sooner than he'd expected. They'd dealt with it as best they could, and the town was still standing. John counted that as a victory, though there was still a lot of work to do.

Getting back into the game—even in this small way—was another step toward making Grizzly Cove the place where all bears could find help and sanctuary. He wanted the place to be more than just a town. More than just an escape. He wanted it to be a place that served their fellow shifters and the Light. Bringing aid to those who needed it and keeping track of the innocents that might otherwise get lost in the shuffle.

They had a quick vote just to satisfy the democratic requirements they had imposed upon themselves, and the motion passed unanimously. John closed the meeting with a lighter heart, though the idea of that little girl, snatched from her schoolyard in Pennsylvania, still laid heavily on his mind. He couldn't help her. Not from way out here in Washington State, but he hoped that they'd get to a point, in the not too distant future, where such things were possible.

"I'll call Rocky and the Lords this afternoon and let them know we're ready to step up," he told his friends, and the meeting broke up soon after. Grizzly Cove was about to put themselves on the shifter map, so to speak. Officially. It was a big step, and John counted it as a positive one.

CHAPTER 1

"Jack, my friend, I have a little job we need doing that's perfect for you." Ezra Tate eyed one of his oldest friends from across the table at Flambeau's Restaurant in the heart of Grizzly Cove.

Jack had traveled to the town to rejoin his two older brothers and meet their new mates. The three brothers had traveled through life together, for the most part, but had gone their separate ways a few months back, each heading out to a different solo adventure in a different part of the country. The only commonality was that they had each been traveling by motorcycle.

They'd been working as mechanics for the past couple of years, but his older brothers had been exhibiting signs of restlessness for the past year or two. Jack felt it, too. They had good lives, but there was something missing.

His brothers, Ace and King, had found their missing pieces. They both had found good women, meant to be theirs, the matings blessed by the Goddess. Only Jack was still a bachelor. He figured that state of affairs would probably last for a while, since he was the youngest. He had a good few centuries left in him—bear shifter that he was— and he hoped, at some point, he'd meet, and mate, his other half, but he wasn't in any hurry.

Ace and King had won the lottery and found their mates against all odds. Jack wouldn't be so lucky. Not so soon after the other two. Mates weren't that easy to find. The whole concept behind this town had been a way for a bunch of old bachelor bear shifters who had served together in the Special Forces to find a way to attract female shifters—preferably bears—to come to their town so they might be able to find a mate or two among those who answered the call.

It hadn't quite worked out that way. Lady bears hadn't come in droves, exactly, and other kinds of magical beings had been attracted to the new bear shifter community—some not so friendly. They had a sea monster problem, at the moment, that they were still trying to deal with. An evil creature attracted to magic, it tried to feed on anyone stupid enough to be caught out on the water where it lurked.

An entire pod of mer people had come to the cove waters, and the town, for safety. A trio of human sisters had come to open a bakery, and all three had found their mates among the bears of Grizzly Cove. Two other sisters—highly magical sisters—had opened a bookshop, and they'd also found mates. Those two *Strega* witches had also gone a long way toward protecting the cove and its people with their magic.

More people were joining the community every day, but except for a few older ladies, not many of them were female bear shifters. Yet, the plan was working. The men of that Special Forces unit were finding mates. They just weren't always shifters.

"What sort of job are you talking about?" Jack asked Ezra as he sipped his beer.

Ezra was a former bounty hunter and current troubleshooter for SeaLife Enterprises, the company that had originally belonged to a Pacific Coast mer pod that had been all but annihilated by a shark shifter who had held one of the new grizzly mates captive as a youngster. Beth was her name. She was now mated to a total badass Special Forces retiree named Trevor. They had taken back control of the company and had been slowly putting to rights everything that the shark shifter—an unlamented bastard named Jonathon—had put very, very wrong.

Jonathon had turned the legitimate investments of SeaLife into shady, and in some cases, even criminal, enterprises all over the country. They'd already stopped cases of human trafficking and prostitution. They'd busted drug rings and car theft chop shops. They'd done as much as they could with the resources they had, hiring Ezra to help. Ezra, in turn, was hiring others who could travel more freely and go undercover where he, and his employers, could not.

Jack knew that if Ezra was offering him one of those very special jobs for SeaLife, the stakes could be very high, but he trusted Ezra—and Trevor and Beth—implicitly. They wouldn't send him off without every last scrap of intel they had. And they wouldn't leave him hanging, if they could help it. Beth was a very wealthy woman, now that she had control of SeaLife. The company had been her father's, but he'd been the leader of his pod, and the money that had gone in to start the conglomerate had come from the pod as a whole.

Beth had put out a call for any scattered members of the decimated mer pod to come to Grizzly Cove, with the Alpha bear's permission, but Jonathon had done his best to kill them all when he'd killed Beth's father, and so far, no one had come to reclaim the share of the giant company that was rightfully theirs.

Jack had heard that Beth was still hoping some would find their way to Grizzly Cove, but until then, she was solely in charge of a substantial fortune. It was also a substantial headache as she and her mate tried to turn the investments back to the right side of the law…and the Light.

"Well, I know you've got more of a nose for magic than the average bear," Ezra said, leaning back in his chair as they lingered over their drinks after a delicious meal. "We've got an operation back east that defies all logic. I've had others go check into it quietly, but they can't seem to get a handle on what's wrong there. The place reeks of magic, but nobody can tell me where it's coming from or what they're doing with it."

Jack frowned. "You know I like a challenge, but what makes you so sure I'm the guy for this job?"

"I sent in Wiklow," Ezra admitted.

"I thought he was strictly on the disabled list these days."

"He is, but I honestly didn't think this would be anything too difficult. Turned out, it was way more than he could handle, in his state. Something chased him off, and he got all spooky on me when I questioned him about it," Ezra admitted with a grimace. "I think I set back his recovery by a decade. Damn it."

"Tough break."

Jack had liked Arthur Wiklow. He'd worked with him in the service. Art had been the kind of guy who could always be depended on to meet a crisis with humor, but injury and tragedy in recent years had left him a shell of the man he'd once been. At least, that's what Jack had heard. He hadn't actually seen Wiklow in person since their military days.

"The gist of it is, he swears there's both good and evil present. He started ranting about black magic and how I needed to get a specialist. Someone who could sense magic but still had the necessary skills to do the job. Someone like you, Jack."

Jack hung his head. "Yeah." He realized he couldn't say no.

Much as he'd like to stick around in Grizzly Cove and bask in his brothers' happiness, that wasn't how his life was meant to be spent. Jack was a born protector. Something deep inside him drove him to right the wrongs he saw in the world. He was both bigger and more magical than his two older brothers. They had always helped him when he'd gotten in over his head, but now that they were mated, he was on his own. Things had changed. He'd have to get used to that sooner rather than later.

He couldn't change who he was or his basic drive to help, but he'd have to figure out how to do it as a solo bear, without the two older brothers who had ridden to his aid all his life. He wouldn't put them at risk like that again. Not now that they both had bright futures with loving mates by their sides.

No, Jack had to learn how to be a solo act, from now on. No time like the present—and Ezra's proposed mission—to start figuring that out. Jack looked up at his old friend and nodded.

"I'm in. Where do you need me to go?"

*

Kiki Richards wasn't really sure what to do about her situation. She only knew that she had to hang on until something changed. Surely, this couldn't go on forever?

This being the very odd happenings in the warehouse associated with her new place of employment. It was a paper-making facility with a large production area and attached warehouse. She worked in the front office, collating test reports for the overseeing authority. It was her job to clean up the test lab reports and put them into the format required by the government. That was the first part of her job. Her boss had said she'd be given additional tasks after she proved herself with that one.

Apparently, the company had been having problems with inspectors, and the previous person who had done this job had been summarily fired. The company might be large, but it was still run by just a small group of people.

This mill had once belonged to the reclusive lumber baron, J.W. Smathers. He'd inherited large tracts of forested land all over North America and several operations, like this one, where the trees were used in various ways. Smathers had cashed in and sold everything several years ago to an even bigger conglomerate called SeaLife Enterprises that headquartered on the West Coast.

The mill where Kiki worked made all sorts of paper goods, from toilet paper to cardboard boxes, to specialty papers that went for medical uses. There were other former Smathers plants that made building materials—lumber, plywood, and particle board, among other things. A separate specialty mill made veneers out of the more exotic species of wood. That one also turned out specialty lumber for the furniture and musical instrument trades.

So far, she hadn't seen any of the SeaLife people, though there had been some communications she'd found in her predecessor's files. One particularly interesting memo notified all branches about a change in CEO for SeaLife, and a new headquarters location farther north on the West Coast, in a town called Grizzly Cove, Washington.

That was certainly a long way from the Blue Ridge Mountains of West Virginia. Kiki had grown up in southeastern Pennsylvania and had gone to Penn State, but she'd known she'd probably have to move around a bit for her career, which she had looked on as an adventure. The only problem was this latest position was adding up to be a bit more *adventure* than she'd ever really wanted.

She hadn't really understood—and still didn't fully understand—what was going on in the warehouse at night, but there was definitely something hinky happening there. Something she didn't want *any* part of. No, siree.

But she'd had to work late last week, to get the reports in order for the government, and she'd accidentally stumbled on something truly odd happening in what should have been an empty and shut warehouse. She'd sensed it before she'd seen it. A growing blackness. A lingering scent of decay. It made her feel on edge. Wary.

Thankfully, she'd heeded her instincts and hadn't betrayed her presence. She'd come searching for a log file that had to be on the last batch of product, but what she'd found had sent chills down her spine. In a cleared space in the center of one of the holding areas, an altar had been set up, draped in black satin, with black candles arrayed on top and people in dark robes standing all around.

She couldn't see their faces, due to both distance and the fact that they'd had the hoods of their robes up, over their heads, but she'd recognized some of the voices as they spoke. They'd been invoking…well…nothing good. The strange words they had used had made her skin crawl.

Kiki had been very careful to back away slowly, so that nobody would notice her presence, and she'd skedaddled home immediately. She'd taken a long, scalding shower immediately on arrival home, but she still didn't feel entirely clean, over a week later.

She'd held her breath the following morning, wondering if anybody had detected her presence. She'd been so afraid they would say something and she'd be in trouble—or worse, in *danger*. She hadn't really understood all that she'd seen, but it had scared her enough that she had debated whether to quit her job on the spot and not go in to work ever again.

Two things had decided her on going back to the plant. First, she had almost no money in the bank and bills to pay. Being practical, she had to keep working *somewhere*. She already had this job, and it paid well. It was also in her preferred field, and if she managed to leave on good terms and get a good reference, it would help her get an even better job down the road. Second, she needed to be sure they weren't suspicious of her. Going in to work and keeping her schedule as normal as possible seemed the best way to gloss over what she had seen.

If they knew she had witnessed whatever that was in the warehouse, then maybe, if she just kept her head down, they'd think she hadn't understood at all and it didn't bother her. Also, if they had seen her, someone might confront her about it, and that would at least get it out in the open, and she could assure them she'd say nothing of the matter and try to convince them that she hadn't thought it all that strange and didn't think it sinister at all. Which was the farthest thing from the truth, but they didn't have to know that.

If they hadn't seen her and she'd gotten away with her accidental eavesdropping, then all the better. She didn't want to rouse any suspicion by staying home or quitting the day after their little get-together. She would just stay as long as she could, build up a little money in the bank, then invent a reasonable excuse for leaving while also securing letters of recommendation, if she could possibly do so.

That plan firmly in mind, she'd brazened out the next week, but nobody had said anything, and no one had looked at her oddly. She'd done all in her power to just go about her business in her normal way, and she thought, just maybe, she'd gotten away with it.

It wasn't until she was leaving work on the following Friday after the *incident*, as she was calling it in her mind, that she realized she'd been living a delusion. Her boss, Bob Boehm, flagged her down in the parking lot and invited her to a barbeque at his home the following day. He told her he'd decided to hold a little party at the last minute because the weather was forecast to be so nice. It was mid-April, and the weather was starting to warm up nicely, spring finding its groove all over North America.

Kiki had accepted the invitation. She hadn't seen any polite way to decline. She'd gone to the barbeque but had felt the same oppressive blackness gathering around the barbeque pit the moment she'd emerged from the house into the backyard. She'd faked a mis-step, twisting her left ankle just the slightest bit, so she would have an immediate reason to get the hell out of there.

Everything inside her said to run. Run fast. Run far. Get out of there!

She made her excuses to her host and limped back to her car, insisting that she'd be okay as long as she could get home to rest her foot. She was shaking when she pulled up at her own little rented cottage. She had decided to hide out there, just in case anybody had followed her from Bob's. Sure enough, as she continued the pretense, limping from the driveway at the side of the house, up the steps and onto the porch, she saw a car driving slowly past, the person behind the wheel immediately recognizable as one of her co-workers. She only gave them the barest glance, hidden by her dark sunglasses.

Her alert level rose another notch, and she immediately set about warding her small home in the only way she knew how. She wasn't much of a witch, but she had picked up a few things over the years. Herbal things, gleaned from her mother in the Dutch country of Pennsylvania. Things that had come from the old country, generations ago.

When people—mostly rich people—had been burned at the stake in the mid-1500s as witches, and their possessions confiscated, some of the real witches in Germany had joined the Anabaptist movement to hide in plain sight. And when, in the mid-1700s, those people had immigrated to America, Kiki's ancestors had gone along. Kiki's family had connections with the Amish community even now, but once they realized the Land of the Free really was exactly that, they'd broken away from the Amish teachings and had lived quietly as neighbors. Kiki's oma and opa—grandmother and grandfather—still didn't draw much attention to themselves. They had always lived simple lives on their farm in southeastern Pennsylvania, and their children had done the same.

But she'd learned the magic traditions from her grandmother and mother and knew what to do to ward her home against evil. Kiki broke out the salt and herbs and first, cleansed her home and then sealed all doors, windows, and other openings, with a salt line and prayers. Kiki wasn't as strong in some things as other members of her extended family, but she could at least ensure no evil came into her home without her knowing about it.

She hid inside the rest of the weekend, praying and even calling home for advice, but she dared not speak too specifically about what she'd witnessed. For all she knew, one of the people at work might be a tech genius and they could listen in on her calls. Instead, she'd just asked sort of general questions that gave her family a small heads-up. They would know something was wrong, but they'd probably wait to act until they heard back from her. At least she'd established contact and had let them know all was not as it should be.

She'd have to figure out a better way to get her message out, but it would take time.

When Monday rolled around, she wore an elastic bandage on her foot and sneakers to work. She apologized to the boss for her clumsiness and told him how bad she'd felt about missing his party. He seemed to believe her, but she couldn't be sure of anything, anymore. The people working around her were all suspect, to her mind.

She was just settling into her office when a commotion in the reception area, which was adjacent to her small room, caught her attention. The young receptionist sounded both frazzled and frightened. Concerned, Kiki went out to see what was going on.

CHAPTER 2

Kiki saw the man first. A giant bear of a man wearing faded jeans and black leather boots that gave the impression he'd just come off the huge motorcycle she could just see out the glass doors behind him. He had a black leather jacket covering a slightly western-looking button-down shirt. She would have expected a T-shirt under that leather, but this man was more than a bit out of the ordinary.

To her very minute magical senses, he fairly glowed with strength of purpose. He had innate magic of his own, of that she was sure, but whether he used it for good or evil was still an open question.

"Can I help?" Kiki asked, moving closer to the front desk. The man looked up, and his gaze caught hers.

Light brown with golden flecks danced in his gaze, proclaiming him something special to her inner vision. He had brown hair, also with strands of gold mixed in. It was on the longish side but still managed to look businesslike and somewhat conservative, even after being squashed inside a motorcycle helmet.

"As I was just telling Cindy, here," the man smiled, oozing charm, "I've been sent by the home office of SeaLife Enterprises to have a look around the operation. My name is Jack Bishop."

15

He stretched out his hand for a shake, and she found herself moving closer to take it. When their hands touched, sparks flew. It was hard to keep her reaction to herself, but she had to do so with Cindy watching. Kiki was ninety-nine percent sure Cindy had been one of those wearing the creepy Halloween costumes the previous week in the warehouse. Kiki didn't trust anybody in the office anymore. Not a single one of them.

But this man was a stranger. A newcomer. He'd been sent by the parent company. It remained to be seen whether or not he could be trusted.

Still, if his handshake was anything to go by, he was intensely magical. And the gleam in his eye said he recognized a bit of the magic in her, as well.

"I'm Kiki Richards," she introduced herself, trying to keep things businesslike and professional. "I'm somewhat new to the company. I came on board to work on government compliance. Maybe I can check with my boss for you?"

"Who would that be?" Jack asked, seemingly reluctant to release her hand, but he did, finally.

"Bob Boehm, head of operations. Is he who you wanted to see?" she asked, trying to be helpful and discreet.

The man tilted his head to the side. "Sure. I wanted to start with whoever's in charge, then work my way down the chain of command."

Jack smiled, putting her at ease. At that point, Cindy seemed to come to her senses and started doing her job.

"I'll call Mr. Boehm," Cindy announced.

Jack was floored by the woman who'd come out from one of the offices behind the reception area. She was gorgeous. And her eyes sparked with intelligence. Her hair was golden, as if sunlight danced among the strands, and her eyes were clear blue. Innocent, yet knowing.

When he touched her hand, his magical senses exploded with awareness, and when he caught her scent, his bear stood up and took notice. *Damn.* He'd had to scramble to hide his powerful reaction to the woman. He'd never before felt this kind of punch to the gut on first meeting a lady. What could it mean?

For one thing, he got the distinct impression that she would be important to his mission here. He hoped, for both their sakes, that she was on the right side of things. Even after such a brief meeting, he knew it would hurt him deeply if she turned out to be a traitor to the Light.

While he was contemplating the luscious Miss Richards, a pale man with thinning red hair came out from the office area. He bustled over to them and started talking right away.

"I'm Bob Boehm. What's this all about?"

Jack noticed the other man didn't hold out his hand for a handshake. In fact, he seemed more belligerent than friendly. Well, if that's the way he wanted to play it, Jack would give it back to him, in spades.

"Jack Bishop, troubleshooter for SeaLife Enterprises. The home office sent me here to check the books and review your operations. You are the operations manager, are you not?"

Old Bob started sweating. Jack hid his smile.

"I wasn't given any notice of anyone coming down from corporate," Bob protested. "I'll need some proof of who you are. Bishop, did you say?"

Jack reached into his top pocket and flicked out a business card they'd had printed up especially for this trip. He handed it to Boehm.

"Call Ezra Tate. He'll confirm that he sent me. I'll wait." Jack looked around as if he had all the time in the world and took one of the cushy chairs over by the window.

Boehm bustled off without another word, leaving the delectable Miss Richards staring after him. The receptionist, Cindy, sounded angry, which seemed odd. Jack took a mental note to keep an eye on her.

Kiki just looked confused and concerned as she watched her boss but seemed to shake it off and moved closer to Jack.

"Can I offer you a cup of coffee?" she asked, a pleasant smile on her face.

"That's kind, but I'm all set," he replied. "Perhaps you can tell me more about what you do here while I'm waiting." He wanted to keep her around. He wanted to know all about her. Not for the mission, just to get to know *her.*

His inner bear sat up and watched the woman with avid concentration. Jack was fascinated by her on every level.

"I suppose..." She looked in the direction of the office area, where her boss had disappeared. "I mean..."

"You're very conscientious to want to wait for confirmation of my identity," Jack told her, figuring that's why she was hesitating. "Why don't you just give me the public explanation? The things you could tell anyone you happened to meet at a party, about what you do for a living. We can start there, and once everything's settled, we can get into the finer points."

She looked relieved, and he gestured to the seat next to him. She sat down, perching on the edge of the chair, looking ready to bolt the moment her boss returned. Jack took that to mean that she wasn't very comfortable with Boehm. Good to know. Jack hadn't liked the look of the man, or the faint scent he'd been able to get from across the receptionist's desk.

So far, he was disposed to not trust or like Boehm, while the luscious Kiki confounded his senses. Her scent was alluring. Seductive. It could be a trap—if she was on the wrong side of things—or it could just be that she was that attractive. Right now, he felt like his bear had sighted a honeycomb, just out of reach. That's how tantalizing she was to his senses. He would have to be cautious until he figured out exactly what was going on here.

"Well, as you probably know, some of the specialized papers we produce here go into the healthcare industry, which is heavily regulated. We run all sorts of quality control tests on the batches. They have to test within certain tolerances, and I organize all that paperwork for reporting to the government. I'm essentially a paper pusher."

"In a paper mill," he teased. "Who woulda thunk it?"

She laughed, and the sound sent tingles that raced straight

to his heart, doing something to that untouched part of him. It felt like rusty hinges were slowly creaking open inside him. A disused part of his soul was coming to life. Revealing itself. Making him aware of it for the first time, ever.

He was smiling as she chuckled. That's how Boehm found them when he came back out to the reception area. Kiki noticed him and stood immediately, the smile leaving her face as if it had never been.

"You check out. Sorry about the lack of welcome. If I'd known you were coming—"

Jack stood, cutting off the other man's words. "No point in informing someone of a surprise inspection." Jack played the dumb hick cowboy part to the hilt, watching the entire situation very, very carefully from behind a façade of bonhomie. "No matter. I'm here now, and you know that I'm on the level. Shall we get started?"

Caught off guard, Boehm scrambled to regain control. "What is it you came here to see, Mr. Bishop?"

That had almost sounded a tad confrontational. Jack was surprised. He hadn't thought Boehm the type to stand up to him even that much. Interesting.

"In short, everything. I want the grand tour of the operation, and then, I'll need an office to work in where I can go over your books." Jack enjoyed seeing the color come and go from Boehm's face. He was alternately shocked, scared, then angered by Jack's presumption. Good. Now, they were getting somewhere.

"I have a conference call in five minutes that can't be put off," Boehm said, surprising Jack, yet again. "Perhaps Miss Richards could start your tour, and I'll join you when I've finished the call." It wasn't a question. More like an insult, but in this instance, Jack didn't mind at all. More time with the lovely Kiki was high on his new list of priorities.

"That's acceptable," Jack told Boehm, looming over the much shorter man.

His inner grizzly enjoyed watching the pipsqueak unconsciously shy away. Boehm might talk a big game, but he wasn't really in Jack's league when it came to the larger fight. Boehm left with a grimace, stomping all the way back to his office and slamming the door.

Kiki looked surprised by the idea of taking Jack on a tour but acquiesced to her boss's wishes without demur. She motioned for Jack to join her and led the way into the office area where Boehm had just disappeared, speaking quietly as they walked.

"Let's just stop by my office. In some of the production areas, we'll need to wear protective gear. I'll pick up my set, and we'll get you some new things from the lab storeroom, if that's all right," she said, leading him into a small office right behind the reception area.

Jack went in and stood just inside the door, opposite the desk, framed with multiple filing cabinets and two computer monitors. Paperwork was all over the desk surface, in neat piles. Lab reports, memos, and big binders of government regulations were everywhere, but in an organized way.

"Excuse the clutter," Kiki said as she went behind her desk. "I was digging into some new regulations and trying to figure out where my predecessor left things."

"How long have you been with the company?"

"Just a couple of weeks, so let me apologize in advance for the tour. I've only been to some parts of the plant once or twice, myself." A look of consternation passed over her lovely face briefly, but she quickly regained her outward calm professionalism.

"Why don't we start with the areas you know best, and hopefully, by the time we get to the areas you're less familiar with, your boss will be free," Jack suggested smoothly, hoping to put her at ease. His instincts were screaming at him to make her life easier. To protect her. To give her a free pass.

Which was exactly what he could *not* do. Everybody in this place had to be suspect until he knew more. Steeling himself, Jack went out of the tiny office as Kiki came around her desk. He had to be cautious here, even as he gave in to the desire of his inner bear to be around her.

She had a hard hat and white lab coat under one arm, a pair of safety glasses in her hand as she joined him in the wide hallway in the executive area. She smiled and started walking toward the back of the building as he fell in step beside her.

"We can go to the lab area first. They have spare safety gear we can commandeer for you. I spend a few minutes at the lab each day because their reports are key to my job. I usually go over in the afternoon with a pile of questions for the techs and lab director," she admitted with a shrug. "I'm still learning, and my predecessor had some odd habits in the way he made notes. I don't always understand his abbreviations and personal shorthand."

"There's always an adjustment when taking over from someone else," Jack replied. He'd never really worked in an office, but he understood the challenge.

She led him through an office area with cubicles that were sparsely inhabited by people on phones or computers, working steadily, even as they eyed him. A few heads popped up from over the cubicle walls to stare at them. There was an air of hostility about the looks he was getting, but he pretended not to notice.

Kiki opened a door at the far end of the office area and led him through into another part of the building. This area had a more clinical look to it. He saw a few people in an open-layout office area to the right of the corridor. Most were wearing headsets as if they were manning some kind of call center. A row of windows preceded the doorway.

"This is the customer service section," Kiki said, pausing by the doorway, a pained look on her face. "I'm not their favorite person because I've had to change some of the ways they handle complaints to comply with regulations."

"We can leave that for later, if you prefer," Jack offered. He'd taken a quick look at the people in the office, and none of them had raised any red flags in his mind—or tickled his magical senses. What was giving him a tingle of magic was farther down the hallway, and he wanted to investigate that before it had a chance to get away.

"Maybe it would be better if you met them with Mr. Boehm," Kiki said, removing her hand from the doorknob. "I can take you to the lab. It's just down here, and I know more about it than most of the rest of the plant."

"That'll be fine," he told her in a calm voice. She was playing right into his wishes, though she probably didn't realize it.

Jack took the precaution of putting up all his personal magical wards. He'd studied, first with a priestess, then later, with a shaman she had sent him to, about how to hide his true nature and abilities from even the most powerful mages. That skill was part of what made him such an effective hunter in these kinds of scenarios. He'd been called on to ferret out mages a time or two in the past, but this time was different because his brothers weren't there to back him up. He'd have to be extra cautious here, because he was on his own.

Trying to seem as boring and human as possible, he followed Kiki down the hall and to the door of the lab. Whatever was setting his teeth on edge was still in there.

Kiki opened the door to the small office area that led to the lab proper. There were desks along one wall for the techs, and a small office for the lab supervisor. The desks were empty, but Carol was sitting at her desk when Kiki walked to the door.

"Hi, Carol. Do you have a moment?" Kiki didn't wait for a reply, wanting to alert the other woman to exactly who Jack was before she said anything rash. In their past dealings, Kiki had come to realize that Carol often spoke before she thought through how her words would sound. Either that or she liked being deliberately rude. "This is Mr. Bishop from the headquarters of SeaLife Enterprises. I'm just taking him on a tour while Mr. Boehm finishes a conference call."

Carol's eyes narrowed as she looked past Kiki to the man who stood behind her in the doorway. There was a slight hesitation before Carol stood and invited them into her office. Kiki held her breath to see what Carol might say, but she seemed to be on her best behavior—very *unlike* the way Carol had greeted the state inspector Kiki had brought through just last week.

Of course, the inspector had been a short, older fellow, who hadn't been all that friendly to begin with. Jack Bishop was tall, handsome and had a charming smile on his face as he walked into Carol's domain. Kiki could easily see why Carol—who was rumored to have run through the male staff like a kid through a candy store—was reacting differently to this hunky guy from the corporate office.

"Jack Bishop, this is Carol Burns, the lab supervisor," Kiki said, making the introductions.

Carol didn't stand up but reached across her desk to shake Jack's hand. Kiki felt a stab of annoyance when Carol captured the man's hand and a little tug-o-war ensued when she held it for much longer than was socially acceptable. All the while, she was staring into his brown eyes as if issuing an invitation. Or trying to see down into his soul.

Kiki mentally chastised herself. She didn't know where such sinister thoughts were coming from, but Carol had been helpful, if not friendly. She hadn't interfered in Kiki's work and had provided the necessary documentation Kiki needed for her reports, when asked. Why Kiki suddenly felt animosity toward the difficult woman—over a man she barely knew—was a mystery.

And it was something she had to nip in the bud. Right now.

"As I said, Mr. Boehm is busy with a call, so he asked me to show Mr. Bishop around. Only, since I'm so new here, I'm not very familiar with anyplace other than your lab and a few other sections of the plant where I go regularly for reporting purposes. I hope you don't mind that I brought him here first."

"Mind?" Carol was fairly purring as she sat back in her high-backed chair, not even looking at Kiki as she spoke.

"Not at all. I'm glad you brought him to me."

CHAPTER 3

Jack didn't like the look of this Carol Burns at all. There was something slimy about her. A slick feel to her presence that indicated strong shielding to Jack's trained magical senses. It's not something others would understand as readily, though this kind of woman would repulse many who were at all sensitive to such things, even if they didn't fully understand why.

She seemed inordinately interested in him, which sent up a red flag in his mind. Were his natural wards noticeable to her? He certainly hoped not. Maybe she was just a man-eater looking for her next meal.

She was definitely giving him the once-over. He didn't like the way her gaze slithered over him, but there wasn't much he could do about it right now. He was undercover, and if this woman was involved in any sort of evil plot, he needed to observe closely and keep his wits about him.

When she'd tried to hold onto his hand much longer than necessary, he'd had to politely disengage while pretending to be just a tad socially awkward. He hoped the ruse had worked. Touching the woman's hand had made his skin crawl. There was definitely something wrong here, and this Carol woman was right in the middle of it.

"So, Jack," Carol said, coming out from behind her desk.

"I can call you Jack, can't I?"

"Sure thing, Carol. I may be from headquarters, but I don't bite," he told her, smiling. "Much."

She giggled, and it wasn't a pretty sound. It sounded more like a rattlesnake's warning rattle to his ears. Oh, yeah, he'd be keeping an eye on this one.

Kiki didn't like the way Carol appropriated the visitor from corporate. Not at all. She was probably just being silly, though. Kiki certainly had no claim over the newcomer, even if he did stir an attraction down deep in her soul.

Why she should feel proprietary toward Jack was a mystery she didn't want to look at too closely at the moment. She was here to do a job, and she didn't want Carol's mercurial mood swings to affect how this important visitor perceived her workplace. That's all it was. Right?

Kiki followed after the lab supervisor and her captive—Carol had what looked like a death grip on his arm—into the lab proper. There, Carol introduced him briefly to the two technicians who were working on various tests that were required by the government to assure quality and consistency in the paper goods they supplied to the medical industry, in particular, which was heavily regulated.

Kiki felt like a third wheel, but she kept smiling throughout the awkward moments and stuck with Carol and Jack while she showed him around her domain. At some point, Carol would have to let him go, and Kiki would resume her appointed role as tour guide. Jack asked some astute questions about the testing regimes, which clearly surprised Carol and made her look at him oddly.

"So, you're not just a pretty face, then?" Carol almost pouted as she teased the corporate representative in a very inappropriate way, to Kiki's mind.

"I prepare for my inspection tours," Jack said, modestly bowing his head. "In this case, I took a look at what the state and federal governments required of this facility in more detail, because I know you'd had some issues with that in the recent past."

Carol shot Kiki a look that should have set her on fire from fifty feet. Then, Carol seemed to recall where she was and with whom. She gave Jack a sickly smile.

"You know Kiki is new here. Her predecessor, Josh Moll, made quite a few mistakes with my lab's reports that cost him…his job." Carol batted her eyelashes at Jack, but Kiki saw something cold behind the other woman's gaze that made her shiver inside.

And what was with the weird pause before Carol said the other guy had been fired? It almost sounded as if she was going to say something else but thought better of it. Which made Kiki wonder again, what exactly had happened to the guy who'd had her job before her?

All of his stuff had still been in her office when she'd taken over, including his coat and a heavy bag that had turned out to contain a custom-drilled bowling ball and his bowling shoes. The head of Human Resources—a reedy man named Oliver Crumb—had told her to dump all of Josh's stuff into a large rolling hamper, which had been deposited in the hallway just outside her door by a bored-looking janitor named Jeff.

Jeff was a strange one. Always lurking, and watching everything. He never seemed to actually do anything. His janitorial skills seemed nearly non-existent, but he was certainly good at watching everybody. He gave Kiki the creeps.

When Carol had shown Jack every last corner of the lab, including where they stored the test tubes and how they disposed of the waste, she wound down and just smiled at him. It was a dazzling smile, Kiki had to admit. Probably designed to charm the pants off any male she fancied. Kiki felt a little triumph when Jack didn't seem to fall for it.

He extricated his arm from Carol's and smiled benignly. A business smile. A noncommittal smile. Perfect, Kiki thought, as Carol's lips thinned with displeasure.

"Thank you for the in-depth tour," Jack said, still being pleasantly businesslike. He turned to Kiki. "Can you show me some of the other areas your job takes you to?"

Kiki studiously ignored what sounded like a low growl coming from Carol's direction. The other woman wasn't happy at being dismissed so easily. Kiki took her cue from Jack and remained businesslike as she led him from the lab area with a final word of thanks to Carol for letting them interrupt her important work.

As they walked down the corridors, heading for one of the production areas, Jack asked quiet questions. Kiki answered as best she could, considering she was still learning her way around the place, but he seemed to be understanding of her situation, being the new girl and all. His questions were mostly about the process and how things worked in the factory portion of the plant, but he threw in some personal ones, as well.

"Are you friendly with Carol?" he asked at one point.

Caught a bit off-guard, Kiki shook her head. "Not particularly. You may have noticed she works more closely with men." Both of Carol's techs were men, and it was pretty well known in the company that, if Carol had a problem, it was usually with another woman.

"I didn't think you were supposed to notice or say things like that in this day and age," Jack chastised her with a smile.

Kiki shrugged. "I'm just stating the facts as I see them. Carol and I work together, at times, but we're not what I'd call friendly."

Jack asked a technical question at that point, and Kiki breathed a sigh of relief at the topic change. They got to the part of the plant that she knew best outside the lab. It was a room where the samples were kept before they were picked up by lab personnel. All the samples from the various production lines were kept in bins, sorted by line, lot, date, and time.

She was explaining the scheme when Henry Baskin, one of the line leads, walked in from the production area with a bagged sample in his hands. Kiki was happy to make the introductions and let the friendly and very experienced factory worker explain how things worked on his production line. With the pressure off her a bit, Kiki tried to think about what she could show Jack next. She was quickly running out of places she'd been and had any familiarity with. She could show him the warehouse, but she hadn't been back to it since that horrible night when she'd observed something sinister.

Henry and Jack chatted while Kiki worried. She really didn't want to go anywhere near that warehouse. She didn't have to visit the place, strictly speaking, in the course of her job, though she'd been trying to track down something her predecessor had mis-reported, which was why she'd gone there in the first place. Really, though, she could ask the production people to get her the information. She had just been trying to cut down on requests to them, which took a while to fulfill, so she could both give them a break and get her work done quicker.

It had turned out to be a bad move all around. She should never have been there to see what she'd seen, and it was best for all concerned to keep thinking that she had no real familiarity with the warehouse operation at all. For that reason, she really didn't want to bring Jack through there. She could keep up the fiction that she didn't know her way around there, but that would make her look bad to Jack, which was something she also didn't want. For some reason, lying to him felt really, really wrong.

Certainly, she'd been raised with old-fashioned values that said lying was verboten under any circumstances. She'd learned how to get along in the modern world, among people who didn't stick to the same morals she'd been raised with, but she tried never to lie or deceive, unless it was under very specific circumstances.

In this case, she was pretending she knew nothing of the warehouse to protect herself from something she feared might be evil. Her folks had taught her that protecting yourself from evil was a top priority, and she felt they would support her ruse in this case and approve of the deception of her co-workers.

Deceiving Jack, now… That felt different.

She couldn't explain why. It just did.

Henry was saying goodbye, and Kiki was starting to wonder what she should do when Bob Boehm walked in the door, saving her from her quandary. He dismissed her offhandedly, taking over the tour, and Kiki gratefully escaped to go back to her office while Bob was getting Jack to suit up in protective gear for a look at the factory. As she slipped out without saying goodbye, she wondered if she'd ever see him again. Then, she wondered why such a fleeting encounter had impacted her so greatly.

Then, she told herself to forget all about the mysterious stranger who had occupied an hour of her day and get back to work.

As things turned out, Kiki didn't get to see Jack again, that day. She went about her work, as usual, though she couldn't help listening carefully each time the door to the office area opened, just in case he was coming back from his tour. By quitting time, he still hadn't reappeared, and she had made it her policy, ever since that warehouse ritual she'd almost interrupted, to leave on time.

She wasn't going to alter that habit now. She wanted her coworkers to think she had never stayed late, and she didn't care if that reflected poorly on her. She got her work done and did it well. She had unsnarled some of the big messes Josh had created and was on good terms with the state and federal inspectors, and paper pushers she dealt with on a daily basis. Bob had to be happy with that.

They couldn't pay her enough to stay late and possibly get caught up in something like what she'd seen the other night. No way, no how. And the fact was, they only paid her a salary that didn't include overtime, so staying late was purely optional. While it was true that, in most offices she'd worked in, everybody worked late to show how dedicated they were to their jobs and earn brownie points with the boss, she wasn't going to do that here. Not after what she'd seen.

And, in fact, nobody in the office area seemed to

habitually work late. Kiki had been watching carefully to see what the standard was in this new workplace since she'd first started. Aside from a few people who worked late once in a while, most of them seemed to leave not long after quitting time. That had made Kiki's decision to leave with the main group much easier.

As she drove home to her little rented cottage, she couldn't help but think back to Jack Bishop. He had been the most handsome man she'd ever seen up close. He wasn't movie star pretty. He was more rugged and sleek all at the same time. Handsome in a way that was hard to describe, though he did have chocolatey brown eyes that were subtly flecked with bits of green and gold. His eyes were almost mesmerizing when she met his gaze.

His brown hair was pretty standard, but on him, it looked luxurious. The slightly shaggy strands, shot through with the occasional strand of golden brown, made her want to run her fingers through them. His facial features were unremarkable taken one at a time, but somehow, when put together, created a strikingly handsome visage.

He was, however, a bit of a giant, but not fat in any way. Well over six feet tall, he was built on the ginormous side, with broad shoulders and honed muscles that showed clearly, even under his conservative attire. His clothing was casual, but neat. He didn't give off the vibe of a man used to working in an office, but he was clearly able to adapt.

All in all, he'd certainly made an impression on her. She was still thinking about him hours later as she was walking down the street to the local pizza restaurant called *Vincenti's* where she had picked up dinner more often than not over the past couple of weeks. She'd gone home, put on her jeans, then decided she didn't want to cook. The Italian place was only a few blocks away, and their food was amazing. It wasn't hard to make the call to take a stroll and get dinner out.

What she didn't expect was to run into anyone she knew. She was new in town, and as far as she knew, she didn't live near any of the people she worked with. So far, she hadn't run into anyone at *Vincenti's*, but that all changed the moment she walked in the door and saw Jack Bishop standing at the counter, waiting to be served.

Jack couldn't believe his luck when he caught sight of the woman who'd just walked in the door. Kiki Richards saw him a moment later, and he caught the look of surprise mixed with pleasure in her eyes before she schooled her expression to polite interest. She waved shyly when their eyes met, then walked over to the counter, where he was already waiting for service.

"Funny running into you here," she said, by way of greeting.

"I could say the same," he agreed with a grin while his inner bear sat up and cheered. His furry side had liked the small woman, though his human side was still a little suspicious of everyone who worked at the plant.

"Have you eaten here before?" Kiki asked him, making polite conversation while they both waited to be served.

The place was busy enough that it would take a few minutes before the servers got to them. Jack didn't mind that at all. He wanted to talk to Kiki away from the office and see if he could figure her out.

He also just liked looking at her. She was a very pretty girl, with that golden hair wafting about her delicate shoulders and those clear blue eyes blinking innocently up at him. Right now, her expressive eyes were wide with surprise at running into him and showed a bit of the nerves she was feeling making small talk. He didn't like that she felt nervous around him, but it could just be the novelty of the situation. She clearly hadn't expected to see him, and he'd taken her by surprise. He would try to put her more at ease.

"No. The guy at the desk in my hotel recommended this restaurant. I'm staying across the street." Jack pointed out the window to the glowing sign of the chain hotel on the other side of the road.

"Well, he made a good recommendation. I eat here a lot.

My cottage is just a few blocks away," she told him as they shuffled a bit closer to the podium where a young woman was seating people.

"Do you want to share a table?" Jack asked. "I hate eating alone."

Kiki tilted her head. "I suspect it's not often that you don't have company," she said, her phrasing both complimentary and a little suspect. "But I'm game, if you are." Her smile was friendly enough, and his inner bear wanted to rumble in approval.

The hostess returned and led them to a booth in the back. The place was reasonably crowded, and the table they were led to was against the back wall, which suited Jack. If the hostess had tried to place them in the center of the room, he'd have made a polite request for a booth along the wall, so that he could have at least one secure side. He made it a habit to always sit where he could see as much of a room as possible and have at least one side where no threats could come from.

Once they settled in, Jack looked over the menu. "I hope you're hungry. I'm just about starved," he told her, preparing the way for the large quantities of food he planned to order. Shifters ate more than non-magical folk, and bears ate more than most shifters. "I'm on an expense account, and if we talk a little about work, I can totally justify picking up the tab for you," he said, smiling at the pretty woman seated across from him.

He hadn't expected company tonight but was glad his path had crossed with Kiki's, once again. He hadn't been able to get her out of his mind all day, even when he'd been in the middle of Bob Boehm's bamboozle. The man had led Jack all over the plant, acting the somewhat gracious host, but hadn't really shown Jack anything important.

Jack suspected there were hidden things going on at that factory. Things done in back rooms he hadn't been allowed to see. Jack was planning to go in and have another look when nobody was around. A little oh-dark-hundred reconnaissance. Possibly in bear form—at least outside. He wanted to try to sniff out any magic that might be around the place, and he could do that better in his fur than his skin.

"I usually just order an entrée," she told him, looking at the menu as he did the same. "Their homemade gnocchi is terrific, as are all the baked dishes."

"I was thinking about starting with some appetizers," he replied, scanning the menu. "A little antipasti?" he asked playfully, looking up to catch her gaze. "And how about some wine, to go with it? I see they have a pretty good wine list, including a few vintages from Maxwell Vineyards. I've become partial to their reds." He ran his finger down the wine list and made a selection. "Since we're eating Italian, how about we try the Maxwell Chianti?"

Kiki was smiling but shaking her head. "I seldom drink alcohol."

"Come on," he coaxed her. "Chianti is practically mandatory at an Italian feast."

"Well…" He could see her starting to give in and felt a moment of triumph. "Just a little, I guess."

CHAPTER 4

Jack got the impression that Kiki lived a rather conservative life. She didn't drink. She dressed somewhat primly at work, and even at home. She was wearing jeans, but they weren't skin tight or a designer label, and the blouse was the same one she'd had on under her business suit. A high-necked number that was about as plain as plain could be. Just a shell, really. In a prim pink that made her look like a kindergarten teacher.

Jack suddenly liked the idea of corrupting her a bit. He wanted to see what she looked like when she really let her hair down. That silky-looking golden hair was still drawn back, off her face, and secured somehow at the back of her head, just as it had been earlier in the day. Did she never wear it loose? Suddenly, Jack wanted to know the answer to that question more than anything, but it wasn't something he could just ask. He'd have to find another way to discover all her intimate secrets. The wine might help there.

The waitress came, and Jack placed his order for three different appetizers, a bottle of the Maxwell Chianti, and what was advertised on the menu as a *fish feast* for himself, with a giant side of pasta. Kiki added her own comparatively small order of baked gnocchi before the waitress left the table.

"I hope you don't expect me to eat half of those

appetizers. I usually take home half the gnocchi and eat it the next day for lunch," she told him, laughing.

"You should at least try some of them," he told her. "I've had those little rolled up eggplant things before, and if these are anything like those were, you'll be glad you tried it."

"Where did you have them?" she asked, slightly altering the trajectory of the conversation.

"New York," he answered truthfully. He'd traveled widely with his brothers, and one memorable trip had taken them all to New York to help out with a werewolf turf war that had been instigated by a local mage who was toying with the city wolves to carve out more territory for himself and his followers. "There's a lot of great Italian places in Little Italy. We'd eat there then stroll to Chinatown for dessert. Or the opposite way around." He shrugged. "There are a lot of good restaurants downtown in Manhattan.

"I've never been there," she said, looking down, but not before he caught the dreamy look of wanderlust in her eyes. This was a woman who wanted to travel, but who had likely never had the chance.

The waitress returned with the chilled bottle of wine and made a production out of opening it at the table for them. It might be a small, local restaurant in a backwater town, but they did things right, he noted approvingly. The waitress offered him the first sip, and he nodded in accordance with the ritual he had learned years ago when his older brother had been on a vintage wine kick.

They'd been hired to ferret out a swindle happening in one of Maxwell Vineyards' distribution channels, and his brother, Ace, had taken to the hoity-toity wine world like the proverbial duck to water. He'd left the grunt work to King and Jack on that mission, but it had all worked out. The miscreant who was diverting cases of Maxwell's best was among the elite *wine sniffers*, as King called them, and Ace had done the actual take-down while the two younger brothers had been the muscle in the warehouse.

As he'd expected, the Chianti was up to Maxwell's

standard of excellence. The Napa Valley vineyard wasn't known as one of the best in the world for nothing. Only the magical folk, living in secret among regular, clueless humans, knew that Maxwell, himself, was an ancient vampire. It was rumored—and Jack knew it to be fact—that vampires could drink wine. The fermented fruit of the vine was their last link with the sun, and it healed them. They still drank blood, of course, but they drank wine in public. Much more civilized, Jack thought with a private smile.

The waitress poured a glass for Kiki, and he raised his to clink against hers in silent toast, inviting her to take a sip. He watched the jewel red liquid flow over her luscious lips. They looked so soft and full. He wanted desperately to kiss those lips, but he knew it was too soon. This fragile little homebody would be scared off like a gazelle under a lion's gaze if he moved too quickly. He counseled his inner bear to patience.

Then, he had to remind his human half that she was still a suspect. Though, more and more, he just couldn't picture Kiki as having a sinister bone in her body. A naïve one, maybe, but not anything crooked or evil. If she was playing him for a fool, she was a master at it. Personally, he thought she was on the level, but he still had to be cautious around her until he figured out more about what was going on in her workplace.

If he'd learned anything today, he'd at least been able to confirm that magic was definitely afoot there. Not wholesome, good magic. More toward the other side of the spectrum, but it was hard for him to see. He'd have better luck in his fur, later, but for now, he would ply the pretty woman with wine and see if she would be indiscreet and help him do his job by spilling all she knew.

"This is really quite good," she said, lowering the glass after a rather large sip.

"Maxwell's is one of the finest vineyards in the country. He'd say the world," Jack corrected himself, putting his glass down.

"You've met the man who makes this wine?" Kiki asked,

her eyes wide.

"Once or twice. We did a job for him a few years ago. My brothers and I are troubleshooters. We've worked for various concerns over the years." That was one way of putting it, Jack thought with inward amusement. "Maxwell is scary but fair. At least, that's how my brother, Ace, summed him up. We all agreed."

"How many brothers do you have?" She took another sip of her wine, appearing a bit nervous as they made small talk while they waited for the food to start arriving.

"Just two, but they're enough." He chuckled, and she joined in, as he'd hoped. He didn't like seeing her ill at ease. The furry bastard inside him wanted to reach across the table and soothe her, but he couldn't. Too soon. Way too soon, he warned his bear side.

"I have three brothers and three sisters," she volunteered abruptly. Kiki wasn't skilled at the small talk, he was coming to realize.

Jack didn't mind. He wasn't usually much of a talker himself, though he had picked up some social skills he used on missions… Like this one. He had to keep reminding himself that he was here to do a job, not romance a woman.

"Wow. Six siblings? That's a lot," he commented, reaching over to top up her glass.

She was sipping nervously, which depleted the glass faster than was probably advisable, but he wasn't going to say anything. If she got drunk and spilled all her secrets, it would save him having to wheedle them out of her some other way.

"My family, historically, were Anabaptists. You know, like Amish?" She seemed even more nervous revealing that tidbit.

Perhaps she'd faced ridicule or rude questions over the years about her background. Well, Jack was the last person to make fun of someone's family history. Not when his parents, who had worked as dealers in the big casinos in Tahoe for a long time, had decided to name him and his brothers after playing cards.

"I don't know much about Amish people, except I think I

remember that they often have large families," he commented, hoping his words were innocuous enough to put her more at ease.

She smiled, and he was glad he'd opted to keep things light. "Yes, exactly," she said, nodding at him. "We're not Amish anymore, but I guess old habits die hard. My family still lives on the farm, and most of our neighbors are still members of the faith, even though our grandparents broke away from the religion many years ago. We still live pretty plainly, though we do embrace technology like cars and computers and mechanized farm equipment for our land." She blushed a bit and looked down. "You must think us very backward with the exciting life you lead. I mean, the farthest I've ever been is Pittsburgh."

"Traveling isn't all it's cracked up to be," he told her.

"Where do you live? What's your home base?" she asked, seeming truly interested.

"Well, if you'd asked me that a few months ago, I'd have said Phoenix, Arizona, but both of my brothers recently married and moved to Grizzly Cove, Washington, where SeaLife Enterprises is headquartered. That's how I got this job," he said, knowing there was much more to the story that he might never be able to tell her.

This girl was human, through and through. Of Amish ancestry, for goodness sake. No way she knew anything about magic, or things that went bump in the night—either rhetorical or sexual. Everything about her screamed prim and proper. Hands off.

"So, both your brothers are married?" she asked, surprising him. He'd have thought she'd ask more about work. That was the safer topic, after all. Instead, she'd chosen to delve into personal information. Interesting.

"Yeah, Ace met Sabrina first. She's from Canada, originally. They got paired up, and when King was on his way to visit them, he stopped to escort Sabrina's best friend, Marilee. King and Marilee hit it off, which nobody expected, and they tied the knot next. I went to see all of them and got roped into this job. The three of us used to work as a team. I have to admit, being on my own on this mission is a bit daunting. I'm used to having my brothers around for backup."

Damn. He'd said more than he'd intended. And he'd used the word *mission.* Had she noticed?

"When my brother, Arthur, got married, and then Brendan and James followed soon after, I felt a bit abandoned, if I'm honest. They wanted the simple life on a farm, but I wanted more. I left for college, and it was really hard to be away from home for the first time ever, a plain girl in a dorm that was a bit of a madhouse, if I'm honest." She smiled and rolled her eyes, her cheeks flushing a becoming pink. "I missed them all, but I managed. I'm the youngest of the first group, then my folks took a break. The twins came along about ten years later. A bit of a surprise, you might say." Her blush deepened, and he was entranced.

The waitress returned with the appetizers and Jack encouraged Kiki to at least try a little of each of the dishes he'd ordered. He ate quickly, noting she'd been right about the quality of this restaurant. Everything was delicious. The ingredients were fresh and top-notch, and the chef had done a stellar job putting everything together.

Jack was sure to keep Kiki's wineglass topped up. She was drinking steadily and was already a little tipsy, if he was any judge. He decided to ask some questions about her workplace, hoping to find out a bit more about the plant while her guard was down.

"I'd never been to a paper mill before today," he said between bites, hoping to turn the conversation in the direction he wanted it to go.

"No?" She looked adorably puzzled for a moment, then her expression cleared. "Oh, I guess SeaLife Enterprises has a lot of different businesses under its umbrella."

Jack nodded. "Exactly. To my knowledge, this is the only paper business in the SeaLife portfolio. Did you always want to work in the paper business?"

"Me? Oh, no. My degree is in Business Administration. I would've taken any job in my field, and this just happened to be the one that was offered," she said, sipping her wine, again. She was going to have a bit of a headache tomorrow, if she wasn't careful, but right now, Jack was just as glad to have the opportunity to question her.

"Do you like it there?" he prodded as he ate steadily. She nibbled on the little tidbits she'd taken from the appetizer plates but drank more than ate, which suited him, at the moment.

"Like it?" She tilted her head a little unsteadily. "Actually, if I'm being honest, no. I did, at first, but there have been some things..." She trailed off, and he let her think for a moment before prompting her.

"What kind of things?" Hopefully, she'd keep talking.

"Really strange things," she went on, and he felt a moment of triumph, even as a little frown formed just above her eyebrows. "Bad things."

"Bad things?" he repeated, hoping to coax her into saying more.

She looked around, as if checking if anyone was listening to them, then leaned in a bit. Her voice lowered, but he could easily hear her with his superior shifter hearing. He leaned closer to her, anyway, knowing the feeling of intimacy might cause her to share more.

"A week ago, I stayed late and decided to check something for myself in the warehouse because everyone else was gone that I would have usually asked for the information." Yes, her words were convoluted. She was definitely more than a little tipsy. But Jack was following so far. "I'd never been to that part of the warehouse before, but I figured I would just go quickly and get the lot numbers I needed, then go back to my office and complete my report. But when I got there..." Again, she looked around. "When I got there... It was horrible."

She reached for her wine and drank a healthy sip. When she didn't keep talking, Jack had to prompt her some more.

"What was so horrible? Was the warehouse disorganized?" he asked, his tone somewhat bored.

"No." Her volume rose a bit with her vehemence, then she lowered her voice even more. "They were standing in a circle around an…an…altar. They were chanting. It was bad. Evil." She shook her head in horror.

Jack tried hard to hide his interest. Now, they were getting somewhere.

"Really?" He tried to inject just enough interest into the single word to make her go on.

"They were wearing robes. Black robes with black embroidery that was glowing red." She paused, shuddering a bit. "The hoods were up, so I couldn't tell who they all were, but I think I recognized some of them. They work in the factory." She took a sip of her wine, shutting her eyes as if to shut out the memory.

"What did you do? Did they see you?" Jack prompted her to continue.

"I don't think so. I went back the way I'd come, and when I got back to my office, I packed up and left as quickly as I could. I went straight home and got out the salt." She nodded in emphasis, as if pleased with her own actions. She was drunk, but he wasn't going to stop her from drinking, now. Not when he was learning things he needed to know.

Jack didn't know exactly what to make of the last comment, though he had some vague recollection that human mages sometimes used lines of salt in their incantations. Maybe that's what it was about Kiki that drew him. Maybe she had magical knowledge, if not actual magic of her own. Although, he couldn't be exactly sure about her yet. She might just be really good at hiding her talents, if any.

"Then, that weekend, Mr. Boehm invited me to a barbeque at his house. I was surprised, to say the least. I had no idea they got together socially, but maybe that's just because I'm so new. Anyway, I couldn't refuse the invitation, so I went. Everything was fine until I stepped into his backyard." She sipped at her wine again. "They were all out by the grill. It felt like the place in the warehouse had felt. Dark. Sinister. Evil. I pretended to trip and twist my ankle so I could leave."

Smart girl. "That was probably wise," Jack said aloud. He was trying to figure out how to play this, but he figured some truth wouldn't hurt. Not too much, but enough to keep her talking. "You know, I've seen some weird stuff in my time. My brothers and I came across a group of devil worshipers a few years ago." Elspeth, the so-called *Mater Priori* and Destroyer of Worlds, was a kind of devil, to his mind. "Bad business, that."

"The worst," she agreed. "I don't know what these people are doing, but I decided, then and there, that I'd just do my job, so I could pay my bills, and I began job hunting that very afternoon. As soon as I find something else, I'm out of here." Her gaze rose to meet his as if she'd just realized she could be in trouble for what she'd said. It was adorable, but he didn't let her see his amusement. "I probably shouldn't have told you that. Sorry." She put down her wineglass and looked at it as if it had betrayed her. "I told you I don't normally drink much."

"That's okay. Honestly, I don't blame you for feeling that way about the company after what you've experienced. Remember, I'm from corporate. I have no allegiance to the current leadership or employees of this particular operation, beyond the general feeling that I want all good, honest workers to be treated fairly, and that the company operates within legally mandated guidelines." He sighed and hoped she was still with him. "I was sent here because SeaLife believes there's some kind of problem. I'm the one who has to figure out what it is. It just may be that your candidness about what you observed will help me do that job, so I thank you for it."

She seemed placated, but he noticed she didn't touch any more wine. The waitress served their entrees at that point, and he asked the woman to bring over a carafe of water with lemon wedges. He figured he'd gotten all he could out of Kiki for tonight—and it was *plenty*. Better to let her sober up and try to avoid a pounding headache in the morning. The food would help.

CHAPTER 5

They set about eating their main course with little conversation, except the occasional comment on the quality of the food or the environment. They were discussing the weather forecast by the time they'd finished their meals, and Kiki seemed a lot more sober. She had sipped the lemon-water with her gnocchi and had only eaten a third or so of her plate before signaling to the waitress that she'd like to take the rest home. Nothing was left of the seafood feast Jack had ordered, and he'd enjoyed every last bite of the deliciously prepared meal.

"You weren't kidding when you said you were hungry," Kiki observed with a grin. "I have three brothers, but I've never seen a man eat that much in one sitting."

Jack rubbed his stomach and grinned back at her. "Then, you have obviously never seen the Bishop boys at the dinner table. I think me and my brothers can out-eat anybody on the planet. There were often fork fights over the last roll in the basket. See?" He held up his hand and pointed to a non-existent scar. "This is where King stuck me with a fork when I was twelve."

Kiki giggled as he'd hoped she would. "I don't believe you." She leaned forward to inspect his hand. "You don't have a scar."

"It healed," he shrugged. What he'd said was the honest truth, but his shifter metabolism and innate magic had made short work of the small wound.

The waitress came over with Kiki's doggie bag and the check, which Jack paid for with the spiffy new company credit card Beth and Trevor had given him for this job. He was officially an employee of SeaLife Enterprises for the duration of this mission, and Trevor had even talked about future work for the company after this task was done. Jack was seriously considering the idea. If he could work from Grizzly Cove, he could at least see his brothers and their new mates between missions. It would never be like it was, with the three of them working together all the time, but it could still be good.

His brothers were intensely happy now, and he didn't begrudge them that at all. No, Jack was truly happy for his brothers. In fact, he hoped to find a mate of his own and settle down like they had—at some point in the future—but lightning had already struck twice in the Bishop family. It would be too much to think that Jack could find his mate so soon.

Although... If he was going to find a mate, he would be hard-pressed to find a woman nicer and sweeter than Kiki. She was pretty, smart, and not much of a drinker. A fact that he was reminded of when she stood a little unsteadily after he'd paid the bill. Jack immediately took her arm to steady her, and she looked up to meet his gaze.

Time stood still as their eyes met and held. The busy restaurant and the noise all around them faded into insignificance.

"Sorry. I guess I'm still feeling the effects of that delicious wine," she said, a little breathless.

"Let me walk you home. It's late, and I'd like to make sure you get there safely." He tried hard to keep the possessive growl of his inner bear out of his voice.

She agreed, and they left the restaurant together. She was carrying the little doggie bag containing the uneaten portion of her meal. She had even put what little of the bread left in the basket that had been served with their meal into the bag, which made him realize that she was a thrifty soul. She didn't let anything go to waste. She'd talked about having to keep her job, even when she knew things were wrong there, to pay her bills. He supposed he'd have to look into her financial situation to verify, but he suspected she was living frugally because she had to watch every penny.

No shame in that. He'd been there a time or two, himself. Not all shifters were independently wealthy. He and his brothers had lived from hand-to-mouth most of their lives, and he respected Kiki's steadfast strength in going back to the factory in spite of what she'd claimed to have witnessed.

He'd have to look further into everything she'd told him, just to be sure, but his gut was telling him she was on the level. If she wasn't, she was some kind of master of deception, and he just didn't think that was the case. Still, he had to be cautious and dot all the i's and cross all the t's. He was on SeaLife's payroll now, and he had to answer to his immediate boss, Ezra Tate, and ultimately to Trevor, and his mate, Beth, who owned the company.

Jack wouldn't skimp when it came to his job. He had an obligation to do the best possible work for his friends and employers. The stakes were high. SeaLife had become a thing of horror due to Beth's stepfather dealing in illegal and disgusting activities, including acts of human trafficking, money laundering, drug smuggling, and even murder-for-hire. Beth and Trevor were trying to set things right, and Jack was part of that. He wanted to help them get things back on the straight and narrow.

But he also found himself falling for the babe in the woods—the pretty paper pusher who had no head for alcohol. He liked Kiki. There was no equivocating. He really liked her. A lot. He wasn't altogether sure he trusted her yet, but that would come, he hoped, as soon as he had a chance to double-check her story.

He walked her home, his senses on alert for anything out

of the ordinary. He caught the scent of evil not far from her door, and a frisson of dark magic made him want to shake out his fur, but it was an older trace. Whoever had been casting spells—or whatever it was they had been doing—was long gone now. The energies left behind by such workings were hours—maybe even days—old.

The feeling got stronger as Kiki slowed her steps and reached into her pocket to retrieve her keys. Whatever had been done, it was Kiki's home that was at the center of the magical working. Of that, Jack was sure.

"Well, this is my place," she said needlessly as they stopped in front of the garden gate.

A short walkway led to a quaint cottage set only a few yards off the street. They weren't too far from the center of town here, but it was a small town, and the area around Kiki's cottage was all very similar. Row houses and small cottages were side by side, each with a small front garden, the houses separated by narrow driveways that led to garages in the rear of the houses. It was quaint. And vulnerable.

"Cute place," he commented, nodding toward the house.

"I liked it the moment I saw it, and the rent was very reasonable," she replied. "I liked the garden most of all. Lots of herbs and flowers."

The garden was wild looking to his eyes. He could see a lot better than regular humans in the dark, thanks to his bear half, and he didn't see anything sinister in the front yard as she unlatched the gate and walked through. He followed, though she hadn't exactly invited him into the garden. Still, he had this sense that he needed to see her right up to her door and safely tucked inside.

He entered the garden and immediately felt the peace of the place. Looking down, he noticed a faint line of white on the ground. It could easily have been mistaken for sand, but he knew without asking that it was a fine line of salt. Kitchen witchery, some might call it, but it was effective, nonetheless.

Whatever malevolent magic he'd sensed outside the boundaries of this garden, it did not penetrate here. The salt, or maybe the garden itself, kept the evil at bay. Dark magic had tried and failed to enter here. It had been gently, but powerfully, repulsed.

Somehow, Kiki—or possibly one of her neighbors, or even the landlord who owned her cottage—had known enough to run a line of salt across the threshold. Then again, Kiki had probably done this herself, since she'd mentioned breaking out the salt after what she'd seen in the warehouse.

Words of magic invocation had probably been spoken as well. Jack couldn't be sure exactly what had been done, but it had definitely been protective magic. The salt line had formed a barrier that nothing intent on doing harm could pass.

The feeling and scent of dark magic had dissipated the moment he'd stepped over the line, even though it had been almost oppressively strong on the other side of that faint, salty line. If he had to piece together what might have transpired, he'd say someone intent on either spying on or causing harm to Kiki had come right up to her garden gate, but the rudimentary protection had stopped them in their tracks.

As they walked slowly toward the front door, Jack noticed the plants, growing wild and free in an unorganized chaos that soothed his senses. This was no rigid garden pruned to within an inch of its life. No, this was more a collection of plants placed in various spots and allowed to grow where they willed.

It was natural. Welcoming. It had an innocent, wild magic, all its own. He could see why she liked this garden. It was like walking out of the human world on the street just beyond the gate into an enchanted forest.

He was getting fanciful. Maybe he'd also had too much of the Chianti? Or, maybe, it was the woman who affected him so greatly. She went up the two little steps that led onto a small covered porch. He noted the weathered rocking chair off to one side where a person could sit and look out at the garden, maybe sipping a cup of tea. Though, where that image came from, he had no idea. Jack wasn't altogether

certain he'd ever had a cup of tea in his life.

Still, the image persisted. He could just see Kiki sitting there in the early evening breeze, watching the last rays of the setting sun, sipping a steaming cup of herbal tea. Was he seeing an echo of something she'd done? Or, more likely, was he just letting his imagination run away with the fairies?

Fairies? Now, what made him think of those immensely powerful creatures? Jack wanted to shake his head. He was getting confused between the magical vision he was seeing—the porch tableau overlaid with a glow of fairy lights.

There was something weird about this place.

Yet another thing he would have to investigate. But not right now. No, as he followed Kiki up onto the small porch and watched her fumble with her key, he wanted only one thing more in this magical evening.

She opened the door and turned to him, a triumphant smile on her face for having managed to get the door open after more than a few tries. He couldn't help himself. Maybe it was the magic of the place reaching out to him. Maybe it was the woman before him, her face framed in starlight and the magical glow of the garden that seemed to intensify the longer he was in it. Maybe it was just natural that he give in to the smoldering attraction he'd felt for Kiki since almost the first moment they'd met.

Whatever it was, it compelled him to dip his head closer. Inhaling her delectable scent, he brushed her smiling lips with his and captured her little gasp against his mouth.

Testing to see if she'd freeze up or push him away, he waited, patient, his mouth caressing hers lightly, until… Yes. She moved into his embrace as his arms came up around her. She wasn't pushing him away. Far from it.

She moved closer, and he took it as implicit permission to kiss her a little more intimately.

Kiki could scarcely believe it. She was in Jack's arms, his mouth on hers, and he was kissing the very breath from her body.

She liked it. She really liked it. Perhaps too much, but she wouldn't ruin the moment by thinking about that now. No, now, all she wanted to do was kiss him back.

She opened herself to the experience and drank in the sensations. His lips were demanding, coaxing, seductive and strong. Nothing about Jack was tentative, and she found she liked that very much. This was a man who knew what he wanted and reached out to take it. Not by force, but with gentle seduction that was both mesmerizing and rewarding.

His kiss coaxed her to give in to whatever he might ask for—physically, mentally, and emotionally. She knew that path was dangerous. She didn't want him to leave her with a broken heart. She barely knew the man, and her standards were high. That didn't prevent her from enjoying the first kiss she'd shared with a man in way too long.

She leaned into him and loved the way his strength enveloped her. He was a big man. A strongly muscled man, as she came to feel firsthand. He might eat like a bear, but there wasn't an ounce of flab on him. His muscles rippled under her stroking fingers as she reached up to his shoulders. Good heavens. He was built like an athlete.

She hadn't expected that. While farm work had made the men she'd known in her youth strong and muscular, Jack was ripped in a way that spoke of discipline and rigorous exercise. She hadn't been able to discern it under his clothing in the office, but touching him was like touching a marble statue of one of the Greek gods. The only difference being that he was warm and vibrant, and his muscles moved, flexing and releasing, under her questing touch.

Heat filled her body at the realization, just as he broke the kiss. She realized, to her embarrassment, that her lips followed his until he moved out of reach. She'd wanted more. She hadn't wanted the moment to end.

"I should let you go," he said, her heart dropping into her shoes at his retreat. Had she done something wrong? Had he realized she wasn't very experienced with men? She felt her cheeks flush with heat and dropped her gaze.

When she didn't say anything, he placed one finger under her chin and tilted her head up. She complied, reluctantly. What she found, when she met his gaze, was a banked fire in the depths of his eyes that matched the fire coursing through her own blood. Seeing that set her more at ease. He wasn't leaving because she'd done something wrong or turned him off. He was leaving because... Because he was a gentleman, she supposed. Hm. That was surprising, as well.

She'd long been told that most men pushed as far as a woman would go and then some, not handling rejection well. But Jack was ending this even before it really got going, of his own volition. What did that mean? She could see the desire in his eyes. She was confident enough to believe he wanted more but was deliberately backing off. So, why?

"I'll see you at work tomorrow," he said, a faint smile playing about his lips. Lips that she'd discovered the feel and taste of now, she thought dreamily.

But his words gave her a clue. Work. He had to work tomorrow and so did she. At the same company, though not, technically, in the same chain of command. Maybe that's why he was controlling himself and not asking for more. That had to be it.

Jack sighed at her continued silence. "I really enjoyed our time together. Dinner would have been very lonely without your company," he said.

She nodded, still unable to speak, really. He'd scrambled her senses with that amazing kiss.

"Um. Me, too." Hm. That didn't make much sense. She tried again. "I mean, I would've just taken my order to go and come back here if I hadn't met up with you in the restaurant. Thank you again, for picking up the tab."

"Thank SeaLife. They're paying for it," he quipped, smiling down at her. "Think of it as a perk of the job."

She frowned, remembering what she'd told him about looking for a new job. "I'm sorry if I said anything I shouldn't have," she said. "I did like the factory until I saw... Whatever it was that I saw."

"Try not to think about it," he counselled, "but keep your eyes open. I was sent here because the management at SeaLife knew something was wrong here. Corporate sent in another troubleshooter a few months ago, but he couldn't penetrate what was going on. I think you might have given me a new avenue to investigate." He touched the frown line between her eyes with his thumb as his hand went to her temple. "Just don't draw attention, and if you do find another job, you should probably take it, if it gets you out of here. I do plan to clean this place up. It may not be pretty, though. It might even be a bit dangerous." He lowered his hand, and she missed the gentle stroking of his thumb on her forehead.

"I'm just glad somebody is going to do something. It's creepy working there now, after..." She couldn't finish the sentence. It seemed so weird to talk about what she'd seen. It was even weirder that Jack wasn't running the other way, calling the men in the white coats to come get her. The fact that he hadn't even blinked when she'd described what she'd seen alarmed her a bit. Then, a thought occurred to her. "Have you run across that sort of thing before?"

Jack backed up a step, breaking all contact between them. She immediately missed his closeness. His warmth. He was looking at her oddly when she met his gaze.

"Tell me, what do you see when you look at this garden?" He gestured toward the haphazard collection of plants in the front yard. "What do you feel?"

"It's messy," she said. "But I like it. It feels peaceful. Natural."

"Anything else?" he prompted gently.

"It feels good. Pure," she went on. "Like nothing bad could ever happen here."

He just looked at her for a moment before he spoke again. "Did you put the salt line across the garden gate?"

CHAPTER 6

This time, she backed up, her breath catching ever so slightly in her throat. How did he know about that? It was barely visible in full sun!

She thought quickly. Everything she had been taught said nothing evil could pass over that line. She'd never really tested it before, but her elders had said they'd used the same charm in bad times, and it had protected them and their house. If Jack had been able to pass over it with impunity, did that mean he was good? She had no idea the power of the ancient charm. More importantly, she had no idea of this man's true power.

He felt big, though. Something about him felt…more. As if there was something simmering just below his surface. She didn't claim to be as sensitive to things as the others in her family, but she had gotten distinct impressions of Other-ness ever since she'd first seen Jack at the office. She didn't know what it meant. She could only hope he was on the right side of things.

Especially since she'd been so indiscreet. She wasn't a drinker. She should have known not to drink that wine he'd ordered. It had led her to say things she wouldn't normally have revealed to anyone she'd known such a short time.

"Did you deliberately ply me with wine to get me to reveal

things I wouldn't have told you otherwise?" she countered, turning the tables on him.

He didn't react the way she'd expected. In fact, he smiled. She'd thought he might back off, but he didn't. He just leaned against the porch post and watched her, that irritating grin on his face that she couldn't interpret.

"Actually," he said after a pause, "I didn't invite you to dine with me with that in mind, but when it happened, I realized I might be able to learn a few things while your guard was down, so I didn't stop it. Maybe I should have." He shrugged as if it didn't matter. "But ultimately, I did learn some things that could be very helpful to my work here."

"Are you one of the good guys?" she asked, hoping against hope that he was and that he'd say so. Of course, what good was his word? He could easily lie to her. Then again, she could usually tell when people were lying.

"I like to think so," he replied easily, that faint grin still playing around his lips. She heard truth in his words, though he hadn't phrased his answer as absolutely as she would have wished.

"How did you know about the salt?" She wasn't letting him off the hook completely. Not yet.

He shrugged. "I've seen something like it before," he told her offhandedly.

"Where?" she challenged.

"Oh, here and there," he replied, saying nothing of importance. "Most recently, I heard about it from one of my new sisters-in-law. She told me someone in town was casting wards with salt circles."

His words set her back on her heels. He'd used the same terminology she'd been taught at her grandmother's knee. Wards and casting. Those were the words used by practitioners of the old ways.

"Are you joking?" she asked, just to be sure.

His expression cleared at once. "I wouldn't joke about such things," he told her. "I know, for a fact, that *there are more things in heaven and earth than are dreamt of in your philosophy.*

So to speak." He misquoted Shakespeare, but she got the idea he was being absolutely serious.

"What are you?" she breathed, wondering again, why he felt so…big. She didn't have a better word for the invisible presence that surrounded him.

His grin returned. "Now, that would be telling." He straightened from his leaning position against the porch post. "Let me leave you with this," he said, slowly backing down the steps. "I came here to put things right. What you told me at dinner is important and will help me figure things out. I'm one of the good guys, and though I suspect your background may be different, you'll probably understand when I say, I am a servant of the Light."

She saw a faint glimmer surround him as he stepped deeper in to the garden, still facing her. She blinked. Was she seeing things? Her sister had claimed to see a glow about certain people, but Kiki never had before. She'd seen it around plants a time or two—and especially since moving into this cottage—but never people. Was that gift manifesting now? Or was it something about Jack, in particular? Was he magic?

And, if he was…he had just claimed to be on the side of the Light. He was good, and the garden was confirming it? She shook her head at her fancifulness. She knew stranger things had happened—especially in her own family—but she'd always been more down to earth than the rest of her clan. Stuff like this usually didn't happen to Kiki. Not plain, simple, non-magical Kiki.

He walked to the garden gate, which wasn't all that far away and opened it, passing over the salt line with impunity. She'd been taught that evil could not pass over a ward like that, but she'd never really tested it herself. Was he really one of the good guys? She desperately wanted to believe he was. So she wouldn't be so alone here, surrounded by people she could no longer trust.

But she still had to be cautious. She was a babe in the woods compared to some of the people in her family. She knew about some magical things, but she'd never really experienced them for herself.

"Keep your doors locked and your wards up," he said softly as he closed the gate behind himself. "I'll see you tomorrow."

She hugged his words to her as she went into the cottage and did as he'd suggested, locking the door behind herself. She felt sort of dreamy as she went around, checking that her rudimentary wards had not been disturbed while she'd been out. All the salt lines were intact, and she added another incantation to each, for good measure. Just in case.

She was in for the night, but the shared meal with her mysterious dinner companion was all she could think about. For those hours out of time, she'd felt...special. Like she was safe and protected.

It was silly to think it. She barely knew him, after all, but there was something about Jack that made her feel like nothing bad would ever happen with him around. Or, if it did, he'd take care of it in his quiet, competent, powerful way.

Few, if any, men of her previous acquaintance had inspired such feelings of both trust and attraction in her in so short a time. Yes, there was one thing she knew for certain after her surprise dinner date. Jack Bishop was definitely something special.

Jack was sort of mentally scratching his head the whole walk back to his hotel. Kiki was something else, and he meant that in the best possible way. She was like no other woman he'd ever met, and he was very much afraid he might be falling, fast and hard, for her. A human. Huh.

Both of his brothers had mated with other magical folk, albeit not bear women. Ace's mate, Sabrina, was a powerful weather witch. King's lady was a werewolf with snow white fur and an extra zap of magic. Special women who had already earned Jack's respect and affection, just for how happy they had made his brothers.

What would they think if Jack brought home a human?

Sure, Kiki seemed to have some knowledge of very rudimentary wards, but she hadn't given him any indication—any feeling—of magic. Even suppressed magic. And he had a special talent for sniffing such things out. That was why he'd been sent here, to do this job, when others had failed.

The cottage had a feel about it. Especially the garden. If he wasn't much mistaken, a fey of some kind had helped in its creation, at some point. He'd be intrigued to discover who the owner of that little home was and what their connection was to fey magic. That was something he hoped to discover, possibly with his brothers' help, since they were sitting on their duffs in Grizzly Cove and had more time to poke around in databases and track down documents than he did.

When he got back to his hotel and secured the room, he fired up his laptop and put in a call to Washington State. First, he called Ezra to update him on progress, so far. Jack also wanted to get Ezra's agreement to get one or both of his brothers in on this, at least from the research standpoint. His brothers were newly mated and probably wouldn't be taking field assignments for the foreseeable future, but they both had skills that could be useful from behind the scenes.

Ezra agreed readily, happy to have a reason to rope all the brothers Bishop into the SeaLife fold, or so he claimed. Ezra didn't wait but added both Ace and King to the call so they could all discuss Jack's intel together and divvy up the workload.

Jack felt much better after talking to all three of them. Ezra was an old friend from their days in the military, but Jack's brothers helped ground him. They'd always traveled as a group, except for the rare instances—more, in recent years—where they took a break from each other and all went off in different directions, in search of adventure.

Well, they'd called it *adventure*, but what they really were doing was looking for mates. They hadn't really said it in so many words, but all three of them had felt the urges of their bear halves to find a special woman and settle down. Ace and King had it worse, being older than Jack, but he'd felt it strongly in the past few years, and their latest solo adventures—embarked on after helping Ezra with a tricky mission in South Dakota—had netted two of the three brothers lifelong companions.

Jack was happy for them, but he was left as the odd man out. He was younger than Ace and King by a good number of years. Shifters had longer lifespans than humans, so while they might appear close in age, there was actually a decade or so between each of them. Jack was a bit jealous of the happiness his two older brothers had found. He wanted some of that for himself, but he knew it wasn't really up to him.

The Goddess they all served played a big part in finding the perfect mate. If it wasn't time, Jack wouldn't find the woman meant for him. Then again, if it *was* time… Well, Kiki was an attractive candidate, even if she was *just* a human. Jack didn't care, and he wouldn't let anybody else give her a hard time, if she proved to be his mate.

No, he'd love her and protect her and spend years making her happy. He wanted that so bad, but he knew fate and the Goddess had a lot to say in the matter. If it was right, he'd discover it soon enough. If not, no amount of hoping would make it so. That was just the way it was, and fretting over it was getting him nowhere.

Jack set to work, going through the paperwork he'd been studying about the factory and looking for data he might have missed, now that he knew some of the players. He paid special attention to Boehm's reports and that of the lab manager. He had all their personnel files, but he couldn't help but feel that the files were missing vital data… Such as which of the people in the factory were serving darkness.

Around midnight, Jack left the hotel and rolled his Harley down the road a piece before starting the engine. He didn't really want everyone in town to know what he was up to. Luckily, there were enough wide open spaces between the small town and the factory that he felt confident nobody had particularly noted his passage.

He also took the precaution of shutting down the motor

and coming at the plant from the woodland side. He stashed his bike under a welcoming tree and quickly disrobed. He left his clothes in his saddle bags and shifted to his bear form. The bear would have better luck blending into the woodland night, and his senses were even sharper when he wore his fur.

First, he did a sweep of the surrounding area to learn the lay of the land. He'd seen topographical maps and other maps that denoted the ownership of the land around the plant. He skirted the perimeter and put his nose to the earth, looking for any sign of magic.

He didn't sense anything far out from the plant, but as he drew nearer, he definitely felt something rubbing his fur the wrong way. He eyed the warehouse area that Kiki had talked about, but the area was too open to chance going much closer. Not unless he had a real reason to do so, and at the moment, he couldn't sense anything going on there worth investigating. The place was empty. The lights out. Everything was as it should be for a plant that was closed for the night.

He did a little more nosing around, but aside from a feeling of something not being altogether right, he didn't sense anything else on his circuit of the property. He'd do more tomorrow night, but all in all, he wasn't displeased with the night's reconnaissance. Jack padded carefully back to his bike and made sure everything was as he'd left it before he shifted. He got dressed and retraced his steps back to his hotel.

The recon had left him with an uneasy feeling, as if something was going on beneath the surface that he just couldn't sense. He'd encountered that kind of feeling only once before in his life, when he'd gone up against someone using black magic. Most others wouldn't notice a difference, but the various flavors and feels of different kinds of magic were kind of a specialty of Jack's.

Evil was one thing, but black magic was the magic of the unseen. It was a stealthy magic. A trickster. Few practitioners of the dark arts took the time to hide their evil in a blanket of black magic. It was a particular skill, and many of the evil mages he and his brothers had come up against in the past didn't care to hide their motives or leanings.

Whoever was doing things at the paper mill, though, they were doing it in stealth mode. That set his senses on alert. This just might be a trickier mission than he'd thought, but he felt sure he was up to the challenge. He just hoped he could keep Kiki out of it and safe, if worse came to worst.

Then again, she might be the one hiding her true nature and dabbling in black, unseen magic. He hoped to the Goddess she wasn't the one causing the trouble. He was already attached to her and would hate to have to shut her down.

His instincts said it couldn't possibly be Kiki. No way. But black magic was like that. It hid in plain sight. It wore innocent clothing to disguise evil behind layers of darkness. It was the utter lack of Light, and the true winter of the soul.

Could Kiki really be hiding that kind of evil behind her innocent façade? It made Jack's soul hurt to think it could even be a possibility, but he had to be ultra-cautious. Those who dealt in black magic could be some of the most deadly and deceitful. Whoever it was, he would have to be on his guard, at all times, and on his toes. He was all alone out here, the only one to stand against this evil. If Jack fell, his brothers wouldn't be there, this time, to pick him up.

No, if he fell this time, it could very well be all over for him. It was a sobering thought, and he vowed to be careful as he got ready to sleep. Morning came early, and he had a lot to do tomorrow.

He couldn't help but think about Kiki as he drifted off to sleep. She was just so darn pretty and came across as breathtakingly innocent. It would be a real shame if he wound up having to kill her.

The next morning, Kiki was already in her office when Jack walked past her door. He peered in unashamedly and waved hello on his way to Bob Boehm's office, just down the corridor. She looked delicious, and her pretty face immediately flushed with heat as he strode past. Good. He liked her reaction. He just hoped it was real.

On that troubling thought, he knocked perfunctorily on Boehm's office door before opening it and walking in. Bob looked up angrily at Jack's intrusion but held back whatever angry words were dancing on the tip of his tongue. Seeing the man's struggle to be nice, Jack smiled.

"I noticed an empty office up front as I passed by," Jack said brightly. "I'm going to park myself there, unless you have any objection. I'll be calling for certain files, now and then. I'd appreciate it if you'd give the clerical staff a heads up."

Not really giving Boehm time to answer, Jack backed out of the doorway and went back to the office he'd spotted. It was right next door to Kiki's. Oh yeah, that would suit him just fine.

He went in and started to rearrange the basic furniture, that had clearly not been used in a while, to suit his own preferences. For one thing, the desk had to be pushed out a bit to accommodate his big frame. He was a bear, and on top of that, he was one of the larger North American grizzlies in existence. Larger than both his brothers, he was the muscle in their trio. Or he had been.

A little pang for the loss of the camaraderie of his siblings hit him, but, he reminded himself, Ace and King were much better off. They had mates. They might soon be starting families of their own. The wild bachelor days of the three of them traveling and working together were over, but Jack couldn't really begrudge his brothers their happiness.

He rolled the tiny office chair out from behind the desk and went in search of something larger. He'd seen an executive style chair in the conference room that would work for him much better than this tiny thing. He made short work of switching out the two chairs and rolled the bigger one back to his new digs.

All the noise next door must've alerted Kiki. She peeked out of her door, and her eyes widened in surprise when she saw him rolling the larger chair down the hall toward the office next to hers. He grinned at her.

"Hi, neighbor."

CHAPTER 7

Kiki gasped when she realized the new noisy neighbor was, indeed, Jack Bishop. He'd commandeered the vacant office next to hers and was apparently rearranging things to suit his tastes. Including snagging Mr. Boehm's conference room chair. She'd accidently sat in it, just once, and had learned not to do it ever again. Mr. Boehm was very particular about his things, and he'd staked a claim on that big chair in the conference room for himself. She'd almost pay to see what happened when he found out that Jack had taken it without so much as a by-your-leave.

Kiki went back into her office and tried hard to ignore the sounds coming from next door. She couldn't help hearing when Jack called various people, asking for paperwork to be delivered to his new home away from home, and within a half hour, folks were dropping by next door, bringing files he'd requested. She heard it all because, throughout, he kept his office door open, and she realized, she was listening intently.

When she figured out she was intentionally eavesdropping, she shook her head and told herself to mind her own business. She had more than enough work of her own to do without keeping tabs on her new neighbor. That thought firmly in mind, Kiki set about untangling another mess her predecessor had left and knew no more until lunchtime.

The only reason she knew it was lunchtime was because Jack knocked on her doorframe and leaned in, smiling that devastating half-smile of his that made her tummy clench. Damn. He was just too good looking.

"Lunch?" he asked. The simple invitation set her nerves aflutter.

"Sure. I was just going to go to the cafeteria," she told him. "I don't have time for much else because I've got a conference call with the state inspector at two."

"No problem. I was going to check out the cafeteria, too. I wouldn't mind having company, if you're willing to be seen with the big bad wolf from corporate." He included a wolfish grin with his remark that made her want to giggle.

"I don't mind," she said, coming out from behind her desk. "Truth is, I don't know many people here yet, and I usually end up just getting something to go and eating it at my desk."

She closed her office door behind her, and they started walking down the hall toward the rear of the building. The cafeteria was at the halfway point between the office and lab area and the plant itself—which consisted of several areas and a giant warehouse, as well as the log yard out back where the raw materials came in—so it was a bit of a walk from where they were at the front of the office building.

"Nobody invited you to join them?" Disbelief rang true in his tone.

"Not so far," she replied, shaking her head.

"What is *wrong* with these people?"

Kiki enjoyed the light banter and his teasing as they walked through the office area. She noted quite a few heads popped up from within the cubicles as they passed by, nosy gazes following Kiki and Jack's progress toward the door leading deeper into the building. She felt a little conspicuous, but she wouldn't let their rudeness ruin her enjoyment of the moment. Jack made her feel special. It had been a long time since a man been so nice to her. Even if it was just some ploy of his to get the information he needed for his own job, she didn't really care. It was nice to feel special, even if she knew it wouldn't last.

How could it? Jack was a man of the world. A heartthrob. Probably a heartbreaker. She was just a farm girl from rural Pennsylvania. Unremarkable except for the fact of her education. In her neck of the woods, her family was thought odd and much too progressive for allowing, and even encouraging, their children to go and study at colleges and universities.

The fact that some from every generation returned to work the farm was seen as an aberration, rather than as the result of someone choosing farm life over city life after having experienced both. Kiki didn't begrudge her neighbors their beliefs. They were good people who did their best, but some of their ideas about education were a little backward, in her opinion. That didn't stop her from being friendly toward them and helping out when she could. Her family had never forgotten their roots and the fact that hiding within that religious community for many years had probably saved them all from being killed as witches in the old country.

Kiki often wished she had just a little touch of the magic that ran in her family. It would have made life easier, she often thought, though her more gifted siblings claimed the opposite was true. Regardless, she had to do the best she could with the plain old human senses and observations she could make, and her conclusion about the office staff was that they were a bunch of nosy ninnies.

Jack opened the door for her at the far end of the office section and politely held it for her. She felt like a queen being escorted by some kind of noble courtier who made every polite gesture and kept her laughing all the way to their destination with astute observations about the things they saw along their path.

By the time they reached the cafeteria, Kiki was feeling totally relaxed in his presence, as he'd probably intended all along. He ushered her to the serving area where they both picked up trays and wound through the line of serving stations.

"What is Carol doing back there?" Jack asked in a low voice that didn't carry beyond the two of them. All amusement had fled from his voice as he looked at the situation evolving behind the servers, in the kitchen beyond.

"I think she runs tests for cleanliness and the presence of bacteria, on occasion. I was told they pride themselves on the cleanliness of the kitchen." Kiki shrugged and grabbed a prepackaged muffin and a small carton of milk. She generally didn't eat a large lunch, and nothing they were serving today appealed to her.

She noticed Jack bypassed the hot food as well, which seemed odd. Judging by their dinner together, he ate a lot. She'd thought for sure he'd pile his tray high with meat and potatoes, but he didn't. He grabbed a banana and some prepackaged cereal along with a matching small container of milk and a bottle of apple juice.

He didn't say anything further until they were seated a good distance from anyone else. He'd chosen the table. He'd also paid for her meal, over her objections. He was still polite and charming, but she couldn't help but notice how distracted he'd become since discovering Carol from the lab doing something in the kitchen. Why was he so interested in that?

Jack got a very bad feeling about the entire cafeteria setup. The fact that the lab hag was behind the counter, doing something with the pots on the stove made every alarm in his arsenal start flashing big warnings. Only the prepackaged foods felt normal to his senses. Everything else had a faint magical taint.

The taint of black, hidden magic.

Damn.

He'd hoped he'd been wrong, but the truth was staring him in the face. That lab woman should not be in the kitchen. That was his first clue. The second was the feeling that each dish on offer had a magical miasma flowing in and around it.

The logical option would be some kind of magical poison that was being fed into everyone in the plant via this cafeteria. How easy it would be to take control of everyone, all at once, with them none the wiser. It was subtle. Concealed. Like all black magic, veiled to all except the one who wove the spell.

The fact that the magic was secreted in the food told Jack he was, in all likelihood, dealing with a potion witch. And the most likely candidate for that was Carol, the lab hag, who was still doing something in the kitchen that she should not have been doing.

If she'd really been running tests, she would have taken a few swabs and been gone in a few minutes. The reality was, she was actually stirring pots on the stove. It looked to him like she was cooking. No way was that part of any test he'd ever heard about. There was no reason for Carol to be cooking while the regular kitchen staff stood by and let her. Unless…

Unless they were already under her spell.

Jack looked around the cafeteria, trying to be casual. Sure enough, the dead gazes of the people eating the cooked foods was obvious, now that he knew what to look for. They were all being slowly—magically—poisoned by whatever it was Carol was doing back there in the kitchen.

And there was nothing Jack could do about it at the moment. He bit back a curse and ate his cereal with deliberate motions. Thankfully, Kiki hadn't chosen anything that was tainted. If she had, he would have had to come up with a way to get her to choose something else, but as it was, she'd gone for the prepackaged stuff, as he had after one quick, sickening look at what was being offered on the chow lines.

"I don't think I like this cafeteria," he muttered at one point. He'd asked Kiki some questions about her work that had kept her talking while he'd been thinking, but she'd wound down, and it was his turn to make conversation. Unfortunately, his stomach churned at the feel of the black magic being consumed—and consuming—all around them, and his heart wasn't in small talk. "Do you want to go outside and take a walk?" he asked, standing when he noticed she'd already finished her muffin.

She looked surprised but quickly sipped the last of her milk and followed him to the big trash cans set up on one end of the large room. They disposed of their trash and headed outside, much to his relief. The mood in that cafeteria had become oppressive to his magical senses. He breathed deep of the clean outside air and headed them off toward the woods that bordered the property.

He felt like he'd just had a narrow escape, and after a few deep breaths to clear his head, he realized that Carol had, most likely, been actively working a spell. What kind of spell? Something to trap him? That felt right, but was it to trap him, specifically, or everyone, in general?

The latter made more sense based on how many people were eating that tainted food. She had probably done the math and realized there were going to be a few that escaped her net. She had to have some kind of contingency plan to get them later. Which put both himself and Kiki in deep danger. He turned to her, keeping his voice low and urgent.

"Remember what you told me about the warehouse?" he said, trying to make his words oblique, just in case someone could hear, though nobody was around that he could see. Still, he wouldn't take chances.

Kiki nodded slowly, her face heating slightly. "I'm so embarrassed. Forget I said anything, okay? It was probably just my imagination running wild."

"That's the thing," he told her, turning to meet her gaze, trying to impress upon her how serious he felt about what he was about to say. "You weren't imagining anything. I don't want you to eat or drink anything anyone gives you from that cafeteria." Her eyes widened, and he revised his instruction. "You know, to be on the safe side, just don't eat or drink anything anyone gives you here. Something is definitely off in that cafeteria, and it's possible you and I are both in danger because we're outsiders."

That was as good a reason as any he could come up with

on the spot like this. She was looking at him strangely but nodded slowly in agreement.

"Honestly, something about the food they offer has never appealed to me," she said quietly, almost experimentally. As if she were testing the words as they came out of her mouth, putting sounds to the more nebulous thoughts in her mind. "I've never eaten anything they make in the kitchen."

Relief flooded him. "Good. Best if you keep it that way," he told her.

"You think someone's tampering with the food or something?" she asked, frowning up at him.

He nodded gravely. "Or something. Look, I can't explain why I feel the way I do, but Carol should not have been back there that long if she was just running a test."

"You suspect Carol?"

"I have to," he said. "She was in a place she had no right to be, and was doing something with the food. Stirring pots and adding things to them. I was watching her."

"You were?" Kiki shook her head. "I didn't realize."

"I'm glad. I was trying not to look as if I was watching, but I was. She was back there the entire time we were in that room. No test swab—even a series of them—takes that long to perform. And, like I said, she was messing with the food, itself. I don't know what she was doing, or what she hopes to accomplish, but she's definitely up to something. For your own safety, you should steer clear of her, whenever possible."

They had reached the woods and walked along the dirt path that ran the perimeter of the property in this area. Jack had noticed it the night before on his scouting expedition and, he realized today, that people from the plant walked this path during their breaks. Even now, a few people could be seen walking some distance from them, on the pathway.

"Do you think she's drugging people? And, if so, to what end?" Kiki seemed thoughtful rather than scared, which surprised him. She was made of tougher stuff than he'd thought.

"I'm not sure what she's doing," he hedged.

"Surely, it's not poison!" She kept her voice low, but he could hear the shocked disbelief.

"I didn't say that," Jack clarified. "It's probably nothing lethal, but more likely, something to influence people."

"A drug, then," she said, nodding to herself. "It would have to be something subtle, but being drugged would tend to explain what I saw that time."

He noticed she was cautious about saying exactly what she'd seen. Kiki was better at intrigue than he would have credited.

"It's surprisingly comforting to think that they were all high," she went on when he didn't say anything. "That's probably why they participated in…that."

The look on her face was something Jack thought couldn't be faked. It held just the right amount of suppressed horror and disgust that she tried to conceal from anyone who might be watching, but the fear of what she'd seen was clear in her eyes. No way could she hide anything sinister behind those baby blues. Right?

Jack realized he'd already made that decision. He was trusting Kiki. For better or worse, he'd taken her into his confidence. Whatever happened, he'd gone with his instincts that said she was an innocent in all this. If he was wrong…well…he'd deal with that when it happened. He just hoped and prayed to the Mother of All that he wasn't wrong. It would break his heart if that turned out to be the case.

"I think you'd better pack a lunch from now on. A can of pop, too. Or whatever you like to drink," he counselled. "I wouldn't take a chance on anything from here."

They were near the end of the small loop in the path, and lunchtime was almost up, so they started heading back toward the building by unspoken mutual consent. Kiki's steps dragged a bit, as if she didn't want to go back inside. Jack knew how she felt, but it wouldn't do to let anyone— especially Carol—realize that they knew, or even suspected, anything.

"Don't let them get to you," he said softly. "And don't let

them see you noticed anything, okay?"

Startled eyes rose to meet his. *Damn.* She looked scared. That wouldn't do.

Jack reached down and took her hand. The alarm in her gaze turned to something else. Something better for the others to see, if they were looking.

"If anyone asks, you're uncomfortable because the guy from corporate was hitting on you, okay?" He smiled at her shocked expression. "Whatever you do, don't let anyone realize you're uncomfortable because of what we think might be going on here. Do you understand?" She nodded. "Good. Now, forcefully tug your hand out of mine and walk away. Don't look, but we've got an audience."

CHAPTER 8

Kiki successfully resisted the instinct to look around to see who was watching and followed instructions. Jack was scaring her. Well, not Jack, *per se*, but the entire situation was frightening. In one way, she was glad to have confirmation that she wasn't crazy. It was oddly comforting to have someone else feel the same way about this place as she did.

In another way, it was even scarier than it had been before. Questions zoomed around her mind, making her wonder what was really going on here. Was it real? Or was Jack humoring her? Perhaps making sport of her?

She didn't think so. She tugged her hand from his and spun around to head quickly back toward the door to the building. She almost ran into Cindy, the receptionist. So, she'd been the one noticing them. Kiki almost groaned. Cindy was one of the worst gossips in the entire place. Surely, the story would be all over the plant by quitting time.

Kiki went in the door and marched straight to her office. She didn't want to talk to anyone, and she was glad when nobody stopped her to chat. Not that many people here were friendly toward her, but they were definitely nosy, and a few had chatted with her, on occasion, seeming to be more interested in interrogating her about her past jobs and how she liked this one than answering any of her questions. She'd learned to avoid most of them. She didn't like being so very obviously grilled for information. Especially when she had no idea what their motive was or what they were hoping to learn from her.

Kiki settled behind her desk, hearing Jack go into his own office next door a few minutes later. She set to work, and before she knew it, a half hour had passed. That's when Cindy poked her head in Kiki's door, all smiles.

"I'm going to get some coffee. Do you want some?"

Never before had Cindy offered to get Kiki anything. Kiki tried to hide her surprise.

"No, but thanks for asking," she replied brightly, as if touched by the offer.

Rather than leaving, Cindy stepped into Kiki's office. "Did I see you outside with the new guy?" Cindy's voice dropped to a conspiratorial tone, and she jerked her head toward the wall separating Kiki's office from Jack's. "It looked like he was holding your hand."

"Uh…" Crap! Cindy was looking for information, and Kiki knew she had to follow Jack's advice, much as she didn't want to paint him as a villain. "You know how these corporate types are. He's a little…um…aggressive in going after what he wants."

Cindy's brows lowered in fake concern. "If he's harassing you, there are people you can tell. Sick Mr. Crumb from H.R. on his butt, and he'll stop."

"No, it's not that bad. I think I handled it," Kiki said quickly. The last thing she wanted to do was get Jack in trouble for something that was far from the truth.

"Well, if he tries anything again, you really should report him. That kind of stuff isn't allowed anymore," Cindy said somewhat self-righteously.

Kiki knew enough about the younger woman by now to know that her supposed concern was a tissue of lies. Cindy didn't care about anyone other than herself. If she was offering support, there had to be an ulterior motive. Clearly, she was just trying to get some juicy gossip.

Much as Kiki didn't like the rumor that would start now, after saying what she'd just said about Jack, she was glad he'd provided the cover story. Even though it would put him in a bad light, he'd given her a ready-made excuse that didn't involve evil feelings and secret ceremonies in the dark of the night.

Jack heard every word of the low-voiced conversation next door. Shifter hearing was better than regular folks'. He could hear the reluctance in Kiki's tone when she did as he'd suggested and all but accused him of being an overbearing asshole. That was all right with him. He could take it. Frankly, he didn't give a shit what these people thought of him, as long as they kept Kiki out of their sights.

He'd been sitting in his borrowed office, pretending to work and trying to reason out in his mind what had been going on in that cafeteria. He'd come to the conclusion that Carol had been casting a wide net, slowly bringing every employee that ate in the cafeteria—which was the vast majority of them—under her spell. Only a very few were clear of her taint by now, probably.

But to what end? What was Carol's goal here? If she was the potion witch, as he believed, then she could probably whip something up in her cauldron to sap the life energy—and any possible magical energy—from her followers. There was also something to be said for the group energy of that many people participating in whatever rituals Carol led in that warehouse. Even if they weren't consciously aware of what they were doing, their presence would help fuel whatever spell Carol was weaving, or whatever evil she was summoning.

Having a bunch of entranced people at her beck and call was not only an ego trip, but also a power base. With that many people under her spell, she could do a lot of damage. Their energies would help her create potions and cast spells that were much more potent than if she'd simply used her own power.

Jack wondered how long it would be before Carol started targeting those who hadn't already partaken of whatever it was she had been brewing up in the cafeteria. He suspected it would happen sooner rather than later. In fact, Cindy's invitation to fetch coffee for Kiki might've been a ploy to get her to drink whatever poisonous potion was going around.

Thankfully, he'd been able to warn Kiki, and she had turned down the offer. He suspected they'd start resorting to more forceful means if they couldn't get her to join the herd, but for now, it seemed she was off the hook. Jack resolved to keep an even closer eye on Kiki. She was his sole ally in this madhouse, at the moment, and he wanted to keep her safe.

The easiest way, of course, would be to get her to quit this job, but he knew it wasn't so simple. She had to have income. She had obligations in town, including to her landlord, whoever that may be. He was still interested in finding out who owned the fairy cottage, but there were more pressing matters, at the moment. Like finding out what Carol's end-game really was. What was she planning? What was she trying to do by bewitching all these people? It had to be something big.

The answer couldn't be anything good.

Jack heard Cindy finally leave Kiki's office, and then, the slow shuffling of papers and click of computer keys resumed as Kiki went back to work. Jack did the same. He had a lot of ground to cover here, and some of it was very mundane, indeed. The files wouldn't read themselves, so he settled down for an afternoon of reading.

By the time five o'clock rolled around, he was more than ready to leave the files behind. He gathered his stuff and followed Kiki as she left the building. He wasn't too obvious about it, but he followed her car on his Harley, keeping back far enough not to draw attention but close enough to be certain she made it back to her little cottage safely.

He was pleased to find that he wasn't followed. Apparently, surveillance on him—or Kiki—hadn't been implemented yet. He had a feeling the longer he stayed, the more suspicious of him the powers-that-be would become, and eventually, they'd have him watched. But, for now, he was free of a tail, and he decided he would stop and have a further chat with Kiki. He really wanted to impress upon her how important it was to tread lightly at work.

He probably shouldn't take the chance, but he was truly concerned for her safety. Something about her made him want to watch over her at all times, though he knew that would be impossible. Still, he wanted to be as certain as he could that she would take this situation seriously and stay as safe as possible.

With that thought in mind, Jack drove all around Kiki's cottage, getting the lay of the land. The little house backed onto a stream. There was a wide garden area between the little creek and the backdoor of the house. Jack decided to park his bike at the hotel and make it look as if he'd gone in for the night if anybody should happen to be keeping tabs on his whereabouts. He'd sneak out of the hotel and go around to Kiki's backdoor as soon as it started to get dark.

Plan firmly in mind, he set about implementing it. The first thing he would do would be to stop at that great Italian place and order some food to go.

Kiki didn't know what to think when she heard a light knock on her backdoor. Nobody came to the backdoor. Nobody had ever approached her cottage from the back, where the trees, shrubs and plants had gone wild in the most picturesque sort of way. She went to the door hesitantly, unsure if she should open it.

"Kiki? It's me, Jack."

Hearing his voice, she opened the door, still confused as to why he might be there—especially at the backdoor. He stood tall under the porch roof, handsome as anything she'd ever seen and holding up a large bag with the Italian restaurant's logo on it.

"I brought dinner, if you're hungry," he told her, his smile was a little devilish. As if he was tempting her to give him a chance.

She was such a goner. All Jack had to do was crook his little finger, and she'd jump at the chance to spend time in his presence. That he'd come bearing gifts was even better. She backed up and invited him in. The kitchen was at the back of the house, and the door opened straight into the little space where she spent a lot of time cooking and eating at the small bistro table in the corner. She went to the table as he came in, filling the small cottage with his exceeding large presence.

"I hope you don't mind my barging in," he said, his whole demeanor absolutely charming.

"No, but why did you come to the back?" she asked, curious. She assumed he was trying to be cautious about them being seen together, but she wanted to hear it from him.

"After today's lunch incident, I figured it was better to lay low. After all, I'm supposed to be some sort of chauvinist masher, right?" His grin invited her to laugh with him, but she truly felt bad about that.

"I'm really sorry," she told him. "But you did say—"

He held up one hand and shook his head. "It's okay. I heard Cindy questioning you. I'm glad you used that excuse. The less they think we might be working together, the better. Being seen as my friend could only cause more problems, because I intend to shut them down. Whatever little scheme they have going on there, I'm going to put an end to it before somebody gets hurt."

"You really think it's that dangerous?" She sat down, her knees going weak at the open acknowledgment of her fears.

"I will never lie to you, Kiki," he told her, his tone turning serious. "I think whatever is going on at the plant is something very sinister." He paused. "And very dangerous."

She'd thought the same, but hearing him say it flat out like that took the wind out of her sails. She just sat at her kitchen table, blinking, trying to take it all in and figure out what she was going to do.

"Let's eat," he said, placing the take-out bag on her kitchen counter. "We can talk more over dinner. If you don't mind my inviting myself to dine, that is." He gave her a small lopsided smile that she couldn't resist.

Kiki smiled back at him, though she was still a bit shaky, and got to her feet. She took down plates and glasses from the cabinets while he unpacked the shopping bag that smelled divine.

"I got the gnocchi for you, but if you'd rather have something different, there's also chicken cutlets parmigiana, those rolled eggplant things, and a meatball hero." He named each as he removed them from the large bag.

"Do you always eat so much?" she asked.

"Lunch wasn't much, and it was a long time ago. I'm so hungry I could eat a horse," he told her with a good-natured grin. "Come on, call dibs on what you want before I attack the rest."

Grinning with him, she took the container with the gnocchi. She was predictable, she supposed, but she was touched that he'd remembered what she'd liked and had taken the time to order it for her. His thoughtfulness was touching.

"I didn't get wine this time," he went on, pulling a two-liter bottle of pop from the bottom of the bag. "Hope you like cola."

"Love it," she replied, already spooning out a portion of the gnocchi onto her plate.

She gave him a dinner plate and utensils, and he proceeded to pile it high with the contents of two more of the containers before taking a seat opposite her at the table. She'd brought over the bottle and glasses while he was dishing up his dinner and got some ice cubes from the freezer for each glass. Napkins and the salt and pepper shaker were the final touch.

They ate silently for a while, but Kiki's mind raced with questions and conjecture. She was busy thinking while he ate, and eventually, it was Jack that broke the silence.

"I noticed the star at the apex of the roof. What's that all about?" His question surprised her.

"It's a thing we do here in Pennsylvania. A lot of the farms have stars on them. That and hex signs."

"Hex signs? What are those?" he asked between bites.

"It's a local thing. Part of Pennsylvania Dutch tradition. Hundreds of years ago, when the first of them came from Germany and the surrounding countries, they started putting hex signs on their barns and buildings. Some say, they are symbols that are supposed to bring good luck or protection. Depending on what the sign is, and what color it is, there are different meanings that evolved over time." She'd grown up with such things and found it interesting to be able to explain some of the traditions of her family—in a generic sort of way—to an outsider.

"So, what does the star mean?" he asked as they continued to eat.

"Stars are generally thought to bring good luck, but they do have different nuances depending on how many points they have. Four points is the Morning Star, the Cross, or the Star of Bethlehem, with all the associated connotations. Five points, like on this house, is referred to sometimes, as a Nautical Star or Compass Star. It's supposed to be the most potent form for protection and good luck. A six-pointed star is probably among the most common with the plain folk. It symbolizes the six days it took to create the world or the six attributes of our creator—wisdom, power, majesty, love, mercy, and justice. It's called a hexagram. There are eight-, ten- and twelve-pointed stars, as well."

"You seem to know a lot about this," Jack commented. His expression invited her to share more.

"My family has a sideline making and selling hex signs to the tourist trade," she admitted. "It's something one of my brothers decided to do a few years back, and we all supported his decision and helped him get the business off the ground."

"Sounds like you have a great family that helps each other. What did you contribute to your brother's business idea?" he probed, snagging more food off the counter and dumping it on his plate.

She laughed, thinking back on that time in her life. "I did just about everything. I cut out circle blanks. I silkscreened the mass-produced ones. I prepped the boards for my brother who did the high-end, hand-painted items. I delivered them to the tourist traps and handled some of the direct mail to his online customers. You name it, I did it. Actually, helping him was what made me want to study business in school."

There was a natural lull while she ate a bit more, but it wasn't uncomfortable. Jack was easy company, and she was very much afraid she was getting to like being around him a bit too much.

"So, what are some of the other symbols?" he asked finally, calling her wandering attention back to the easy conversation they'd been having.

"Hearts for love, of course," she answered immediately. "Tulips for faith, and *distelfinks* for luck and happiness."

His brows drew together in puzzlement. "What in the world is a *distelfink*?"

She laughed and explained. "Sorry. A stylized bird. That's just what we call them."

"What about the colors? You said something about different colors having different meanings."

She was pleased he'd remembered and surprised that he seemed genuinely interested.

"Well, black makes up a lot of the outline of most designs. It stands for protection. It also binds everything together," she told him. "White is purity or the power of the moon. Orange is for abundance. Red for passion and art. Yellow for health, love, or the sun. Green for fertility, growth, or success. Blue for peace and calm. Purple for royalty and sacred things. And brown for the earth and strength."

"And this all comes from the Amish?" He looked skeptical. "I thought they were all heavy-duty Christians."

"Oh, they are. But they came from a culture that had a lot of old-world traditions, and the culture is sort of frozen in time. Imagine a society of three hundred years ago when people were closer to the earth, sun, moon and stars. They farmed the land, and there were no cars or televisions. No man on the moon. No airplanes in the sky." She sighed. "It's hard for people to imagine, but the Amish have successfully shut themselves away from most of the modern world. They still live on their farms and follow the ways of their parents, grandparents, great-grandparents, and on down the line."

"That's pretty amazing," he said, his voice going contemplative. "I've never spent any time in this part of the country, so I guess I never much thought about how those folk might live."

"My family used to be part of it, and I still can't really imagine living that way," she admitted. "I don't think I could have been happy being denied a university education. Plus, I would have been married years ago and probably had a bunch of kids running around already." She made a face. "While I have nothing against kids—and I want some of my own, for sure—I don't really agree with starting so young and having so many in such quick succession. But that's just me. I guess it's fine, if that's what they really want—and some do, I'm sure."

Why was she talking about having kids? Kiki felt her cheeks heat with a blush because of the topic. Having babies made her think about making babies, and the last thing she needed to talk about with this man was any allusions to sex. For heaven's sake! Jack was walking, talking sex on a stick! She didn't need anything to help her imagine what it might be like to do the deed with him. On the contrary, she needed help *not* thinking about it.

CHAPTER 9

Jack was charmed by the shy blush on Kiki's face. She was, hands down, one of the most interesting women he'd ever met. She knew about a lot of things that he found fascinating, and the glimpse she'd given him into the beliefs and mysticism of the local farming communities was something he'd never expected. He had figured the Amish were somewhat fanatical Christians, and that was it.

What she'd revealed to him was that they had even older beliefs about symbols and portents. Her revelations had also told him a lot about her family and her own beliefs, which gave him hope that she wasn't as narrow-minded as many human beings. There was clearly more depth to her beliefs and customs than he had thought.

Shifters, for the most part, believed in the Goddess. Maiden, Mother and Crone, She was the Lady of Light. She was the goodness in all creation. The infinite opponent of evil.

Jack was Her servant. Always had been. He and his brothers had chosen young to always be on the good side of the equation, and they'd spent most of their lives, to date, fighting the good fight. They'd joined the military and served in many far-flung places in the Special Forces. When they'd finally gotten out of the service, they'd continued to do what they could whenever they encountered evil.

That had been happening more and more in recent years. Change was coming to the world, and it wasn't necessarily a good change. Just about everywhere the brothers had traveled, they'd come up against servants of evil trying to get away with something. Usually, their plots involved harming innocent people. When that came to light, the brothers always went into action.

As the last of the food he'd brought disappeared, Jack realized he soon wouldn't have any further excuse for lingering in her presence. He had plans for later tonight. He was going to prowl the perimeter of the factory again, in his bear form. He hoped to venture closer and get a more detailed look at a few areas of interest.

That was later. Right now, he was enjoying his time with Kiki. She really was the most fascinating woman. She stood and put a kettle on while he gathered up the dirty dishes and brought them over to the sink.

"I'm making tea, but I can make coffee, if you prefer that," she said softly, standing beside him in the small kitchen as they both worked.

"Tea is fine," he told her as he began washing the dishes.

"Oh, you don't have to do that," she objected as he grabbed the sponge and soap and began working on the tomato sauce stuck on the plates.

"It's no problem," he told her. "I'm the youngest, so my brothers always stuck me with these kinds of jobs. Honestly, washing dishes is one of the nicer things they made me do."

She chuckled. "Let me guess. You were the one who had to clean the bathroom, too?"

He touched his nose with a soapy finger and winked at her. "Got it in one," he said, congratulating her on her guess. "Anything gross or disgusting was my job when we all shared quarters. I'd like to see them get away with that nonsense now that they're married, though." Jack smiled at the thought. His new sisters-in-law didn't seem like the kind of gals who would take any crap from his brothers.

Kiki worked quietly, making the tea, and brought out a big jar of honey. Jack's mouth started to water. It was true about bears loving honey, and he was no exception. But this jar didn't have any sort of commercial labelling on it. It was just a big clear glass jar.

"Is that local honey?" he asked, following her motions as she set everything out on the table.

"Better than local. It's from my family's farm. We keep a number of hives and collect some of the honey and beeswax every year. This is one of last year's," she told him proudly. He couldn't wait to taste it.

"That's great. I really love honey," he told her. She would soon learn the truth of that when he put a giant ol' dollop in the tea she was pouring for them both.

Jack finished with the last dish and put it on the drying rack, then wiped his hands and returned to the table. He sat opposite her, the big jar of honey between them, in pride of place at the center of the little round table. Kiki finished pouring the tea. Chamomile, his nose told him. He knew the plant, though he'd never had it as a tea before.

Kiki lifted the jar of honey and placed it in front of her. Both hands on the jar, she said some words. Germanic sounding words. Her eyes were closed briefly as the poetic words from long ago and far away spilled from her mouth.

Jack didn't know what, exactly, she was saying, but it had the feeling of a prayer…or a charm. Some kind of benevolent blessing. He was intrigued as she opened her eyes and smiled self-consciously.

"Sorry. It's traditional to say the bee blessing so they always come back."

She then opened the jar, and the delicate scent of wildflowers and fruit trees wafted to his sensitive nose. The honey smelled like the purest sunshine to him. He couldn't wait to taste it.

"I've never heard of a bee blessing," he said, just to buy himself some time so he didn't make a fool of himself over a tablespoon or two of honey.

"It's one of those things from the old country," she told him. "I don't know where it all started, but my brother looked it up one time and told us that there was a famous bee blessing found in the Vatican Library. They said it was written in the ninth century and had come from the monastery in Lorsch, Germany. It's similar to ours, but I think the language has drifted quite a bit from that Old High German version in the Catholic book." She offered him the jar and a big spoon, talking while he refrained from taking too much. "There's an Anglo-Saxon charm that's similar, that they say keeps honey bees from swarming. I like that one because it refers to the bees as victory-women, which some have interpreted to be Valkyries or shield maidens. I like that idea." She smiled. "All those lady bees wearing little horns and brandishing a sword as they go about fighting the good fight every day."

"The sword being their stinger and the horns, their antennae?" he asked, puzzling out the image she painted with her words.

She grinned brightly at him. "Exactly!" He handed the jar back to her, though he really wanted more of that scrumptious honey. "All those little warrior women, buzzing around, doing their jobs and bringing home the bacon."

"Or the pollen, as it were," he said, smiling at her over the rim of his steaming tea cup as he raised it to his mouth.

It smelled great. Slightly magical but wholesome and good. The steam alone stroked his senses with a gentle flow of garden magic. That's when it came to him. If he had to describe Kiki's nascent magic as anything, he'd call her a garden witch.

Or, maybe, it was this house and the honey and herbs in the tea that was making him think that way. So far, Kiki hadn't shown him that she had any magic of her own to call on. She knew a few basic charms, but those were things anybody could do. The magic in the salt ward and the honey blessing wasn't coming from the caster of the spell, but from the ingredients put into them. The salt. The honey. Those were the tangible forms given power by the spoken words. The magic was in them, not coming from the person saying the words.

Real witches and magical folk gave of their own power, or consciously siphoned it from other places and formed it to their own will. Good mages took the power from the natural things around them, with permission, from the elements of earth, air, fire and water. Timeless things. Powerful things that would lend their strength to a mage of good will.

Evil folk took power from dark places. They sought it from other realms where evil ruled. They forcibly took it from other people, who they drained dry of both magical power—if they were mages—or blood. Sometimes, both.

Blood magic gained its power from the murder of innocents and was one of the most heinous of all acts. Black magic was the power of deception, cloaked in mystery and hidden from all until it snared its victim. They were two sides of the same dark coin. Something Jack and his brothers had fought against most of their lives.

Jack didn't sense any of that here. No, this golden honey carried the power of the sun and the little female warrior bees Kiki liked so much. The tea, too, was wholesome and filled with the happy, calming influence of that little unassuming chamomile flower. There was no danger here.

Jack took a sip. The magic of the honey burst on his tongue, soothed by the calming chamomile. A perfect combination.

"This is delicious," he told Kiki, as their eyes met over the rims of their cups. "Did you pick the chamomile yourself?" He'd noticed the strainer filled with loose tea. That wasn't store bought.

"It's from our farm, too," she told him, smiling. "We keep an herb garden in the back by the kitchen door. There's a tea section filled with plants and flowers that make good teas. There's a medicinal section with plants that can be used in home remedies. Then, there's the cooking garden, with the usual herbs and spices. We try to grow as much as we possibly can, and we never use pesticides. Everything is organic, though we do use some modern machinery for the larger fields, unlike most of our neighbors."

"Sounds like paradise," he said.

"It is, in a way, but it's also kind of isolated," she admitted. "I mean, I loved growing up there, but I'm not sure I could handle doing nothing but farm work, day in and day out, for the rest of my life. I suspect I'll eventually settle in a little town somewhere and keep a garden for my own use, but a large farm is full-time work, and I've already been there, done that."

"Would you keep bees?" he asked, curious.

She nodded, sipping her tea. She put down the cup, and her eyes went dreamy. "A few hives, definitely. A small hen house for a few chickens. If I had enough space, maybe even a horse or a few alpacas."

"Alpacas?" Jack laughed at the thought of it.

"They have the softest, warmest wool, and no lanolin. You can just shear them, clean it and spin it. Easy-peasy," she explained. "And they're really cute. A neighboring farm to ours raises them, and I've always wanted to have a few of my own. They're herd animals, so you can't have just one. You need a few so they don't get lonely."

Leave it to Kiki to worry if the livestock got lonely. She had a tender heart that he was really coming to appreciate. He finished his tea, sorry that the last of the sweet honey was gone. It had revived him and calmed his senses at the same time. He felt refreshed and grounded. Definitely ready for what he had to do later that night. But first, he had to take his leave, which was getting harder and harder by the moment.

The more time he spent with Kiki, the more he wanted to spend in her company. She was like a slow-acting drug he was quickly becoming addicted to. He stood, pushing back his chair and taking his empty tea cup to the table. He had to leave now. It was almost time for him to start his other mission of the evening.

"Just leave that in the sink. I'll wash up, since you so

kindly took care of the dinner dishes," she said, standing and coming up behind him while he was at the sink.

He turned, and she was so close. It was a tiny kitchen, after all. He took her cup from her hands and placed it carefully on the counter beside him before acting on the instincts that were clamoring for him to take her into his arms. He moved slowly, so she would see him coming a mile away and could stop him with the slightest movement, if that's what she wanted.

Kiki didn't move away. In fact, she stepped closer to him. Much closer.

As Jack wrapped his arms loosely around her waist, she leaned into him. Something clicked home in his heart and soul. Some sense of perfection he'd never felt before. She smiled at him, and it felt like his entire world had been lit from within by the sunshine in her heart.

Regardless of the fact that Kiki was human, with no discernable magical powers of her own, she was magic to him. Everything about her felt special and new. He would have to examine the bubbly feeling in his body later. For now, he wanted to kiss the living daylights out of her while he had the chance.

Jack lowered his head and matched his lips to hers, and then, the magic really began.

Kiki loved the way Jack kissed her. She'd been craving another one of his amazing kisses all day. It had been an altogether strange day, and she still wasn't sure what to think about everything that had happened at lunch and after, but she knew one thing for sure. Even if he was some kind of crackpot—which she didn't really think was all that likely— Jack certainly knew how to kiss.

His hands went to her waist, one dipping lower to cup her ass. She leaned against him, enjoying the hard, hot feel of his body against hers, through their clothing. His other hand rose upward, along her spine, caressing her back as his lips claimed hers in a kiss that tasted faintly of the sweet honey of her home.

It had never tasted so good.

She kissed him back, her hands shaping his shoulders then rising up into the short strands of hair at the nape of his neck. He was so powerfully built it was a pleasure just to be free to touch him. She was used to brawny men who worked farms in her area, but she had never seen a man so well put together as Jack. He was like something out of a fantasy. Like one of Michelangelo's sculptures come to life. Only bigger. And more muscular.

He was so warm she could feel the heat of him through the fabric of his shirt. She yearned to have nothing between them, but she didn't know if he felt the same. His kiss spoke of passion, but it also held a modicum of restraint. She didn't know why she thought that, but she wasn't surprised when he drew away by slow degrees, ending the molten kiss before it could go much further.

To say she was disappointed would be the understatement of the millennium. She hadn't been with many men, but her body was fairly screaming at her to take Jack by the hand and lead him to her bedroom.

She couldn't, of course. Not when he was pulling away. Shutting her down before she could even work up the nerve to really get going.

"I've got to go."

Was it her imagination or did he sound annoyed by the very idea?

"You don't have to," she told him, daring greatly. She had no idea where this newfound boldness had come from, but she liked the feeling of empowerment it gave her.

He lowered his forehead to rest against hers. "Yes, I do." He sighed, and she could feel the regret in the tension in his muscles. "You'll never know how sorry I am to go."

She tilted her head. "Not as sorry as I am." She was getting brassy now. She liked her new bold ways.

He'd lowered both hands to her butt, and now, he pressed his lower body to hers, letting her feel the excitement he couldn't hide. She sucked in a breath. Wow. He really was a big boy...all over.

"I can't hide how much I want to stay, but I came here to do a job, and to do it, I have to go." He sounded so full of regret, she had to smile. Then, his words started to penetrate.

"You're going to do some investigating? At this hour?" She frowned up at him. Kiki didn't like the sound of that at all. He was going to be putting himself in danger, she was almost certain of it.

"No better time to catch them with their pants down than when they aren't expecting it," he replied, removing his hands from around her waist. "I also have a ton of reports to go through, and they're waiting for me back at my hotel. To top it all off, I have to report in to the home office. It's three hours earlier where they are, and they want daily updates."

"Whatever you have planned," she said, her hands on his chest as she began to draw away, "promise me you'll be careful."

"I'm always careful," he told her, winking as she stepped away from him.

Why was it so hard to let him go? She'd only known him a couple of days. Why did it feel like she was practically losing a part of herself to step away from his tall, hard body?

"I want a promise in return," he said, reaching for his leather jacket, which he'd hung around the back of his chair earlier.

"What kind of promise?" she asked, meeting his gaze with a bit of suspicion.

"Just..." His voice dropped low, his expression serious. "Stay inside tonight. Lock all your doors and keep away from the windows. Whatever is going on at the plant isn't something straightforward. It's devious and tricky. Don't fall for it. Don't let anyone in here, and you should be safe. The garden alone will probably be enough of a deterrent, but you never know."

"The garden?" She didn't understand.

"Surely, you've felt the magical nature of the garden

around this cottage?" he asked, surprising her with the direct, if puzzling, answer.

"I…" She thought about it. "I knew it was special, but…" How did he know so much about magic? Only her family talked openly about such things and then, only amongst themselves. "Magic?" she asked, hoping he would elaborate.

Jack shook his head as he put on his jacket. "We can talk more about it tomorrow. Suffice to say, I believe in it, and I can sense it more than other people. That's one of the reasons I was sent here." He moved toward the backdoor as he spoke. "You know, there was another guy corporate sent before me, but he couldn't get anywhere. He knew something was wrong here, but he couldn't figure out what it was. That's when they asked me to take on the challenge. So far, I've been up to it, but I have no illusions that this will be an easy problem to solve. We're in the first stages of the investigation. I have to be cautious, and so do you. Promise me you'll stay in tonight, okay? So I can do my job without worrying too much about you."

"If it means that much to you, all right. Not that I have anywhere to go tonight, anyway. I hadn't planned to go out."

"Not even to dance in the fairy garden?" he joked, his smile inviting her to laugh.

"I promise I won't dance in the garden," she assured him. "Tonight, at any rate."

Her grumbling reply made him laugh. He stooped down to smack her lips with his in a kiss of farewell, and then, he was out the door, closing it behind himself.

"Lock it, Kiki," he said, through the door.

She threw the bolt and knew he could hear the metallic sound on the other side of the wooden door. "Satisfied?"

"No, but I'm glad you locked the door," he quipped. A moment later, she heard his heavy boot tread as he walked down the porch steps and into the back garden. She rushed to the window over the sink and saw only a tall shadow melting into the wildness of the plants, and then, he was gone.

CHAPTER 10

It was one of the hardest things Jack had ever done, leaving Kiki like that. Especially after she'd invited him to stay. He hadn't expected that. Knowing she'd been raised strictly, in a community that frowned on premarital sex, he hadn't thought she would be so willing to invite him in.

Reenacting the night before, he rode his bike out to the woods surrounding the plant. Hiding the bike under a large conifer, he disrobed and shifted, intending to nose a little closer to the building this time.

Everything started out the same as the night before, but as he drew closer to the buildings, his senses went on high alert. There was magic nearby. Not the good kind, either. Slowing his steps, Jack paused often to listen and observe. He paid special attention to his surroundings. He could feel it when he drew closer to the foul essence of whatever magic had been wrought here.

Suddenly, he stopped short. The sounds of the night were dulled. He looked all around but saw nothing out of the ordinary. Then, he looked down. Just visible in the gloom was a line of something dark and wet against the deep brown of the ground. They were just under the trees, not far from where the trees gave way to grass and the grounds of the plant site.

Someone had been through here, walking just a few feet into the surrounding forest, and they hadn't just been taking a stroll in nature. No, they'd been spreading a foul potion along the floor of the forest that would take hold if not interfered with in the next few hours. Jack knew this hadn't been here last night, so it was something new. Something that had been placed here within the past few hours.

It was a dark ward. A black magic thing that would sink into the earth and cause harm to the fabric of the forest, itself. Already, the leaves and plants on the ground where the potion had been laid were withering and dying. If allowed to take hold, this substance would poison the earth wherever it had been laid.

Jack set out to follow the trail and see what the parameters were. He was betting this was some kind of ring, but rather than protecting against evil, it was made of evil and put there for other purposes. To keep good out? Perhaps. Or to poison anyone who was foolish enough to cross the line. Such things could also alert the spellcaster to breaches in the dark ward. Once set, it would take a high-powered mage to undo, but the potion was still wet. It hadn't sunk into the earth, yet. It could still be redirected and weakened to the point where it would be of little to no use to the mage who had cast it.

It took time, but Jack confirmed his suspicions. The dark line formed a wet sludge-like ring around the plant. Jagged in spots, it nonetheless formed a magical ward that was on the verge of setting into the earth itself. Jack thought hard about everything he knew, or had ever heard, regarding the breaking of potion-set wards and knew he needed help.

Not help from other people but from the earth and forest, itself.

Jack knew just what he had to do. Still in his mighty bear form, he hunted the herd of deer he'd scented nearby. Approaching them from downwind, he looped around to herd them in the direction he wanted them to go. Their innocence and purity of spirit would protect them from the evil line of magic. Creatures such as they were not susceptible to the dark magic that could warp malleable humans and the magical races.

The deer could cross that disgusting line and trample it beneath their elegant hooves. Jack just had to time it right and get them moving in the right direction. The moment they scented his bear form, they'd run. Thankfully, the winds were working with him.

He could see them up ahead, nosing around among the trees. He watched and waited, looking for the right opportunity. The right positioning of the herd and its leaders. Almost…

There. Jack charged, herding the deer like a collie. They were more than ready to go in any direction he pushed them, and as they crossed that seeping evil line, their hooves did just what he'd hoped, breaking the circle and dispelling the magic.

From inside the building, Jack heard a female scream of anger. Hiding behind a tree while the deer ran over the remnants of the line again, farther away from his position, for good measure, he saw the door fly open, and the potion witch storm out. If he'd been in human form, he might have laughed. As it was, his inner bear wanted to growl at the evil woman, but in either form, Jack felt a deep satisfaction at having destroyed her dark work.

She stalked toward the woods, and he realized he'd probably overstayed his welcome. Slinking into the shadows, Jack did his best to blend into the night as he backed away. Carol Burns stomped right up to where the evil barrier had been churned up and dispelled by the herd's many hooves and let out a sound of pure frustration.

Jack suspected a whole lot of cooking and witchery had just gone up in smoke. He was glad she'd been set back in her twisted goals. It would give him more time to figure out what, exactly, was going on at the plant and why this woman had chosen it as her personal playground.

His inner bear was glad to be rid of the slimy feel of the black magic. Carole had spread that vile stuff all around the perimeter of the plant, but the herd had done a great job in breaking the ring and robbing it of its power. The spell had been broken, and Jack's inner bear rejoiced. The bear had really hated the feel of Carol's spell. Like, *really* hated it. *Loathed* it, even.

Which made Jack start thinking. It was most likely that the potion Carol had strewn all around the forest had been meant specifically to bar those folk not already under her spell from crossing the perimeter around the plant. Why did it rub his fur the wrong way so badly? He was a shifter. More than that, he was a bear shifter, which made him more magical than most. The spell shouldn't have bothered him so much in his bear form…unless…

Jack moved silently through the trees, heading for the darker patch of forest near the other end of the warehouse. The deer hadn't been through that area, and he wanted to make certain it was dissipating everywhere. He also wanted to see if his suspicions about the dark slime of the potion were correct.

Skirting closer to the dissipating line of the dark ward now that Carol had gone back into the building, Jack observed all he could about the slowly disappearing potion. It was fading into the earth, its energy dispersing, but it left behind a telltale odor that his bear senses recognized once the rest of the disgusting brew was absorbed by the earth.

Blood.

Not only was Carol a mage of the unseen dark arts, but she dabbled in blood magic for her potion casting. This just got better and better. Or, actually, worse and worse.

Blood path mages were the worst sorts of degenerate creatures Jack had ever had the misfortune to encounter. They preyed on the innocent, powering their spells and themselves, at time, with the blood of others.

They weren't vampires. No, bloodletters were an ancient race of Others who had their share of degenerates, Jack was sure, but the few vamps he'd come across in his work had been those working to eliminate the bad ones. They'd been warriors on the side of Light, just like Jack.

Okay, not *just* like Jack. For one thing, they really did need blood to survive and how they got it was somewhat of a gray area for Jack. They had powers of seduction unrivaled in any creature Jack had met, though he supposed if he'd stuck around in Grizzly Cove a little longer, he might have met a sea siren. They were rumored to be the ultimate seductresses, but vamps had their own charms that usually brought their prey to them willingly.

Jack had a bit of a problem with that whole concept, but that wasn't the issue here. Carol wasn't a vampire of any kind. She'd been out and about during the day. He'd seen her in the daylight, and she'd shown no signs of the usual vampire pallor. Plus, he'd seen her eating food in that kitchen. Vampires couldn't do that. Not easily. The only thing they could truly ingest, besides blood, was wine.

Shaking his furry head, Jack tracked around the perimeter of the plant, watching to make certain the vile line Carol had cast was well and truly gone. Once he was satisfied the black magic was fully dissipated, he took one last look at the warehouse and found, much to his surprise, the janitor standing outside one of the large bay doors, looking almost directly at Jack.

Shit. Had the man seen him? Jack thought it was a pretty good bet, he probably had. Jack moved, watching the man's eyes. Sure enough, the gleam of his eyes tracked Jack's movements, and he looked a little too interested to suit Jack. *Damn.*

The janitor probably shouldn't be in the warehouse at this late hour. No one should be. The fact that Carol had her run of the place was to be expected now that Jack knew what she was, but the janitor? He could be an accomplice, but Jack wasn't sure. There was something about the way the man just watched that struck Jack as odd.

He didn't seem to have any reasonable reaction to seeing a giant grizzly in the woods. Jack knew for a fact that there were no wild grizzlies in the area. He'd have scented them right off, if there were. So, seeing him in his fur should have evoked fear or wary interest, neither of which Jack scented coming off the man.

The wind was right, and he could smell interest, but absolutely no fear. He also didn't smell evil. Of course, black magic practitioners were the best at hiding their true natures, so that wasn't any sort of guarantee.

What the man did next was even more perplexing. He took out a small notebook and started taking notes. He'd look up every few seconds to keep an eye on where Jack was, but he kept scribbling in that little book, as well.

Something about the way the janitor just watched and made notes, made Jack very uneasy. He left the area, quickly melting back into the darkness under the trees, then made his way carefully back to his bike and then shifted and dressed.

Back in his hotel room, a short time later, he fired off an email to Grizzly Cove. He needed a deeper background check on that janitor, and he also wanted Ezra to know what Carol had been up to earlier tonight. The information on its way to the other side of the country, Jack finally was able to grab a few hours of sleep. He had work to do tomorrow, so a certain amount of sleep was imperative. Jack had learned, in these uncertain times, that he never quite knew which way the wind might blow tomorrow, so getting rest when he could was always a good idea.

The next morning, Jack woke around dawn. To his surprise, a response was waiting in his email inbox, even though it was still the middle of the night on the West Coast. Ezra must have been prowling around last night, or at least reading his email after work hours.

The reply piqued Jack's interest. Apparently, the janitor's background check had indicated he had a former employer who was known to be a highly placed agent of the *Altor Custodis*. Jack and his brothers had come across the *AC* before, a few times. They were an ancient order of watchers.

The *AC* didn't take part in the action, but rather, just watched from the sidelines, taking notes—as the janitor had done last night—and making reports. They were dedicated to identifying and watching anyone with magic. Mages, of course, but also vamps, were, and every kind of Other being in existence. If the *AC* knew about them, it was for certain that there was a file on them and their kind somewhere in the legendary *AC* archives that went back centuries.

Jack didn't like the *Altor Custodis* or their mission. What business was it of theirs if someone was a shifter or a bloodletter or danced naked under the full moon? To Jack, the *Altor Custodis* were just a bunch of pervy peeping Toms. Of course, of late, there had been evidence that some of them were much worse than that.

There had been warnings from the Lords in recent years that the *Altor Custodis* organization had been infiltrated by *Venifucus* agents at the highest levels. Just the idea of the *Venifucus* having access to all those *Altor Custodis* reports… Thousands of years' worth of surveillance of Others—many of whom would likely oppose the goals of the *Venifucus*. Not only would the *Venifucus* agents know where to find people who might sympathize with their evil cause, but they'd also know the habits and possible vulnerabilities of those who would stand strongly against them. They could both recruit new members from the archives and target possible opponents.

Jack didn't like the idea of that at all. Nobody who stood in opposition to the *Venifucus* did.

The ancient order of the *Venifucus* were interested in power. Grabbing power, in all its forms, by any means necessary. Ultimately, they wanted to bring back their *Mater Priori*, the mother of their order, Elspeth. She'd been a fey creature of immense power who had started the last great war of the magical races. That war had resulted in what mortals still called the Dark Ages. Those were the decades and centuries when Elspeth had been gaining ground, and darkness spread over various lands like a pestilence.

When she'd finally been defeated, she had been banished to the farthest realms, from which, it was hoped, she could never return. Nobody fighting her at the time had been able to harness enough power to actually kill her, so the decision had been made to try to trap her and banish her.

It had worked. Others of all races had stopped her in a concentrated push to combine forces and end her wickedness in the mortal realm. Centuries ago, shifters, bloodletters and even mages had all worked together to accomplish that great goal, but in the intervening centuries, with the rise of man to prominence in the mortal realm, they had all but forgotten those ancient alliances.

Shifters had gone back to their own Packs and Clans, no longer counting bloodletters among their friends or allies. Mages had retreated to their towers, isolating themselves in their schools of wizardry and scholarly pursuits. Hedge wizards had gone back to their homes, practicing their more subtle brand of magic among their villages and towns…and the world had evolved to what it was now.

A place of science and technology ruled by mortals, with Others relegated to either fairytales or nightmares. It was a good world. It was the world Jack had been born into, and he liked it, for the most part. The only problem was that the followers of Elspeth, Destroyer of Worlds, had not disbanded after her defeat as everyone had thought. No, they'd gone underground, waiting and watching, infiltrating and learning even darker black magic to survive in this new world.

And now, they were rising.

Ezra had written that he knew a guy he would call in the morning. Apparently, Ezra had a contact within the *AC*, itself. He'd also sent a phone number and name. Ezra had strongly suggested that Jack get in touch with this contact before going back to the plant. It was too early to call anyone, even if they were on the East Coast, which he could tell from the area code, so Jack set about doing his own research based off the information Ezra had provided.

What he found only made him more concerned. Ezra had provided Jeff the janitor's work history. Only the one name had sent up an obvious red flag for Ezra, but Jack thought a few of the other employers listed on Jeff's paperwork sounded familiar, as well. Sure enough, when he dug a little deeper, he found that one of the corporations Jeff had worked for in the past was owned by a werewolf Pack in Manhattan. Another business Jeff had left more recently was a partnership between one of the oldest vampires in New York and a mortal restauranteur. Jeff had been a cleaner in that establishment until he was fired for unspecified reasons.

Jack knew that sometimes bloodletters partnered up with mortals to invest in businesses that helped them maintain the façade of mortality. Restaurants were a good fit because the vampires could show up, get a private room, order food, and nobody would be the wiser that they hadn't eaten any of it.

If Jeff really was an *Altor Custodis* agent, he had placed himself well to spy on both the vampire who partially owned that restaurant and the werewolf Pack. Added to the prior job Ezra had flagged, the evidence was mounting against Jeff. One coincidence, fine. Two started to stretch credibility. But, three… Yeah, Jeff wasn't the dopey innocent he appeared on the surface.

Jack sent Ezra the information he'd dug up and looked at the clock. Still early but not too bad. Jack could probably get away with calling the man Ezra had suggested in the next half hour. Before that, Jack made himself some coffee, using the hotel room's mini coffee maker and supplies, and ate one of the protein bars he kept in his bags. That would keep him going for a while, and by the time he was finished, it was a more reasonable hour to make that contact.

Dialing the number, Jack waited patiently for someone to pick up on the other end. He didn't have to wait long.

"Harper Sagtikos?" Jack asked by way of greeting. "This is Jack Bishop. I think maybe our mutual friend, Ezra, might've warned you I'd be calling."

"Actually, I'm friends with Gus, but he connected me with Ezra, and I'm happy to offer any counsel I can provide," came the reply over the phone. The man's voice was deep and rich. Warm, somehow, and…filled with power. Even over the phone, Jack could feel it.

"Gus, huh? So, does that mean you're a shaman?" Jack asked, adding up the evidence. Gus was Grizzly Cove's resident shaman and a rare spirit bear.

"I was Gus's teacher, though I still have much to learn myself," the powerful voice replied. It wasn't so much volume, but intensity. This man had that in plenty. Just like Gus.

"Well, then." Jack had a lot of questions he'd like to ask and wasn't sure where to start. "I'm in the middle of a situation here, and I need some magical advice."

Jack went on to explain everything he'd found so far. He told Harper about the potion witch and the brew in the woods the night before. He talked about the fey garden and the star on Kiki's house. He revealed everything he knew about the situation. Truth be told, it was far more than he'd wanted to reveal, but even by phone, this shaman's power was potent. He had a way of eliciting information with subtle questions until he knew everything Jack knew about the situation here.

CHAPTER 11

Harper was full of practical advice about how to deal with a potion witch. He also gave Jack an unexpected primer on the old-time knowledge of the Amish and Germanic people who settled in Pennsylvania long ago. Jack was a bit surprised by how much stock the shaman put in the old folklore that had come along with those people to this new land.

"You can use some of that protective magic. I know you bears have a lot of natural resistance to most things, but if you're dealing with black magic, it's always what you can't see that you need to be wary of," Harper told him. "Ask your friend, Kiki, about those hex signs. They're not just pretty decorations. Some of them hold true power. Like symbolic wards rather than the salt barriers you told me about that she put around her home."

"I had no idea," Jack admitted, feeling a bit slow as Harper revealed knowledge of things Jack had never even thought about before. Harper was in teaching mode, and Jack recognized the value of his words. He listened avidly.

"The old ways aren't just old wives' tales," Harper went on. "The belief persists in simple things because there often is power in them. Like throwing a pinch of salt over your shoulder for luck. You'll even see famous chefs doing it on television these days. But why? They may think it's a quaint custom, or part of their act, but the truth is salt forms a powerful protective barrier against evil. Like the star on Kiki's cottage and the fey garden around it. These are powerful protections that hide in plain sight. Unlike the dark magic you're fighting, these things can be seen but not always recognized by those who think magic is just a fairytale."

Harper went on with his practical advice for longer than Jack expected, but Jack hung on every word. Here was a man who knew his stuff, and Jack recognized the expertise Harper held. Thankfully, the shaman was willing to share his knowledge, and Jack knew he would need every bit of it to prevail against this enemy. Black magic was something he'd come across, but not all that often, and never in such a potent form.

Carol had had years to learn her craft and had likely been planning whatever it was she'd been doing at the paper plant for a long, long time. She'd managed to send the last investigator Ezra had sent here away with his head spinning in confusion. Jack vowed the same would not happen to him. He had a job to do, and he was going to do it.

Thanks to the long phone call, Jack was a bit late getting to the office, but Kiki was sitting serenely behind her desk as he passed her office door, and Jack breathed a sigh of relief. He didn't think the potion witch would move overtly against Kiki—and whatever few others who hadn't already fallen under her spell. Not just yet. If nothing else, Carol had already proven that she was able to bide her time until she could catch her prey in her very evil trap.

Harper had been of the opinion that Carol had been setting up that very special luncheon for months, slowly upping the dose of whatever potion it was she had been feeding everyone. Little by little, she'd been casting a long-term spell that bound the people who ate the poisoned food to her. Such things, Harper had said, took time. Often, lots of time. Subverting a human being's free will wasn't as easy with black magic as it was with more overt spells.

Now that Harper had told Jack specifically what to look

for, he noticed the way each person he passed in the hall behaved. He could easily spot Carol's influence on pretty much everyone who had been at the plant long-term. Only Kiki was new and completely untainted. Thanks be to the Mother of All.

When Jack's work took him down to the accounting area later in the morning, he kept his eyes open. He was deep into a filing cabinet in a back corner when Carol swanned into the office area from the direction of her lab. She had an entourage following her around, like she was some sort of rock star. Jack kept still and went unnoticed, but he watched all with interest while pretending to be absorbed in the file he was holding.

He didn't realize he'd been holding his breath until Carol and her bevy of followers exited through a side door that led to one of the smaller production areas. Though what business she could possibly have in that section, he had no idea. As far as he knew, that production area wasn't tested at all by her lab. They supposedly had their own, much simpler testing section, since their product didn't come under federal or even local regulation.

Jack made his way back to his office, stopping at Kiki's on his way. He leaned in the doorframe and just watched her until she looked up and saw him standing there. She really was one of the most beautiful women he'd ever met. She had a radiant innocence about her, as if her spirit were shining through from the inside out.

Harper had laid Jack's last doubts about Kiki to rest. Jack still wasn't as familiar with her brand of folk magic, but Harper's words had gone a long way toward reassuring Jack that it was all good, not something he'd have to be concerned about as they worked together.

"Jack," she gasped, smiling even as he startled her. "You're like a cat, you're so quiet."

Jack shook his head as he walked a couple of steps into her office. "Not a cat, but I'll try not to startle you in the future." His inner bear wanted to growl at the comparison to an inferior feline. Although, he had to admit, some of the bigger cats weren't that bad.

"Do you mind working through lunch with me? I could use your help deciphering some files I've been looking at this morning." His voice was pitched loud enough that Bob Boehm, who was rather conveniently lurking in the hall just outside the door, could hear.

"Not at all. I packed a lunch," she said. Did she also realize they were being spied on? Jack couldn't be sure. Either way, he was certain their words would be reported back to Carol, one way or another, so having a secure story was all to the good. "I have enough for two, if you like schnitzel and noodles."

"I love schnitzel," he told her heartily. He wasn't exactly sure what schnitzel was, but he figured, if Kiki made it, it had to be good. Her beaming smile was well worth the risk. "I brought some deli sandwiches with me because I don't want to waste any more time going all the way down to the cafeteria. My boss called this morning, wanting an update, which is why I was a bit late getting in." There. Let good ol' Bob report that to Carol.

"Isn't SeaLife's headquarters on the West Coast?" she asked.

Jack nodded. "He got up very early to catch me before I came in." Jack tried to inject the right amount of concern into his voice for Bob's sake. "He wants results, and he's starting to lose patience."

Kiki reached into a bottom drawer and took out a sort of covered pot-thing with a cord attached. "I'll start warming this up and clear a space on my desk. Bring in your files, and we'll go over them while we eat."

"What is that?" he asked, gesturing toward the colorful contraption.

"My mother sent this to me last week. It's a lunch box that plugs in and heats up the food. Isn't it great? Mom saw it online and had it sent to me as a gift." She stretched to plug in the cord.

Jack started to wonder if maybe Kiki's mother wasn't a tad clairvoyant. Otherwise, why send such an...*appropriate* gift to her daughter right before she needed it. The only microwaves were in the cafeteria, and for all Jack knew, they were contaminated, too. That's why he'd opted for stopping at a deli to get sandwiches. But Kiki had a way to heat her own food, which was perfect.

"I'll just get the files and my sandwiches, and be right back," Jack said, listening for Bob's scrambling footsteps as the man backpedaled down the hall so as not to be caught eavesdropping. Kiki probably hadn't heard it, but Jack's shifter senses made Bob's inexpert stealth moves easily heard.

Jack pretended not to notice Bob as he slipped into his own office, farther down the long hall. Jack just went about his business, doing as he'd said. He retrieved his bag of sandwiches and the files and headed back to Kiki's office. They sat together across her desk and shared the meal.

It turned out he hadn't been lying. He loved Kiki's schnitzel, which was basically breaded and fried meat served over a bed of noodles. It was delicious, and Jack insisted on giving her one of his sandwiches to make up for taking half her lunch. They ate and looked over the financial documents he'd snagged earlier.

He didn't really need her help with the files, but it was a handy excuse to share lunch with her. As they worked, ate, and chatted, he realized just how comfortable she was to be around. He also began to understand that she saw patterns where others might not. Her mind was quick, and her grasp of the numbers they were examining was better than he'd expected. Better than his own, in fact.

Of course, he was more a man of action than a desk jockey. Jack could do paper-based investigation when he had to, but he was better at field-work.

"There's definitely something a little off with these numbers," Kiki said in a low voice, turning the sheaf of papers she was looking at toward him across the desk. Jack looked where she was pointing with her pencil. "See how this doesn't add up?" She flipped through the pages to another section. "This doesn't either. The numbers don't tally with the totals in several spots like this."

"Can you mark them all for me with a sticky note or something? I'm going to need to send a copy of the pertinent parts to headquarters so they can dig into the official reporting. I'm willing to bet that the numbers we see here aren't the numbers that were reported to the home office," Jack said, his inner bear hot on the trail, right alongside his human half.

"Sure," Kiki agreed easily, already reaching into her desk for a pad of sticky notes. "And I think you're probably right."

They worked on finding the parts of various financial reports that didn't add up for the rest of the day. When quitting time arrived, Jack was sure to walk Kiki out to her car.

"My bike is just over there," he told her. "If you don't mind, I'm going to follow you home. I just want to be sure you get there safely."

She looked relieved. "Thank you. I don't mind one bit. In fact, I'd really appreciate it."

"Good. I'll hang back until we're out of sight of this place then move up behind your car. Don't worry if you don't see me at first," he warned her. "I'm going to be stealthy." His grin sparked a responding one on her lovely face.

He stood there like a goof, basking in her smile a tad longer than he probably should have, but when he realized the silence had dragged on a bit, he just shrugged and headed for his bike. He watched Kiki out of the corner of his eye as she got into her car and backed the little vehicle out of the spot.

He followed at a distance until they were clear of the plant, but he kept a close eye on the little car. Once he was sure they weren't followed, he moved up so she could see him in her rearview mirror. He hoped that made her feel a bit safer as she made her way to her little cottage.

When she pulled into the driveway at the side of the house, she rolled down her window and motioned for him to stop. Jack was glad. He'd been prepared to leave her once he was sure she was safely home, but another part of him—the more basic part—wanted to spend more time with her. They'd been together all afternoon, but somehow, that wasn't enough to satisfy him.

He rolled his bike to a stop beside her car in the driveway, tucking it in beside the house where it wouldn't easily be seen from the road. He then went to close the gate that she had opened on her way in. The driveway separated her cottage from its nearest neighbor, as did the green picket fence that ran around the circumference of the property, including the gravel drive and fey garden inside.

Jack had sensed the magic of the place as he'd driven through the gate. Once inside the boundary of the fence, it was as if he was within a benevolent ward that brought with it peace, calm and security. He looked at the little house, noting again, its whimsical design and décor. It really was a magical little place in the best possible ways. He sensed benevolent, protective magic from the house.

It was a sleepy sort of protection, though. As if the spells had been laid long ago, and the house was well settled into its role as haven and hidey-hole for those within its walls. As if the house had a rudimentary awareness of the people who came and went while the house and its magic…remained.

"Do you want to sit in the garden for a bit or would you like to come inside?" Kiki asked, coming up beside him once she retrieved her purse and sweater from the car.

"I guess we should go inside, just in case anybody drives by. There was something I wanted to ask you about that I didn't want to bring up at work." Jack followed her into the house, noting the small living room at the front of the house. She led him into that room, inviting him to sit while she kicked off her shoes and went into the kitchen to get soft drinks for them both.

"What was it you wanted to talk to me about?" she asked

as she brought in two cold cans of soda, handing him one as she took a seat opposite him on the wide sofa.

"Hex signs." He blurted the words out without thought, momentarily distracted by how close she was…and yet how far. It wouldn't take much to breach the measly amount of space between them and take her into his arms. Nope. It wouldn't take much at all.

But he had to stay on topic here. Harper Sagtikos, the shaman teacher, had told Jack to ask Kiki about hex signs, and he would do so. Even if having Kiki sitting so close, with no desk between them, was a little more than just *distracting*. He'd had a hard enough time keeping his mind on work all afternoon while they'd been in her little office. It had been all he could do to stop himself, at the time, from climbing over that little desk and pinning her into her office chair, only to kiss her breathless.

He'd had a taste of her now, and he wanted so much more. Impossibly more. Which was something he couldn't act on until he was certain she was safe. To do that, he had to finish the job and end the threat posed by the potion witch. He just wasn't sure where to start.

At least he knew who the enemy was. He'd uncovered that much information. He still had to do some more verification and investigation to see just how far Carol's influence went. Black magic was tricky. Like an iceberg, it was never just what was visible on the surface. By its nature, most of it was concealed below the surface, ready to shift and spring at any moment. Jack knew he had to be ultra-cautious, but he was pleased with the progress he'd made so far. Another few days and he should be about ready to plan Carol's take-down.

"What about hex signs?" She was looking at him with a puzzled expression on his face, and he knew he'd let the silence go on a bit too long.

"I've been reading up," he said, unwilling to discuss Harper's existence with anyone other than Ezra. "I was just thinking maybe we could get a few more your house, maybe even your car or office. A little added layer of protection."

"Funny you should mention that," Kiki said, rising. She moved toward the little table by the door, where she picked up a large padded envelope and brought it over to the couch.

"Patches?" he read the name from the envelope, surprised it was addressed to someone called Patches and not Kiki.

Kiki blushed. "It's a nickname my family calls me."

"I sense a story behind that," Jack teased her just a bit.

Her blush deepened, and she sat down, busily re-opening the package. "It may have had something to do with my years as a scout and my desire to earn as many of the merit badges as possible. I admit, I was a little obsessed by the whole thing. It got so there was little room on my sash for any more patches, so my siblings thought it was cute to start calling me that."

As she opened the package, out tumbled a stack of disks of various sizes from a few inches in diameter to about a foot. Painted on one side, the wooden disks had all sorts of arcane symbols on their surfaces. Hex signs. Potent magic he could feel wafting from the pile of disks in a subtle, comforting wave. Protective. Loving. Family.

"My brother sent all this. It arrived this morning," Kiki told him.

Jack shook his head, marveling. "Is anybody in your family clairvoyant, by any chance?"

"Well…" Kiki lowered her eyes. "Mom has an uncanny way of knowing things sometimes," she finally said.

"Did she mention to your brother that a gift like this might be nice?" Jack challenged with a grin.

"Actually, when I called to thank him, he said something of the kind." Kiki smiled back.

"Well, score one for the good guys," Jack said. "May I look at them?" he asked, before reaching out. It was always wise to be careful with magical objects belonging to someone else.

"Sure. Mom suggested I should share these with friends," she told him. "Which is why my brother sent so many."

They spent a good twenty minutes going through the hex signs. Kiki was a wealth of knowledge about what each symbol and combination of symbols and colors meant. They sorted out which signs she would put where and even started putting a few of the larger ones up around the house.

As they were put into place, Jack could feel their subtle magic settling into position. There really was something to these things. He never would have credited it, if he hadn't seen and felt their magic for himself.

There was a selection of smaller hex signs. Some as small as a refrigerator magnet. Those, Kiki would bring into work the next day and put around her office. She had lots of metal filing cabinets and doorframes on which to place them. She had a somewhat larger medallion-sized hex sign that was perfect for her car, and a few left to spare. She selected some for Jack and insisted that he take them and put them up where he slept. There was also a small one she wanted him to put in his motorcycle's saddlebags.

He accepted with alacrity. There was no way to tell her that his natural bear magic was potent enough to protect him from almost anything. It seemed to mean so much to her that she give him this gift of protection. It was sweet, really.

Kiki was so glad her family had sent their little care package. She felt good being able to give Jack a piece of her heritage that might actually protect him in some small way. Not that the big man needed her protection, but every little bit could help in this sort of situation.

She still could hardly believe that she was involved in something that reeked of dark magic and was potentially dangerous. She'd thought so before, when she'd narrowly avoided that scene in the warehouse and then the barbeque after, but she'd almost convinced herself she'd been hallucinating when nothing else happened.

Now, though, she knew she hadn't been dreaming. Jack felt the same and had witnessed things—things she'd seen, as well—that made her realize that this threat was very real.

"Why don't you stay for dinner?" she asked, once they'd sorted through the hex signs and conversation lulled. It was getting dark out, but she didn't want him to leave.

She didn't ever want him to leave.

CHAPTER 12

Whoa. That thought had come from out of the blue. From the place where her intuition sometimes sent messages. But she couldn't believe this one. She'd only known the man a few short days. No way could she know enough about him, yet, to make that kind of decision about him. No way could she want to keep him forever based only on a few days' acquaintance.

Perhaps it was the danger of the situation. She'd read that, sometimes, dangerous situations led people to bond more quickly and closely than otherwise. There was just one problem with that theory—they hadn't really been in that much danger together. With any luck, they wouldn't be in danger at all. So far, it looked like Carol was giving Jack a wide berth, and nobody had tried to subvert Kiki since that barbeque. Maybe they'd decided to leave her alone.

One could hope.

But she knew that was foolish. They might've let her go for a little while, but before long, they'd try something else. Carol had almost everyone—if not everyone—at the plant under her spell already through that adulterated cafeteria food. Kiki had no reason to disbelieve what Jack had claimed about Carol tampering with the food.

When Kiki had thought about it later, she realized it had

made a sick sort of sense. The food at the barbeque had probably also been tainted, which was why she'd felt such an aversion to the grill area. Just as she'd felt a more subtle aversion to the cafeteria food ever since she'd started working at the plant.

"I'd love to stay, as long as I'm not putting you out," Jack replied politely. "Is there anything I can do to help?"

"I probably should have warned you before I asked, but I have a freezer full of leftovers, and I intended to make a dent in that tonight. Do you mind leftover chicken and dumplings?" she asked as she rose from the couch and headed for the small kitchen, Jack following right behind.

"I'd love some. Tell me how I can help," he insisted, moving to the sink and washing his hands in preparation while she went to the freezer and took out the carefully wrapped food that she'd put up just a few days before. Somehow, she must've known to cook extra because there was plenty—even for Jack's enormous appetite.

They worked together to thaw and heat up the food, then shared the meal together in the cozy intimacy of her kitchen. The mood was mellow and heated at the same time. Kiki realized she liked everything about Jack, and she hoped he would allow their relationship—or whatever this was—to progress a little further.

She'd been bold with him before, and it hadn't really worked, but oddly, she hadn't felt embarrassed about being shot down. He'd left her feeling as if he'd wanted to stay but couldn't. Not *wouldn't* but couldn't. It made a difference.

Kiki wasn't sure how this night would play out, but she started hoping that, maybe this time, he wouldn't leave quite so quickly. She would try not to be too obvious about it. A girl did have her pride, after all.

Jack's inner bear was clamoring for him to reach out and stake some sort of claim on Kiki all throughout dinner. His human half felt a similar urge, but he worried if that was really the best thing *for her*. She might know about hex signs and old-world magic that was passed down in her family as folklore, but she probably had not the first clue that there were shifters out there, much less that she'd been working with one all day.

How could he honestly think about anything long-term with her unless she knew the truth about him? His inner bear didn't understand why he didn't just show her his furry side and be done with it. The bear insisted that she was special. That she'd understand and not be scared. How could she be scared of him when he cared so much for her safety? She would know that he would never hurt her, no matter what form he wore.

But the bear side thought in very straight lines. It didn't always understand human subtlety. Scratch that. The bear was never subtle.

Shrewd. Instinctual. Brutal, at times, but never subtle.

Jack had to use his human half's finesse to handle this situation. He honestly didn't know how much longer he could go on denying his instincts. Both halves of his nature were pretty clear on the idea that Kiki was something special. To what degree she would fit into his life—or his future—was still unknown.

He had toyed with the idea that she might be his mate, but it was a dream almost too good to be true. Some shifters searched for a century or more to find that one perfect mate destined to fill their lives with joy and love, by the grace of the Goddess. The Mother of All.

Jack was Her servant. He believed in Her power and Her goodness. He had always hoped and prayed he would find a special woman to share his life with, but he wasn't sure lightning could strike the same family so many times in a row, so close together.

Only a short while ago, his brother Ace had met his mate. Then, King had met his perfect match a little after that. They were all happily mated now, living in Grizzly Cove, where they had relocated after a lifetime spent drifting from place to place. Jack didn't really know where he fit any longer, but he had figured he'd sort through all those things while he worked on this mission for Ezra.

So far, though, he hadn't had much time to think things through. His brothers were happily mated, and Jack was odd man out. Was it just wishful thinking that Kiki might really be his mate?

It didn't feel that way, but this was all so new to him. Never before in his life had his instincts pointed him so strongly toward a woman. That had to mean something. Didn't it?

Jack wished, not for the first time, that he could talk to his brothers. They used to have really good heart-to-heart conversations every once in a while, and as the youngest of the three, he'd usually learned quite a bit from his older and wiser siblings. Not that he'd ever let them know it.

He could really use some of that wisdom and guidance in this situation, but it wasn't the kind of thing he felt comfortable talking about over the phone. Feelings and how to interpret them was something to be discussed around a campfire, preferably after consuming an entire roast and more than a few beers. Gosh, those had been the days.

His brothers were older than he was, though they all looked close in age due to the way shifters aged. Most shifters lived a few centuries and spent the majority of their lives fit and aging at a very slow rate compared to humans. There were decades between Ace and King and himself, though it probably looked as if they were born only a few years apart.

It was his time to be on his own and stop relying so heavily on his siblings. Jack knew that, but it didn't make it any easier to be out here in the world, working without the safety net of having his brothers around to back him up. Part of growing and evolving was learning how to trust his own instincts. For far too long, he'd relied on Ace and King's judgements. This time, Jack was on his own. It was scary, to be sure—though he would never admit that to his brothers— but it was also liberating.

Jack was finally becoming his own man. His own bear.

Not the youngest part of a trio. The dreaded *baby bear* of the grouping. He'd fought more than his fair share of battles over stupid shifters calling him that. Of course, Ace hadn't liked being the *mama bear*, either.

Jack gathered his wandering wits and moved into the living room with Kiki once they'd set the kitchen to rights and cleaned up the dinner dishes. She'd made coffee, and they were sitting on the couch, again—this time with much less space between them than before—as the atmosphere grew more intimate.

Night had fallen in earnest. Jack should probably be making a move to leave, but somehow, he couldn't bring himself to go. It was more than just wanting to make sure she was safe tonight. It was a desire to just be with her. Whether they were talking or working or—Goddess help him—making love together the way he dreamed, he just wanted to be here, sharing the same space, looking at her pretty face and breathing in her delectable scent.

Everything about her was attractive to him. The way she moved, the way she smiled, her scent, her sense of humor...everything.

Kiki had sensed, as the evening progressed, that something had changed between herself and Jack. He wasn't rushing to leave tonight. Dare she hope that he might stay, this time, if she issued the invitation? She didn't want to go out on that limb again, and get shot down, but if he didn't make a move soon, she might just make some moves of her own.

Everything about Jack seemed to dare her to be bold in ways she'd never imagined herself behaving. He brought out the inner wild child that she'd never really known she'd had. She liked the way he made her feel. He gave her confidence in herself as a woman, just by the way he smiled at her. He'd encouraged her intellect as they'd worked together all day as equals. Partners. She'd really liked that.

He seemed to believe in the folk magic she'd grown up

with, which was both surprising and very welcome. She loved her family and their old-fashioned ways. She would have been bitterly disappointed in anyone who belittled their beliefs. Jack's attitude, though, had been surprising. He seemed to not only tolerate, but respect her family's efforts to keep her safe. He'd taken the hex signs very seriously, indeed, which had pleased something deep-seated in her soul. She didn't fully understand it, but she felt it all the same.

Just as she felt the most amazing attraction for him that she'd ever felt for any man. Jack tempted her as no man had ever tempted her before. She wanted to know his touch, his intimate embrace. She wanted to feel him moving inside her and learn the ecstasy he could bring her. She suspected it would be a life-changing experience, without peer or precedent.

Even if being with him ruined her for any other man, she didn't care. She wanted to make love with Jack. It was fast becoming a necessity that she know what it was to have him in her bed...and in her body. She was very much afraid that he would also find his way into her heart and soul. If he left her then—and, really, she had no indication that he might want anything long-term with her—she knew she would never be the same. As it was, she knew she would never forget him.

A man like Jack came around once in a lifetime, if a woman was very, very lucky. Or blessed. She thought, maybe, she was a bit of both, at the moment. Especially when Jack leaned closer, and she caught the scent of his body, warm, musky and unbelievably enticing.

"You're going to have to promise me that you'll be extremely careful at work over the next few days," he told her now, his gaze earnest and serious.

"I will," she promised readily. "I have no desire to get tangled up with whatever is going on there, I assure you."

"Good. Because it's going to take me a few more days to wrap up my investigation and get the final data I need to bring this whole house of cards tumbling down. I'll give you warning, and I don't want you at the plant when everything hits the fan, okay? I want you safe. Here. This cottage is the safest place I've seen in this area, so this is the place you should hunker down."

She was touched by his vehemence. "I promise." The look of relief on his face indicated a level of concern that spoke volumes to her hopeful soul. "But, whatever happens, I want you to promise me you'll be careful, too."

Jack moved closer to her on the couch as her hand went to his chest, resting over the reassuringly strong beat of his heart. They were being drawn together, as if they were two magnets with opposite polarity. Yin and yang. Male and female. Jack and Kiki. Like it was inevitable.

"I won't take chances," he said, his gaze searching hers. "That's why I'm moving so slow. I want to get all my ducks in a row before I strike, and when I do, it's not going to be pretty. Which is why I want you in the clear. Things could go sideways, and I need you to be safe."

She wasn't sure what kind of confrontation he was expecting, but it sounded like he had some kind of worst-case scenario in mind. Kiki knew Jack was some kind of corporate troubleshooter, but the fact that he hadn't blinked an eye at the odd things that were occurring at the plant made her wonder just what kind of trouble he usually handled. She thought he might be more of a paranormal investigator than a guy who found problems with accounting and spreadsheets—though, to be fair, he had done a bit of that, as well.

Everything about Jack intrigued her. She'd never met anyone like him before. There was an aura of danger around him, but not to her. Never to her. He was dangerous for those who would cross him and whatever evil was going on at the plant. She didn't know how she knew that, but she trusted her instinct.

And, right now, her instincts were telling her that, if she pushed him just the tiniest bit, she might be able to rouse the wildness that simmered just beneath Jack's surface. She wasn't scared of his wild nature. She knew, deep down, that he would never harm her, even though the power he seemed to wield was enormous.

Being this close to him, her otherwise weak magical senses could feel the strength of him on the plane where magic lived. The plane where much of her family operated... But not her. Never her. Kiki hadn't been born with the gift the way the others in her family had. She'd always felt like the odd one out because of it, but it wasn't that she had no magical senses. It was just that they were weaker than everyone else's, so they all discounted her paltry ability.

Jack, though... She sensed things about Jack. She felt earth magic when she was around him. Or, maybe, she thought with an inward grin, maybe she just felt the earth move when he smiled. His smiles had a way of reaching right down in to her soul and mesmerizing her.

"I promise I'll stay here, out of trouble, but what about you?" she asked, truly concerned for his wellbeing. Her hand rose to clasp his hard-muscled shoulder as she moved even closer to him.

Was it getting warm in here?

"I can take care of myself," he told her with one of those bone-melting, soul-stealing smiles. She couldn't take any more. She closed the remaining distance between them and sought his mouth with hers.

Damn. She had put the moves on him, much to her amazement. Kiki had never been so bold in her life, but those thoughts were swept aside as inconsequential as he not only accepted her kiss, but took control of it.

Time stood still. All she could hear was the beating of their hearts. All she could feel was the hot, wet warmth of his mouth on hers, the strong feel of his arms around her, tugging her close against his hard body. And, on another level entirely, she heard choirs of angels singing of power and majesty. A magical chorus singing without words of ancient power and eternal Light.

Jack could hardly believe he had Kiki in his arms. He'd been reticent to start anything with her that they couldn't finish, but she'd surprised him by making the first move. She'd broadcast her intention, and he'd seen it coming a mile away, but he'd been absolutely powerless against the desire that rode him hard, pushing him toward this fragile human soul who knew little of the real world. The dangerous world that he lived in.

He had sensed from almost the moment he'd met her that this…whatever it was between them…was inevitable in many ways. Timing could have been better. He didn't like the fact that she was working in the middle of a danger zone, for one thing. He was going to fix that, but it would take time. He just had to keep her safe until he could clean up the whole stinking mess at the plant.

This physical and emotional connection he felt toward Kiki was inconveniently timed, but he wouldn't trade this feeling for the world. She kissed like a dream come true, and she fit in his arms as if she'd been made to fill them. He'd had his suspicions about what she might come to mean to him, and he still wondered if maybe the Goddess was smiling down on him, right now, but as their kisses grew bolder and he moved his hands to the hem of her shirt, physical sensations outpaced his internal spiritual conjecture.

She felt so good in his arms. No way he could let her go now. The only thing that could stop him making love to Kiki tonight was if she called a halt. Otherwise, he was all about throwing caution to the wind and indulging them both tonight. Tomorrow would come soon enough, and he'd deal with whatever it brought when the new day dawned.

Tonight, he promised himself, was going to be about Kiki…and Jack. Together. In every sense of the word.

CHAPTER 13

Kiki felt her head whirl and realized it was from more than just the amazing kisses. Jack had lifted her into his arms and turned toward the hallway that led to her bedroom. Thank heaven!

He carried her as if she weighed nothing, his arms sure and strong. Everything about him took her breath away. He kept their mouths joined as he walked slowly toward her bedroom. He wasn't in a hurry. His lips teased hers as he gave her the most exquisite feelings she'd ever felt in a man's arms.

Jack paused at threshold of her room and lifted his head to gaze into her eyes. She was breathing hard, and she noted the slight flush on his cheeks. He wasn't unaffected by their shared passion. That was reassuring.

"Kiki, I…" He started over. "Will you let me make love to you tonight?"

She felt her tummy wobble at his serious question. He wasn't going to let things unfold in a way where her consent might come out of passionate desperation rather than careful thought, but it didn't matter. She'd already made up her mind long ago. If she got the chance to make love with Jack, she knew she was going to take it, and here he was, just waiting for her to say the word.

"Yes, Jack. I want that," she said softly, reaching up to cup his cheek. "I want you."

She might have imagined the fire in his eyes at her words, but she didn't think so. He carried her across the threshold and into her bedroom. Thank goodness she'd made the bed that morning and tidied up, almost as if she'd been hoping one thing might lead to another.

He put her on the bed then just stood there for a moment, gazing down at her. The heat in his eyes warmed her, and she got the feeling this was as big a deal for him as it was for her. She hadn't allowed many men this close to her. In fact, only a very few. This kind of physical intimacy was something that was rare and precious to her, something she didn't seek out with just anyone.

Jack was special. She hadn't known him very long, but her instincts told her that he was something—someone—she might never have a chance to know again. Kiki had decided, days ago, that she wanted to know him as intimately as possible, if given the chance, and now, here he was, in her bedroom… If only she could get him to take that final step and come join her on the bed.

Deciding he might need a little extra incentive, Kiki moved her hands to the little buttons on her shirt. One by one, she slipped them free of the buttonholes, baring more of herself to him. She watched Jack's eyes, which had widened at her movements. He seemed to be holding his breath, watching her demure striptease, as one by one, the little buttons came undone.

She slipped the shirt off one shoulder, then the other, revealing her lacy pink bra. That seemed enough to spur Jack into motion. He sat on the edge of the bed and helped her slide the shirt down her arms, allowing it to tangle behind her back, holding her hands captive while he lowered his mouth and kissed the swells of her breasts, flowing slightly over the cups of her bra.

He then drew her pointed nipple into his mouth, right through the pink lace, making her moan. She liked the little hint of bondage, though she knew Jack would release her

124

arms if she asked. For now, she liked feeling just that little bit of helplessness and danger. It wasn't real. Somehow, though she'd only known him a short time, she trusted Jack on an instinctual level.

He kissed her deeply, something a bit wild in his kiss. Kiki moaned and met him stroke for stroke. They were communing on an unspoken level, very clearly, about passion and desire…and what they both wanted to happen next.

When he finally broke the kiss, he also let go of the shirt tangled around her wrists, allowing her to move her arms, once more. But that was only so he could reach around with both hands and unhook her bra. Kiki brought her arms forward so he could slide the straps down her arms.

She was bare to his hungry gaze. She didn't feel vulnerable but rather, powerful. His appreciation was clear in his eyes, his care for her evident in the gentle way he reached out to touch her, hesitant at first, then more assertive as she leaned in to his caresses.

Hungry for more, Kiki reached between them to push at his clothing. He seemed to get the message because he sat back and quickly disposed of his shirt before coming back to her. He kissed her deeply, pressing their bare torsos together and rubbing lightly, making her very aware of the hard, chiseled perfection of his chest.

His arms were things of masculine beauty. Strong biceps and muscular forearms, plus those amazing shoulders looked like they could hold up the world. His abdomen was sculpted and ripped. She'd never seen a man so perfectly built and physically superior in every way. Not close up. He had the body of a Greek god, yet he was hot to the touch.

Jack was a real man. Not a marble statue. Thank goodness. She might appreciate the beauty of a work of art, but she knew Jack and his amazing body would never leave her cold. On the contrary, he lit a fire within her that she'd never experienced before.

He lay her back on the bed and kissed her again, each kiss drugging her senses, pulling her further downward into the languorous dream world where reality slipped away, and all that existed was her and Jack. She felt coolness on her legs and realized he'd freed her from both her pants and panties in one long sweep. Her shoes had already clattered to the floor, some time ago, and now, the only thing still between them were his pants.

That would not do. They had to go.

"You're still wearing too many clothes," she told him in a breathy voice she hardly recognized. She tugged at his waistband for emphasis, and he grinned.

"Your wish is my command, milady," he teased, getting up to stand at the side of the bed while he slowly stripped off his pants for her.

The black briefs he wore under the pants were a nice surprise. Sexy. He stripped them off at the same time as the pants, taking it all down in one long slide. When he stood back up, and she got her first good look at him… Oh, *my*.

Daring greatly, she reached out to take him firmly in hand. Jack moved closer. Clearly, he liked what she was doing, so she took things up a notch. Sitting up, she leaned forward to kiss the tip of him, and he shuddered. When she took him into her mouth, he groaned. It was a rumbling sound that was almost a growl. Sexy, squared.

This man was full of surprises, and she liked every single one of them she'd discovered so far. She couldn't wait to learn more about how he made love. What he liked, what he would do to her. All of it. She wanted it all.

"You're killing me, Kiki," he ground out between clenched teeth as she sucked.

He pushed her away gently and put one knee on the bed. Rearranging them so that they were facing each other, laying on their sides, he reached out and cupped her breast with one hand.

"I don't want this to end too soon," he cautioned her.

Kiki leaned up and pushed at his top shoulder so that he rolled onto his back. His eyes widened at her move, but he let her take charge.

"Slow is for later. Right now, I need something faster," she whispered as she straddled his hips. "I hope you don't mind."

"Mind?" His words were tinged with laughter as his eyes flared with hunger. She reached into her nightstand drawer and retrieved a condom. She hadn't had cause to use any since moving into the cottage, but she was glad now, she was prepared for this contingency. He smiled at her when he saw the little packet. "Go for it," he told her, his words a bit strangled as she slid down his body and put the condom on him. He made a little squeak of sound, followed by that sexy rumble that made his whole chest vibrate.

Without further ado, she reached between them and, positioning herself over him, took him inside in one long stroke that left them both gasping. Sweet heaven! That felt good.

From there, she began to ride. Taking him hard and deep, she ground herself against him. Fast, then slow, then faster again. She lost track of time and space. The only thing that existed for her was the magical man beneath her, his hands on her hips, encouraging and supporting her movements.

When she came apart, he let her shudder over him for a short while before he flipped them so that he was on top, charging home within her. She hadn't thought she could go any higher, but Jack proved her wrong as her orgasm spiraled even tighter, reaching for some oblivion she had never seen before. She'd never even known this level of bliss existed.

Kiki cried out his name as she teetered over the edge, exploding into a starburst of fireworks within her body and soul. Jack came with her this time. She felt him shudder, and the growl that rumbled from his chest was even more animalistic, shocking her with the sensual earthiness of the sound.

After long, heavenly moments, he disengaged their bodies then rolled them to their sides as they came down, together. He touched her shoulder then slid his hand down to her waist, pulling her close. His touch was gentle, yet possessive.

She loved the feel of his fingers on her skin.

"You okay?" he asked, his voice a low rumble in the quiet of her bedroom.

She nodded. "Mm-hm." She couldn't really find the energy to put actual words together, but she hoped he'd be able to tell from the silly, satisfied smile on her face that she was way more than just *okay*.

They lay there, like that, for a long time. Finally, Jack got up and went into the small bathroom that was right next door to the bedroom. When he came back, he got back in bed beside her, positioning them so she could snuggle against him. He put his arm around her as he lay on his back.

"Rest a bit," he told her. "If you're agreeable, I'd like to try that again later."

She rose up to look into his eyes, loving the easy humor she found there. "I'm agreeable," she told him, dipping low to place a kiss on his lips. She eased back when he would have taken the kiss deeper to whisper against his lips. "But I don't want to wait."

Like magic, it started all over again. This time, the buildup was slower…and even more intense. She hadn't thought it was possible, but Jack proved her wrong. All night long.

*

Early the next morning, Jack went back to his hotel to get a change of clothing. He didn't want to leave Kiki's warm bed, but he hadn't gone to her house last night prepared to stay over. He needed fresh clothes if he was going to keep the change in their relationship private.

Not that he wasn't thrilled to pieces that she'd allowed him into her bed, and into her confidence last night. Under any other circumstances, he'd be shouting his pride in their new relationship from the rooftops. Only, under current conditions, it could draw too much of the wrong kind of attention from the super-wrong kind of people.

Carol had to realize the *guy from corporate* Jack was

portraying would be trouble, especially if she couldn't manage to get him under her spell. Jack didn't want to give Carol any reason to believe that she could get to him through Kiki. That would only put Kiki in more danger than she was already in, just by working at the plant.

As Jack walked down the hallway toward his hotel room, he went on high alert. Someone was in his room. The feeling Jack was getting wasn't one of danger, however. It was more of curiosity and patience. Trusting his instincts, Jack opened the door to his room cautiously, staying in the doorway, rather than walking straight in.

"Sorry for the intrusion," the man inside the room said, turning to smile at Jack. "Ezra said to make myself at home, and you weren't around last night, so I figured I'd wait to see if you came back to your base or if I should call out the cavalry on your behalf. I'm Ben Steel."

The man didn't step forward or offer his hand. He just stood his ground and waited to see what Jack would do.

Jack's inner beast wanted to rend and tear. How dare someone invade his territory? But Jack's human side appreciated the man's words and held the bear back.

"Give me a moment to verify?" Jack said, already whipping out his phone. He dialed Ezra, not caring that it was the middle of the night in Grizzly Cove.

"Jack," Ezra answered on the first ring. He hadn't been asleep. "You had us worried. Ben said you weren't at your hotel."

"I'm here now," Jack bit out. "And your guy was in my room. I assume he's yours?"

"Yeah. Sorry. Ben Steel. He's my *AC* contact. Now, he's your *AC* contact, too," Ezra said. "He should know better than to invade a bear's territory though. I suspect he's testing you to see how close to the edge your bear is. *AC* operatives are known to play stupid ass games like that, at times." Jack could hear the disgust in Ezra's tone, and it touched a chord within Jack, calming his inner bear.

"I'm putting you on speaker," Jack warned Ezra a moment

before he lowered the phone and tapped the icon that would allow Ben Steel to be part of the conversation.

"Hey, Ben, you should know better than to invade someone else's territory," Ezra said, humor in his tone.

"Sorry. I just didn't like the idea of sleeping out in the hallway." Ben sounded totally unconcerned.

"Don't push him, Ben. Jack's one of the good ones. Now, you two have a lot to discuss, and my mate is getting impatient. It's the middle of the night here, and I've got better things to do," Ezra claimed. Jack could hear the amusement in his tone. Ezra hung up without further ado, leaving Jack and Ben facing each other.

Jack put his phone away. "Well." He looked at Ben and shook his head. "Let's start over. I'm Jack Bishop, and this is my hotel room."

"Ben Steel. Sorry to intrude. You weren't here, and I figured waiting was the best option available at the time." Ben shrugged, and Jack could hear no subterfuge in his tone. Ezra vouched for the guy, which made Jack more likely to trust him.

"What information do you have for me?" Jack would feel his way with this new contact.

"Mind if I sit? I've got some files on my laptop you'll probably want to see." Ben gestured toward the couch and coffee table in one corner of the room where he'd set up his computer and had likely passed the night.

"Be my guest," Jack said, a bit of irony in his voice as Ben moved toward the couch. Jack followed.

"The most important point for you to know is that the janitor, Jeff Pikeman, is an *Altor Custodis* agent of long standing. He's been with the order since his teens and has gone from job to job, filing reports as he goes. Oddly, he only filed a preliminary report on this job, nothing more, which is out of character for him." Ben sat and pulled up the files on the laptop as he spoke. "His previous pattern was to file reports every two weeks, but he's been on this job for months, and aside from that initial check-in, he's gone silent."

"He could be under the influence of the potion witch. Just about everybody at the plant already is," Jack observed as he stood near the couch. He could see the screen of the laptop over Ben's shoulder.

"Ah yes, Ezra filled me in on what you'd learned about Carol Burns. Not too surprisingly, there is no *AC* file on her, but..." Ben typed a few commands on his keyboard and brought up some new files. "The Saginaw-Burns family—which I know she is part of, because I checked—has a long and well-documented history of witchcraft and demonic worship. They're suspected of running one of the premier schools of dark magic in the world. Her great-grandfather, Richard Burns, is still alive and believed to be the head warlock in charge of the educational operation. He's got to be several hundred years old, by now, and suspected of extending his life through the use of blood magic. He's the family patriarch, and I personally think he's high up, if not actually on the high council, of the *Venifucus*."

Jack whistled through his teeth. "Carol is well-connected, then," Jack surmised. "Do you think she's got back up readily available, or is she out here on her own? I'd hate to take her on, and then find out she's got a cadre of black magic commando wizards on call."

"Too early for me to say one way or the other right now. I had hoped you could get me into the plant today, so I can take a look around for myself," Ben told him. "I've made a study of the Burns family and many of their protégés through the years."

"If this old guy is hundreds of years old, he must have trained up quite a few dark practitioners, right?" Jack asked.

"Surprisingly, few have survived to the present day. One thing most people don't talk about in connection with old man Burns is how few of his students actually survive his training." Ben made a grim face. "Like I said, he's keeping himself alive by feeding off others. Who better to drain than another magically gifted being—especially one that has some modicum of trust with you?"

131

"That's disgusting," Jack observed, wondering why anyone would dare to go near the old man, knowing they could easily disappear forever, their magic stolen and their lives extinguished to keep the old warlock going.

"Black magic is hidden because it's often so unpalatable that even most dark mages won't go near it," Ben said philosophically, then shrugged. "Either way, I know most of the Burns family associates who are thought to still be alive. If any of them are at the plant, I can probably sniff them out."

"That's a start," Jack replied. "I'm going to grab a shower, then some breakfast, and I think we need to wake up a few folk in Grizzly Cove. There's still some paperwork I need their help with. After that, we'll both go in to the plant, and I'll introduce you around as my associate from corporate."

CHAPTER 14

When Kiki woke, it was just shortly after dawn, but Jack was gone. He'd told her he might leave the last time they'd made love, just before they both fell asleep. He'd kissed her so beautifully and told her that, if she woke and he wasn't there, it was because he'd gone back to his hotel to get a change of clothes. He'd said he'd leave his cell number on the kitchen table for her and that she should call him when she woke.

As she made her way into the kitchen, she smiled to see the little slip of paper from the memo pad that usually lived near the phone. He'd scribbled his number and had simply written "call me", signing his name in the same bold scrawl.

She dialed his number, and he answered on the second ring. Butterflies took flight in her stomach on hearing his deep voice over the line.

"I just got up, and you were gone," she said.

"You found my note."

Damn, she was getting excited just from the low rumble of his voice over the phone. She'd never seriously contemplated having phone sex before, but he was giving her definite ideas.

"Sorry there's been a change of plans," he told her, nipping that burgeoning fantasy in the bud. His tone was clipped and almost businesslike. "A colleague from corporate was waiting for me when I got in," he explained, and her heart started going at its regular pace again. Then, a horrible thought occurred to her.

"Does that mean you're not coming in today?" Or ever again? Was he being taken off the project? Panic edged its way toward her mind.

"No, we'll be in, but it'll be a bit later in the morning. Possibly not before lunch. We have a big conference call with the home office to do first, and I'm not sure how long that will take." His voice dropped lower, and she could hear a door close in the background. "I'm out in the hallway so we can talk privately," he told her. "Will you be okay on your own? You realize how dangerous the plant is right now, I hope? I don't like the idea of you going in alone."

She was touched by his concern. "I realize the danger, but you know, Carol has been coming in later and later. She's usually never in before eleven these days. I think she does a lot of her…you know…other work…at night, and therefore sleeps in a bit. Bob Boehm hasn't said anything to her, so I assumed they had some sort of special arrangement."

Jack gave a wry chuckle. "It's special all right. He's completely under her spell."

Kiki still had a little trouble talking about such things openly. Magic and spells and that sort of thing were not something her family talked about lightly. Talk like that could get you in real trouble with the neighbors, so it was best not to speak so plainly when dealing in mystical matters. Still, she knew what he meant and was really surprised by the fact that someone outside her own small circle of family believed in such things.

"I'll be okay for the morning. And I'll bring a few things for protection that should help," she added. She was too well trained by her family to tell him exactly what she had planned. Besides, she had no idea if the little talismans and kitchen magic she knew would work. She wasn't one of the truly magical ones in her family.

"We'll try to be in before Carol. Eleven, you said? We'll

aim for ten-thirty." His tone turned intimate. "You'll never know how hard it was for me to leave you this morning."

Kiki gasped. The way he said it made little nerves fire in her midsection. It was a verbal caress.

"I missed you when I got up," she admitted.

"Hopefully, I can make it up to you. Maybe tonight?" he asked, sounding hopeful.

There was no question in her mind. She would accept him in whatever form, time or place he asked. She was smitten, and she was willing to see where this relationship led.

"Sounds like a good plan," she told him, agreeing.

Jack sighed, blowing out a breath she could just about hear over the phone line. "It's going to be a long day," he said, laughing a bit at his own impatience. "But I know it'll be worth it."

Oh, yeah. If tonight was anything like last night, it would be totally worth it.

He rang off with a few more words about timing and the plan for the day, and then, she went about her morning routine with one rather important addition. It was time to get crafty. She went out into the garden and began picking flowers and twigs that had special meanings she had been taught from a young age.

Kiki called on all the lessons of her family heritage, though she'd seldom used it before. In the hands of some of her siblings, these herbs and flowers, along with the ritual words, could be very powerful. She knew that first-hand. She'd seen it with her own eyes, time and time again. The fact that she'd never been able to replicate her siblings' successes didn't mean the herbs and flowers themselves didn't have potent ability to protect and defend against evil.

She was counting on that innate magic to do something to help her ward off evil. After all, it couldn't hurt to wear a sachet of herbs under her clothes, or have one in her car, her pocket, or purse, and it might just help. That thought in mind, Kiki spent the extra hours of the morning preparing a few of the magical sachets she'd been taught to make as a young girl. She spoke the traditional words, though she had no way of knowing if her recitation had any effect, but a ritual was a ritual, and she would follow the steps she had been taught.

Within an hour, she had a handful of small sachets that she distributed throughout her things. Pocketbook, briefcase, sweater pocket. She even tied one around her neck and tucked it inside her shirt, where it wouldn't be seen through her clothing. She also put her star necklace on—the same silver star she'd been given as a teenager by her loving parents. It was the traditional five-pointed star, ringed by a circle, with a single point at the top of the circle where the bail for hanging the pendant off a thin silver chain was located.

A pentacle. That's what it was called by neo-pagans and followers of Wicca in the modern era. Kiki's family didn't label their beliefs. They were just the old ways. The things that they'd had to hide in centuries past or risk being burned at the stake as witches.

The necklace fit easily between her breasts, where it always resided whenever she wore it. She'd taken it off when she'd moved into this cottage because it didn't really fit some of her work outfits, which had lower necklines and a probability that any chain she wore might become dislodged from under her clothing as she bent over her filing cabinet or moved stuff around her office. She didn't usually advertise her beliefs by allowing people to see the pentacle. She'd been trained from a young age to do the exact opposite, in fact.

But, now, things were different. She needed what little protection such talismans might offer. She was facing down what had to be evil. Though she'd never been on the front lines of such battles before, she'd heard stories passed down through her family, and occasionally, one of her siblings might encounter someone or something that had to be dealt with. At such times, they left her out of the action because of her distinct lack of magical talent.

She'd felt bad about being left out. Bad that she couldn't

help when her family needed her. The whole thing had just made her feel *less*, all her life. Now, here she was, ill-equipped to deal with whatever was going on at the plant, but having to do so, nonetheless. She could call her family to come bail her out, but what would that prove? That she wasn't up to the challenge, yet again.

Kiki was tired of being a failure. A non-magical daughter of a highly magical family. She felt strongly that, if she didn't take a stand now, she never would. Jack was here, and he seemed to know what he was doing. She would rely on him to get her through this adventure, and she would help him in whatever small ways she could. She had faith in him, and in the Almighty, to help them defeat whatever evil might block their path to the Light.

By the time she was finished with her gardening and sachet-making, it was almost time to go to work. She got ready as she normally did, but with the important additions of her morning's work secreted here and there about her person and in her things. It may not work, but somehow, just knowing that she'd made the effort made her feel better. Kiki set off for work, looking forward to the moment Jack would get there. She'd feel a thousand times safer with him nearby.

Jack and Ben arrived at the plant around ten forty-five in Ben's rented car. They'd laid out a plan of action before leaving Jack's hotel. Ben would check in with his *AC* contact and see what was going on there, first. Depending on what they learned, they would lay more detailed plans to counter Carol Burns and her vile potions.

They had both agreed that they must eliminate the potion witch, if at all possible, before she poisoned everyone in the entire plant. Jack had pointed out that she might have already done so, but Ben said he wanted to see what the janitor had to say first, before he'd concede that point. There might still be a chance to use the inside man to help them achieve their goals. It all depended on whether or not Jeff the janitor had fallen under Carol's spell.

When they walked in, Jack had no trouble introducing Ben as his *associate* from corporate. The receptionist was helpful in getting Ben I.D. tags so he could go anywhere in the plant, and Jack escorted Ben back to the office area, peeking in at Kiki's door to say hello on his way to his own office.

"Good morning, Kiki. May I introduce Ben Steel? He's my associate from SeaLife Enterprises, come to assist with my mission here."

On the surface, Jack was saying all the appropriate things, well aware that others in the area were listening. He had no doubt that the receptionist had called down to Bob Boehm and maybe even Carol Burns the moment he and Ben had left the reception area.

Kiki stood behind her desk and offered her hand to Ben in a businesslike manner. "Pleased to meet you. Kiki Richards. I'm basically the compliance department, such as it is."

"I'm a big fan of compliance," Ben said, winking in a way that made Jack want to growl. How dare the man flirt with his woman?

That thought came straight from the heart of the bear that lived inside Jack. He did his best to contain the growl that wanted to come out, but he couldn't help the shift of weight that brought him closer to Kiki and nearly body-checked Ben's access to her to shake her hand.

No doubt about it. Jack was getting very possessive of Kiki. Not only that, but his inner bear was getting territorial, which could only mean one thing… A thing he shouldn't think about right now, while so much was on the line. He couldn't afford distractions at the moment. He had to focus on the fight ahead. Once the potion witch and her evil were dealt with, he'd have time to think about personal matters, including one very beguiling human woman who made his bear stand up and want to claim her…forever.

In the meantime, he had to stop Ben from thinking Kiki might be available for his attentions. Believing that directness was usually better than subtlety in such situation, Jack just told it like it was.

"Stop flirting with my girl and let's get to work," he grumbled at Ben, letting just a hint of his bear's growl of displeasure filter through.

Ben stepped back from the desk, chuckling. "Whatever you say, big guy." Ben's hands were held up, palms outward, in a show of surrender, but he was still laughing.

Jack watched until Ben was back in the hallway, then he leaned over the desk and gave Kiki the good morning kiss he'd missed earlier in the day. By the time he left her office, her eyes were dreamy, and he had to work on hiding his own reaction to being near her.

He ushered Ben to the office next door, and they got to work. There were roles to establish during what was left of the morning and then, the real work would begin. But first, Jack had to make one thing absolutely clear.

"Just so you know, she's mine," he growled in a low voice that wouldn't carry beyond his office.

Ben smiled. "I sort of figured that out, but are you sure she knows?"

Jack could only sigh, holding in the snarl of frustration that wanted desperately to come out.

Kiki could have walked on air, her joy making her buoyant at Jack's possessiveness. Some women might've found it insulting, but Kiki took it as a sign of affection. Both her father and her brothers were protective types, and she'd grown used to having the males in her life looking out for her. She wasn't too proud to admit that it had been scary being out here, on her own, facing the kinds of problems she had never faced before.

Jack's presence at her side and watching her back made all the difference. She liked that she could count on him to put her safety first. They'd only known each other a short time, but her instincts—which she had always found to be utterly reliable—told her that Jack was the real deal. A man with a conscience, a code, and a respect for her abilities second only to his desire for her safety.

He was the real thing. The kind of man she wanted to spend the rest of her life with.

It was far too soon to tell if their relationship was heading in a more permanent direction, but she certainly hoped he was feeling some of the same things. She was truly uncertain about where their attraction and nuclear-powered flames of desire might lead them, but she had vowed to enjoy every moment she had with Jack. She believed very much that he might possibly be the one great love of her lifetime. If that was the case, she wanted to cherish every moment of their time together.

He made her feel so good about everything. About life. About herself. She knew the situation at the plant was bad, but with Jack around, she felt like they had a real shot at fixing things.

That he now had help in the form of mysterious Ben Steel reassured her. She didn't know exactly what to make of the man, but he had the same still, watchful quality that Jack did, only more so. Ben gave her a very strong first impression of being the still waters that ran very deep. Ben's gold-tipped light brown hair and blue eyes were striking, but of course, no man could compare with Jack. Not in her eyes.

Jack's energy was just as deep, but a bit more leaked through to the surface of his movements and words. Ben was quieter. More still. Watchful and restrained where Jack was boundless energy that spilled over from a deep core of ancient power.

Her own thoughts startled her, but even as she realized that, she also understood the profound truth of them. Jack had deep-seated magic in his very soul. She could sense that much at least. Ben was…different. Not as obviously powerful to her senses, he still had a core of strength that she hoped would help protect Jack on this perilous mission.

Jack took Ben around the plant himself, giving him a private, and very thorough, tour. He introduced him as his *associate from corporate* whenever they encountered anyone, but mostly, they were left alone. Jack was able to pass on a few observations of various areas when nobody was in earshot, and eventually, he left Ben with a clear view of his quarry.

"That's Jeff," Jack said quietly.

"I recognize him from the file photo, though he's aged a bit," Ben murmured back.

"I'll leave you here, if that's agreeable, and meet you back at my office. Can you find your way?" Jack asked.

"No problem. I'm going to see if Jeff will have lunch with me off-site or at least outside," Ben said, even as he very obviously gauged the situation. Jack could see the small signs that this former Special Forces soldier was observing everything in view and assessing his options. "We have recognition signs that need to be passed and then, I'll ask him for a report. If all goes well, don't expect to see me until after lunch hour."

"Very well. See you then," Jack said, leaving Ben to his covert work and heading back toward the front of the building...where Kiki was. Jack didn't like being too far from her at any given moment.

True to his prediction, Ben didn't return until after lunch. Jack had passed the hour with Kiki, eating their packed lunches in her office. He didn't want to leave her when lunchtime was over, but he had to hear what Ben had found out. Reluctantly, he left Kiki in her office and went to his, next door.

Ben was already there, and he was frowning in thought when Jack entered. Closing the door behind him, Jack then went to take his seat behind the desk, and they settled in for a long discussion of all Ben had learned from his contact.

"First, I have to say," Ben began, "I'm not altogether certain about Jeff's loyalty. He said all the right things, but there's something... Well, there's something not quite right with him." Ben sighed. "I've been told a few times by people I respect that I'm a Sensitive," Ben admitted, surprising Jack.

"You're sensitive to magic?" Jack asked.

Ben nodded tightly, clearly uncomfortable with the concept. "I'm sensing something about Jeff that just doesn't feel right."

"Have you ever encountered black magic in your work?" Jack didn't wait for an answer but went on. "It's a rare specialty that hides its true nature. It doesn't feel the same to me as regular dark magic. There's a more sinister quality to it," he explained. "It's also way more subtle. I only sense the tip of the iceberg with black magic because, like the iceberg comparison, the majority of it remains hidden beneath the surface. It can be tricky."

Ben's mouth formed a grim line of tension. "I'm no expert on magic. My so-called sensitivity is something discovered late in life, and I only became aware of the unseen world when my military career ended. Compared to you, who were raised with the knowledge of your abilities, I'm a novice who is still learning, but I can say that what I'm feeling off Jeff is like nothing I've felt before. It could be that black magic you're talking about."

Jack sat back in his chair and sighed. "Then, we all have to be very, very careful."

"For what it's worth, I think Carol is on her own here. I didn't see or sense anyone who might be a magical ally," Ben reported. "Like I said, I know most of the Burns family associates on sight, and I didn't see any of them here. Some of the things Jeff said also lead me to believe that Carol is striking out on her own, looking to make her own place. This, it appears, is where she's chosen to make her stand as a solo witch."

"Why is that, you think?" Jack asked, thinking hard about the implications of Ben's words.

"Well, as I mentioned, practitioners in her family line don't always last long with her grandfather, and his willingness to kill others to fuel his own artificially-extended life. Maybe she realized he'd be coming for her unless she grew powerful enough to fight back effectively. The strong ones in that family are the ones who survive. Broadening her power base here would fuel her powers significantly and make it much harder for the old man to feed from her."

"It's sick, but it makes sense," Jack said after letting that thought percolate for a moment. "I only hope we caught her before she got too powerful for us to handle."

CHAPTER 15

"One thing I did get from Jeff is that he has been watching. He's even been keeping notes, he claims, though he refused to let me see them. He said he was going to write up a big report at the end, and that's why he hasn't checked in for a while," Ben told Jack as they sat at his desk. The door to the office was closed, and they were keeping their conversation low, so that nobody could hear.

Ben had also set up some sort of electronic jamming device so that nobody could listen in remotely using electronic means. Jack hadn't really thought about that, but then again, he was used to working with his brothers, and King usually took care of stuff like that. Listening devices were more of a human thing, anyway. Jack wouldn't have been worried about such things on his own because he wasn't going to say anything aloud that a bug might pick up.

With a partner, though, that all changed. So, it was a good thing Ben had come prepared. Jack knew Ben had been some kind of Special Forces soldier. He carried himself well for a human, and he was solid muscle with good reaction time. He moved like a man who knew how to fight, which reassured Jack that, if push came to shove, Ben would likely be able to handle himself in a fight.

There was also the faintly metallic tang to his scent that

indicated he carried a number of weapons. Gun oil was just barely detectable to Jack's sensitive nose, as was the shadowy scent of honed steel. Knives and firearms, no doubt. Jack was glad. Ben might need some advantages if Carol moved against them before they were ready.

"We're going to call all this in to Ezra tonight," Jack decided. "If the scat hits the fan here, I want him to know what's been going on."

"Good idea," Ben concurred.

"There's also a specialist in the cove that might have more information on how we can combat this particular problem. I'm going to suggest strongly that Ezra get her on board," Jack thought aloud.

"A woman?" Ben asked, one eyebrow rising skeptically. Jack had to remind himself that Ben was human, with human sensibilities. He wasn't used to shifter women, many of whom were even more fierce than their male counterparts, though much slower to rile.

"A potion witch," Jack clarified, thinking about Mellie. He'd met her briefly when he'd visited his brothers and their new mates, but he didn't know the *strega* potion witch well enough to just call her on his own. "I figured we should try to fight fire with fire. Or, at least, learn how to fight this kind of thing from someone who knows Carol's type of magic best."

"Good thinking," Ben said, nodding, his lips pursed in a thoughtful frown.

They spent the afternoon going over files and discussing plans. Jack really wanted to spend his evening with Kiki, but he knew the mission had to come first. He would do the meeting with Ezra and Ben, but as soon as that was done, he was planning on spending the night with Kiki again—if she'd let him. He suspected she would, despite the fact that he hadn't been free to spend much time with her at all today.

Perhaps that was for the best, though. It was better not to let the enemy know that they had any special relationship. The last thing Jack wanted to do was make Kiki more of a target. He knew there was some risk to her simply because she'd so far evaded attempts to put her under Carol's spell with the rest of the workforce, but he figured, with his office right next door, he'd be able to hear if anything untoward happened in Kiki's domain, even through a closed door. His hearing was exceptional, and he had always been able to sense magic if it was being used nearby.

Ben, too, was a self-proclaimed Sensitive. If the two of them missed something happening right next door to them, then they had seriously underestimated the enemy. If that was the case, they were in a whole lot of trouble.

Planning took up most of the afternoon. Ben and Jack didn't leave the office at all, and they didn't hear or sense any signs of trouble from next door. In fact, Kiki had been quiet for the past hour or more, as if she was deep into reading or writing one of her reports. Jack smiled as he stood, stretching his muscles before he stepped out from behind the desk.

"I think that's all we can do for now. Let's get Kiki and head out. We'll have dinner together, and then, I'll drop her home before our conference call," Jack improvised, ignoring Ben's knowing look.

Jack went past Ben, who was still sitting in the chair on the guest side of Jack's desk, and went to the door. He opened it and peeked out, surprised to find the hallway exceedingly quiet. He couldn't hear any background noises from the office area just down the hall, which was unusual. Going on instant alert, he signaled back to Ben, who came to his feet immediately.

"Something's not right," Jack said in the quietest tone Ben would be able to hear. "Be on your guard."

"Ready," Ben said not a moment later. Jack glanced back to see a lethal black pistol held familiarly in Ben's beefy hand. Jack nodded once. "Just don't shoot me if I need to go furry."

"Wouldn't dream of it," Ben replied immediately. "I'm loaded with silver."

Damn. The human wasn't taking any chances. Silver was poisonous to many different kinds of supernatural folk, including shifters. It didn't kill Jack's kind outright, but it was one of the few things that could take a bear down and keep him down for a good long while. Getting the silver out was a high priority, and any missed bits could poison a shifter's blood, possibly unto death.

Jack nodded tightly, acknowledging Ben's statement. "I'm going to check on Kiki. You keep watch."

"Right behind you," Ben replied. Jack was glad to have at least some backup right now, even if Ben was human, and they'd never really worked together before.

"Something smells off," Ben reported the moment his feet crossed over the threshold and he was in the hallway with Jack. "Like ozone and…"

"Brimstone." Jack grimaced as a growl sounded low in his chest. Something had happened out here in the hall while they'd been obliviously sitting behind his closed office door. *Shit.*

He rushed to Kiki's door and opened it without knocking. The magical residue hit him in the face, and he had to brace his feet to keep himself from stumbling backward.

"Some kind of ward that dampens sound and sensation," Ben said, his tone dark. "I can feel it now that we're outside your office. Fuckers sealed us off behind a ward so we wouldn't know what was going on around us."

"Kiki's gone, and she didn't go voluntarily," Jack growled, not caring that the furious bear inside him was aching to get out and rend and tear those responsible for taking Kiki away. "She wouldn't have left her purse or her jacket, and it looks like there was a struggle in here," he went on. Ben was at his back, facing the hallway, acting the part of alert backup, though Jack feared those who had snatched Kiki were long gone.

"Damn," Ben said after shooting a quick glance over Jack's shoulder and seeing the wreckage in Kiki's office. "What do we do now?"

Jack heard a loud crack and realized he'd tightened his grip on the doorframe so much that he'd splintered the wood. He finished the job and threw the chunk of wood in his hand down the hallway in disgust.

"We get her back."

*

Kiki couldn't believe what had just happened. One minute, she'd been minding her own business, working in her office. The next, Carol had walked in without knocking and demanded Kiki go with her. Kiki had refused, of course, and then, things had gotten violent.

Carol had grabbed one of Kiki's hands and pulled her out from behind her desk while Bob Boehm had entered the small office behind Carol and grabbed Kiki around the waist. He'd picked her up, even though Kiki had done her best to kick and scream the place down, but they'd done something, and Jack didn't hear.

The air around her had felt dead, muffled, as if sound wasn't carrying beyond her immediate position. Jack's door was still closed, and he didn't hear her. Panic set in, and she'd fought like a wildcat, kicking out, even as her hands were pulled behind her back. She managed to make a huge mess of her office, so at least Jack would know something had happened when he finally came out to check on her. She knew he would. And then... Then, he'd rescue her. If at all possible.

As she looked at Carol's self-satisfied expression, Kiki feared that they had greatly underestimated Carol's abilities. She only hoped Jack would figure that out before he did something rash.

As they dumped her in to a big canvas wheelie bin and rolled her down the hallway toward the warehouse, Kiki prayed as she had never prayed before. Bob had tied her hands together behind her back when he'd been manhandling her and now, as she rolled around at the bottom of the canvas hamper, her arms felt like they were being wrenched out of their sockets. She screamed, but nobody seemed to hear.

The hamper itself seemed to be muffling any sound she made. Could it have been bespelled in some way? If everything Jack had said about Carol's abilities and proclivities was true, then there was little doubt she'd be able to make it so that Kiki's cries would go unheard.

The wheels of the giant canvas bin made noise Kiki could just about hear. Dampened by the carpet in the office area, the sound of the wheels changed when the bin was pushed onto the tiled floor of the lab area. Kiki thought maybe they'd stop when they reached Carol's lab, but no. The hamper was pushed through the lab area and into the production area, then into the warehouse itself.

The place she'd avoided ever since that late-night episode where she'd seen some sort of evil ritual taking place. She'd never wanted to go back to the warehouse. Not after what she'd seen. It seemed all her resolution not to return to the scene of the ritual had been for naught. When Bob lifted the wooden cover off the hamper and she could see where they had taken her, she was right back at that exact spot where the altar had been set up that fateful night.

The altar was back. Kiki's stomach sank into her shoes as she took in the scene. It certainly looked as if the place had been prepared for another ritual—this time, during the day. Carol had grown bolder since Kiki's first days on the job if she was willing to do this sort of thing during working hours when anybody might see.

Of course, if she already had everyone at the plant under her spell, Carol could afford to be bold. Nobody would interfere. On the contrary, they'd probably all be lining up to partake in the ritual. Sheep to the slaughter, Kiki thought, only she hoped the image that conjured wouldn't turn out to be literal.

"Bring her up to the altar," Carol instructed Bob, looking down into the hamper where Kiki was on her knees, trying to keep her balance.

Bob reached down and lifted her with his hands under her

arms. Someone else grabbed her legs, and together, they carried her to a chair that had been set up in front of the altar. Kiki tried to kick free, but the janitor's hands—she finally recognized Jeff as the guy who held her feet—were surprisingly strong.

They deposited her in the chair none too gently, then Bob fasted her ankles to the chair so she couldn't get up and run away. Her hands were still bound behind her back, so she had to sit forward a bit to ease the pressure on her shoulders. She was completely uncomfortable, but she was certain Carol either didn't give a damn or was glad of causing Kiki pain.

"What are you doing?" Kiki asked as Carol began laying a line of…something…in front of Kiki and making her way around the altar. Whatever the substance was, it poured like water but looked like tar once it was on the ground. Kiki felt echoes of the evil that had created it, sending shivers down to her bones.

Carol didn't answer. She was too busy speaking vile words under her breath that Kiki couldn't bear to hear. Evil words. A ritualistic chant calling on dark powers. The bitch was casting a black ward around Kiki, herself, and the altar.

Kiki felt panic take hold. This could not be good.

When Carol had finished making her circle and closed it back in front of Kiki with a resounding magical snap of the ward going up, Kiki wanted to cry. She was sealed inside this ring with a madwoman, a black altar and whatever Carol planned to do. Kiki couldn't move, and though she'd been fighting her bonds all along, they hadn't gotten any looser. She was a sitting duck.

Carol lifted her head once the ring was complete and took a deep breath. Her smile was pure evil as she turned to look at Kiki.

"Now…we wait." Carol surprised Kiki with those words. She thought for sure the next item on today's sinister agenda would be Kiki's death, but for whatever reason, Carol was waiting for something. That made Kiki curious.

"What are you waiting for, exactly?" she dared to ask.

"Your boyfriend," Carol answered easily, making Kiki frown. "He's the real prize here. I want him, and I believe he'll come to get you. He's foolish enough that he'll probably trade himself for your safety. I've seen it before. Shifters can be so stupid."

Shifters? Kiki didn't quite understand what Carol was talking about, but whatever she was getting at, she apparently believed Jack was the prize she was really after. Kiki was just bait in a trap to get to Jack.

Somehow, that didn't make Kiki feel any better. She loved Jack. She hadn't been prepared to really admit that to anyone, just yet—even herself, apparently—but to hear Carol threaten him had brought everything into much sharper focus. She loved Jack and didn't want to see him fall into this trap, even if it meant more peril for herself. She had to figure a way to warn him.

"Nothing to say?" Carol asked Kiki with a sickly smile. "That's okay. I never liked you anyway, you know. You're too insipid. This is going to be fun." Carol's eyes widened as her smile turned psycho.

She leaned over and pulled a knife off the altar. Kiki could see the highly-decorated hilt as Carol held it up to the faint lights of the warehouse. It was silver with all sorts of arcane symbols. Some of them, Kiki recognized, but they were all wrong. The star in the circle was upside-down. The two points on top forming devil's horns, according to the teachings of her kin. Evil.

Likewise, some of the other symbols were recognizable as something she'd seen in her family teachings, but reversed or changed slightly to be something…not good. Kiki shied away from the sharp tip of the blade when Carol brought it close to her face. Carol laughed, and it sounded more like the cackle of a witch out of some dark fairytale.

"I just need a little bit of blood," Carol said in a sing-song tone, tracing the tip of the evil dagger down over Kiki's cheek and then on to her neck. She paused with the tip at Kiki's jugular. "It would be so easy to plunge my athame into your neck and end you right now. I've wanted you dead for a while—ever since you interrupted my ritual that night." Kiki sucked in a breath while Carol chuckled. "Yes, I knew you had seen us. I let you go to see what you'd do. As it turned out, that worked to my advantage because, somehow, you lured a shifter into my web. For that, I'll let you live a little longer." The deadly blade moved lower. "I need you alive a bit longer to seal the deal with the bear."

"What's this?" Carol asked, using the tip of the blade to lift the silver chain that had been secreted under Kiki's blouse. Kiki felt the pentacle rising out of her shirt until it was visible to Carol. Kiki's eyes sought the other woman's, wanting to see her reaction. "You've got to be kidding me. You're a witch?" Disbelief colored Carol's words, and Kiki found it insulting.

She realized in that moment that she could not let Carol know that she was the weakest of a long lineage of truly powerful magic users. If Kiki died here, Carol might very well go after her family, and Kiki couldn't bear the thought of that. Instead, she tried to invent a story that Carol might believe.

Kiki shrugged one shoulder. "I dabble," she said. "A good friend of mine in school was Wiccan, and he got me interested. It was my way to rebel, I guess. Believe it or not, I used to dress Goth."

Carol let the chain drop, leaving the pentacle outside of Kiki's shirt as she gave Kiki a sideways look. Kiki wasn't sure if Carol believed her or not, but she left the pentacle in place, which made Kiki feel like she'd at least won a small victory. And, for some unknown reason, Carol hadn't spotted, or didn't care about, the little ribbon around Kiki's neck that held the herbal sachet she'd picked that morning.

"You can keep the trinket for now, but it won't do you much good against my power," Carol gloated as she returned the blade to Kiki's skin, tracing down the opening of her blouse. Pausing, Carol dug the blade into the skin just over Kiki's heart, collecting a bit of her blood on the tip.

Leaving Kiki for the moment, Carol went around behind the altar. Kiki had to strain to see what Carol was doing behind her, but it looked like she was putting the little drop of Kiki's blood into a bowl that was on the altar. Damn. She was probably making some kind of potion, though what it might do, Kiki had no idea. She only hoped Jack would figure out what was going on before he barreled in here, guns blazing.

CHAPTER 16

Jack tracked Kiki's path using his nose. Her scent was faint, but not too faint for his shifter senses to follow. Ben came with him, guarding his back while Jack forged ahead slowly, not wanting to blunder in to find himself in the middle of a trap. Everything about this seemed fishy, but he knew one thing for certain. Whatever was going on, Kiki wasn't playing him false.

She might be the bait in a trap set for him, but not of her own volition. He knew her well enough to know that, for certain. He also had the steadfast belief that a woman—even a human woman with little magic of her own—could never betray her mate that way.

And, from the reaction of his inner bear to her disappearance, he was pretty darn sure she was, in fact, his mate. He'd felt it before. He'd hoped it was so. But, until this moment, he hadn't really been able to see the truth. Kiki was the woman meant for him. He might've been a bit mistrustful of his instincts to this point, but he was all on board now.

The thing was… He had to approach her cautiously. He didn't want to scare her off.

First, of course, he had to deal with whatever Carol was planning and free Kiki. Then, he'd have time to woo her and convince her to be his mate forever more. With renewed resolve, he focused on the hunt…and on avoiding any traps his prey might have set for him.

The first of those traps appeared not three minutes after he thought of it. Jeff the janitor stepped out of a supply closet and moved closer. He held a gun in his hand and a dead look in his eyes.

"This is loaded with silver hollow points," Jeff said in a flat tone. "The hollow tips are filled with pure silver powder. This shit will even kill a bear, Carol says. A shifter bear."

"Will it now?" Jack asked conversationally, wondering where Ben had disappeared to. One moment, he was right behind him. The next, Ben was gone, and Jack was facing off with a clearly entranced *AC* operative with far too much knowledge and far too little free will.

"Carol says, if you come quietly, she may even let the girl live. You could exchange places with her," Jeff told him. "I just have to take you to her. That or shoot you," Jeff said, his tone absolutely chilling in its utter flatness. "Your choice."

Jack didn't react as Ben came out of nowhere and grabbed Jeff from behind, relieving him of the gun before Jeff could get a shot off. Jack moved closer to help, but Ben had his *AC* comrade well in hand. Zip ties bound Jeff's arms, then his legs, in short order.

"You've done this before," Jack observed.

"Too many times," Ben agreed, stuffing a clean rag he'd grabbed from the janitor's closet into Jeff's mouth and tying it in place with another. "We can leave him in there for now. I don't want to hurt him if we don't have to. It's not his fault he was stupid and got caught up in Carol's spell." Ben closed the closet door on the trussed up janitor, wedging a chair under the knob for good measure.

Jack growled his agreement. "Your buddy, Jeff, saw me in the woods a few nights ago. He must've reported the bear sighting back to the witch, and she loaded him with ammo that could take down a shifter."

"We have to assume she knows what you are—or at least, she suspects," Ben agreed. "That changes the complexion of this situation a bit."

"It's a trap. Of that, I have no doubt," Jack said, nodding once.

"Forewarned is forearmed," Ben told him. "I don't think she knows about me. Maybe I can be your ace in the hole."

"Maybe." Jack tilted his head, looking at the other man. "But you look nothing like my brother, Ace."

Ben grinned, as did Jack. This kind of humor was something he'd only ever shared with his brothers, but it was good to meet others—real warriors like Ben Steel, former U.S. Navy SEAL—who could also appreciate a little joke under pressure. Jack might just have made a friend.

Jeff dealt with and out of the picture, they pressed on, moving even more carefully. Ben was a ghost at his back, not too close, but not too far, either. Jack was impressed by the human's stealth and ability to blend into the background. It was clear Ben was highly trained and very experienced with covert missions. He was as light on his feet as any shifter and as quiet as a mouse, which Jack appreciated.

As they came to the final door before the warehouse area Kiki had pointed out, Jack called a halt. He wanted to fill Ben in before they moved any closer.

"Remember that ritual I told you Kiki had reported?" Jack asked in a voice just above a whisper that wouldn't carry beyond Ben's ears. Ben nodded. "This is the area of the warehouse where it happened. My bet is that Carol is set up in her ritual space, which means she has the high ground. I'm going to take the direct approach. You, *Ace*, are going the roundabout way. Copy?"

Ben nodded again. "Keepin' it covert," Ben agreed. "Roger that. You want Jeff's gun?" One side of Ben's mouth lifted in a half-grin.

"Better not. It could have been tampered with by the witch. Nice as it would be to rub her nose in it, I'll decline." Jack watched Ben frown as he unloaded the firearm, planting the bullets in the sand of a cigarette butt holder placed near the doorway. He tossed the gun into a rain barrel a little farther away.

"That'll keep it safe enough for now," Ben mused when he was done. "We'll come back and clean that up later."

With that, Ben took off for the corner of the huge building, seeking another way in. Jack had given Ben the blueprints for the entire plant last night, so they both knew there was a few other entrances Ben could choose from, depending on what he found on the other side of the building.

Jack was on the more direct route. The same route they'd taken Kiki. He could smell her delicate scent, just barely, in the air. Jack opened the door, knowing he was stepping into a trap, but he didn't see any other way. His bear wouldn't let him do more reconnaissance. It wanted to see her and make sure she was okay. It wanted to free her. Now. No room for argument.

Jack trusted his bear to see him through whatever was going to happen. If he'd failed to understand the true danger of their opponent, that was on him. He'd known Carol was dealing in black magic. He'd thought he'd taken her measure, but the fact that she'd been able to kidnap Kiki out from right next door to him meant he'd been wrong. So very wrong.

He only hoped he had enough strength inside him to withstand whatever Carol could dish out. The direct approach might get him killed, but he'd take Carol out—and free Kiki—if it was the last thing he ever did.

Jack walked into the warehouse. At first, he didn't see anything out of the ordinary. There were shelving units just beyond the door, starting about fifteen feet from the small parking area where a forklift and a scissor lift were kept ready and waiting for use in this part of the warehouse. Jack proceeded with caution, moving quietly and quickly among the towering rows, keeping his eyes peeled for any sign of Carol or her followers.

He went down the aisle between the rows of shelving units that stretched up into the sky, knowing that somewhere ahead, oppressive magic was being used. He could feel it, the closer he moved. Black magic, shielding its own presence, but in such strength here that it could be felt, even as it sought to hide itself. Damn.

Carol was way more powerful than Jack had suspected. He'd allowed himself to be deceived by outward signs, when he should have been looking deeper all along. Black magic was like that. It was deceptive. Tricky. Deceitful.

Jack felt like a big fat sucker for having fallen for it. He'd known better, but he'd been distracted. He'd taken his eyes off the prize, and now, Kiki was in danger. It was his own damned fault.

No use crying about it now. Action was required to fix this shitty situation. Jack just hoped that, in a head-on contest, he could prevail against Carol and her little army of zombie followers.

Using caution, Jack peered through the last few rows to see if he could discern what was going on in the big open space just beyond the last row of shelves. He caught glimpses that set his temper off. Kiki was there, her ankles bound to a chair, her arms twisted—no doubt, also tied up—behind her. She wasn't gagged, but he couldn't hear anything she said, though her lips were moving as she talked to Carol.

There was a black ring on the floor around her and Carol…and what looked like an altar at her back, swathed in black satin. Jack's inner bear wanted to rend and tear, stalk and kill. It wanted the witch who dared touch his mate dead.

The human side counselled the bear to patience. Kiki looked okay for now, though every moment she was in Carol's clutches was an agony for his protective soul and only served to make him angrier. He could harness that anger and use it to their advantage. He had to. Kiki's life was on the line.

He watched as Carol went behind the altar and stirred a bowl there with a red-tipped dagger. Red-tipped? He couldn't scent anything inside the circle, but he knew it had to be blood on the tip of that knife. Kiki's blood. Incensed, he stepped out from behind the shelving.

All heads turned to look in his direction as he deliberately made noise to announce his arrival. Anything to make Carol pause in her evil deeds.

The move worked. She looked up and smiled, right at him. He couldn't hear what she was saying through the barrier she had put up around herself, the altar and Kiki, but he understood the look in her eyes. She thought she had triumphed. Maybe she had, maybe she hadn't. As far as Jack was concerned, the jury was still out on that one.

He stepped forward, Carol's minions—the workers from the plant—spread apart, forming a lane for him to approach. It was a creepy version of the parting of the Red Sea, only it wasn't water, it was people. People under a potion witch's control. The next best thing to zombies.

When they closed in around him after he stepped into their midst, still leaving that lane open to the altar, he tried not to wince. Jack could deal with these people, but he'd rather not hurt any of them. For one thing, he didn't know how many of them had entered into this willingly. It could very well be that they'd all fallen victim to Carol's magic.

They might be innocent dupes, unwittingly forced into doing what they'd been doing to support Carol's lust for power all this time. If he could break the spell, he might be able to free them. Jack would much rather do that than possibly injure, or even kill, anybody.

Carol lowered her dagger, stepping out from behind the altar. He could see her lips moving. She was talking to Kiki, who looked like she started screaming when she saw him. She was trying to warn him, bless her. He couldn't hear her words, but the intent was clear. She was telling him to run, to get out. She was screaming about how it was a trap.

Sweet, sweet, Kiki. She wasn't yelling for him to come save her, but for him to get away and save himself. He would have to make her fully aware—after this was all over, of course—as to why that was impossible. He could never leave her in danger. He would give his life for hers. He had been born to protect her. It was his honor and his privilege.

Now, he just had to explain that all to her and get her to agree. After he dealt with this little witch problem first, of course.

"Well, would you look at that," Carol spoke to herself, it seemed. Kiki could see some kind of disturbance out in the warehouse among the gathered people who worked at the plant, but she didn't know what was causing it. "Seems my little trap worked like a charm."

Carol sounded smug. Which meant she must think that Jack had fallen for her ploy. Kiki searched the crowd as it parted before her, leaving a lane open to… Jack.

Her heart fell. He looked angry and determined. He also looked so good to her she wanted to cry. She wanted to scream out to him and tell him to run. That it was a trap. That Carol was after him, for some unknown reason.

Kiki tried to yell, but he didn't seem to hear her.

"Oh, shut up, will you?" Carol shouted, sounding disgusted, behind her. "He can't hear you. He can't hear me either, right now, but not for long. I can make myself heard through my ward, but don't bother screaming. He'll never be able to hear you again, once I'm through."

A chill of fear ran down Kiki's spine as Carol moved to Kiki's side and lifted that creepy dagger. Carol pointed the tip of the knife to her own throat and spoke a dark word. Suddenly, Carol's words echoed almost painfully around the circular ward when she spoke.

"Welcome to my little party, Jack. You should have played nice, and I would have rewarded you before I drained your power and made you my plaything." Carol's voice dripped with something cloying and dark. Kiki wanted to retch.

"I don't know what you think you're doing, but you have to let the girl go. She doesn't know anything about anything, as I'm sure you realize by now." Jack's voice sounded far away, as if coming to Kiki's ears down a long tunnel.

"If I do, you'll come to me willingly?" Carol sounded as if

she didn't believe him, her voice scornful. "I wasn't born yesterday, grizzly man. You'll submit, or I'll kill her. Slowly. While you watch, helpless." Carol sounded way too happy about that scenario. "Letting her go isn't part of my plan at the moment." Carol raised her arms like a conductor at a symphony concert. With an audible whoosh, she then dropped them to her sides.

For a moment, nothing happened. One heartbeat. Two. On the third, all the workers from the plant turned on Jack, like zombies going after the only living soul on the planet. Kiki screamed, but she knew Jack couldn't hear her. He had his hands full fending off an attacking horde.

He seemed to go down under a pile of people and then… Something stirred. A pale green and yellow-gold light came from the center of the knot of people, resolving into a golden brown filled with the energies of the earth. Something was happening. Something Kiki didn't fully understand.

One minute, Jack was in big trouble, and the next, the people that had been menacing him were flying through the air, launched outward from the center of power by those same golden brown energies. Magic. Visible for the first time in her life to Kiki, without a boost from one of her family members. She could actually *see* this magic, which meant it had to be amazingly powerful since she was such a poor witch.

The power grew outward from the center, and where Jack had been standing, there was now a giant—absolutely freaking *huge*—grizzly bear. Kiki blinked, not quite believing her eyes.

"Oh, goody. The fur ball has come out to play," Carol crowed. "What do you think of your boyfriend now?" Carol seemed to be taunting Kiki, but she could only shake her head. "Oh, poor little Kiki. You didn't know anything about shifters, did you? Honey, I hate to break it to you, but your boyfriend is a bear. Literally." The sarcasm dripping from her voice set Kiki back. Did she really mean…?

Kiki looked at the bear, now rushing toward her, sending

BIANCA D'ARC

the workers flying in every direction if they got too close to him. She noticed that he carefully kept his claws away from the people. He was going out of his way not to hurt anyone more than necessary. Sweet Lord! Jack really was the bear!

And the bear really was Jack. Good heavens.

Jack went full bear and raced forward, only to be brought up sharp by the evil black line of Carol's ward. Try as he might, the ward blocked him. Jack paced back and forth around the curve of the circle in front of Kiki. He had to find a way through. That's all there was to it.

The ward itself had hurt when he clashed with it. He could smell singed fur and knew the ward had burned where he'd touched it. The pain was nothing at the moment. The priority in his mind was to get to Kiki and free her of Carol's threat.

Jack had to throw the people who continued to come at him away. He did it as gently as possible, but he knew some of them would wind up with broken bones simply because of the way they landed. They were moving slow, like zombies under Carol's control, which helped, but they just kept coming. All the while, Carol had time to do more spells.

She might be primarily a potion witch, but that didn't mean she couldn't cook up more nastiness for him to deal with on his way to defeating her. Just as he thought that, Jack noticed a lull in the crowd as they parted to let another of their number through. It was Bob Boehm, and he was carrying a rifle.

Jack had little doubt the ammunition in that firearm would prove to be as painful to shifters as the stuff that had been in the janitor's gun. It wouldn't kill Jack outright—not unless Bob made a very, very lucky shot—but enough poisoned holes in his hide would probably disable Jack enough so that Carol's minions could subdue him. If that happened, they were toast.

"You can run, bear, but then my friend Bob there will just shoot Kiki instead. I have the ability to let things pass through my ward, if I so choose, and I would definitely

162

choose to let him shoot little Kiki in your place," Carol taunted him, giving him no real choice. He would protect Kiki with his last breath. If that meant standing in the way of a bullet to save her from taking it, he would, even if that bullet was nearly guaranteed to stop him in his tracks.

Bob was far enough away that Jack couldn't leap on him before he fired the shot. Carol had taken Jack's shifter abilities into account when she'd laid this trap. Jack stood his ground, in front of Kiki's chair, so close, yet so far away with the evil ward keeping them apart. Jack was big enough in his bear form that he totally blocked Kiki's sitting form. At least he had the satisfaction of knowing that he'd take the bullet, and it wouldn't harm her.

What came after, he still didn't know. The situation looked grim, but he would take it one step at a time and hope he'd find an opportunity to turn the tables. Somehow.

Bob stood, taking careful aim. He was back toward the edges of the crowd that had parted to give him a clear shot, but Jack could see him clearly. Bob's eyes were glazed. He was fully under control of the potion witch.

A second later, a shot rang out.

CHAPTER 17

Jack heard the shot but felt no impact. Then he realized, the shot hadn't been from the rifle but rather, a handgun. He searched the periphery of the room, where the shelving units were stacked all around and spotted the flash of moving metal. Ben.

Ben had taken Bob out before he could make the shot. And, even as Jack watched, Bob toppled over, clutching his leg. He'd let the rifle fall to the concrete floor. Ben snagged its strap with a picking hook used in the warehouse and dragged it away from Bob's prone body. Jack doubted Carol could see Ben in the dim light of the warehouse, but Jack saw it all with his superior vision. He even caught the hand signal Ben made before he moved on to another hiding spot, telling Jack he'd called for backup.

Jack wasn't sure what kind of backup Ben might have in this part of the country, but even human military or police were better backup than nothing. Jack just hoped he found a way into the circle so he could take Carol out before anyone else was put in jeopardy.

With the immediate threat taken care of, Jack could concentrate on trying to break through Carol's black ward. He pushed up against the barrier, hoping sheer brute force would get him through, but all that did was singe more of his fur. His innate magic protected him from Carol's magical taint, but it did take something out of Jack to stand in direct opposition to her spell.

He'd have to find another way to get to Kiki, but for the life of him, he couldn't think of anything at the moment. Of course, Carol wasn't going to give him much chance to sit still and ponder the situation. Even as he contemplated, he saw her moving back behind the altar. She had more tricks up her sleeve. He just had to hope he could counter at least one of them in such a way as to give himself the opening he needed to get through to Kiki.

Kiki could hear what was going on outside the ward, though she knew Jack couldn't hear her. Carol had tight control over what entered or left the circle of her evil protection.

When Bob showed up with a rifle, Kiki almost stopped breathing. Jack blocked her vision and she knew he meant to protect her with his own body. On hearing a shot, she screamed, but the bear didn't move.

She could barely see from this distance in the dim light of the warehouse, but it sure looked like Bob fell over, from what little she could make out over the shoulders of the giant bear. Someone had shot Bob!

She cringed. She'd been raised to believe it wasn't right to be happy to see someone hurt—possibly killed—but she couldn't help but feel a bit of joyful satisfaction that Bob had been stopped from shooting Jack. She didn't know who had shot Bob, but if she'd been a betting woman, her money would have been on Ben Steel. He'd looked like a soldier to her civilian eyes. From his clean cut hair to his upright stance, that steady gaze of his had made her feel like he had seen a lot in his life…and had probably done even more.

Jack tried to force his way through the ward, but though his strength was impressive, Kiki could see that the magic of Carol's dark ward was hurting him…and draining his strength. There had to be a way to get that ward to fall.

165

As Carol worked at the altar behind her, Kiki searched her memory for anything her family might have taught her about this kind of thing. She wasn't much of a witch, but she'd been raised among several very strong magic users. She knew a bit of the craft, just from being around them.

Unfortunately, she knew from bitter experience that even if she spoke the right combinations of words and chanted at the top of her lungs, she didn't have the internal magic necessary to do anything against Carol. Her only—albeit small—successes in the realms of magic had been when she was able to harness the everyday magic of ordinary things. Common folk magic that didn't require the energy of the user to spark the spell.

Simple charms…earth magic…herbal remedies…

Kiki's gaze met those of the bear that was…somehow…Jack. At that exact moment, knowledge came to her. She knew what she had to do.

Their eyes locked, an eternity compressed into a single glance. She loved this man—who could turn into a bear, apparently—but that didn't change who he was. She could see the desperation and fear in his eyes, along with the resolute strength that made her love him all that much more.

He'd put himself between her and Bob's rifle. He'd been willing to die for her. A truer act of love she had never seen. It was only right that they solve this problem together, and, if the Lord above was smiling on them, they would spend the rest of their lives exactly the same way…together.

Kiki tried to tell Jack with her expression that she had an idea, but she wasn't sure how much got through. Better to just do it. He was a smart man—a smart bear—he'd figure it out soon enough. And she had to do something before Carol unleashed whatever nastiness she had brewing in that bowl on the altar. The fact that Carol was distracted with her potion-making was also a huge plus as Kiki squirmed on her chair.

She eyed the circle of black goo all around her. The thought of touching that sinister darkness was repugnant, and

Kiki sensed the power of it could probably kill her, frail human that she was, outright. Jack had to be immensely powerful to withstand so much contact with the ward.

Kiki knew she must break the circle and collapse the evil ward. She had just the thing to do it, too. In her pocket. The sachet of herbs picked in that magical garden outside her cottage only this morning. Pure, potent and blessed with the words she had spoken as she made the sachets, it just might work to counter the evil blackness on the floor of the warehouse that kept Jack and her apart.

The only thing that gave her pause was that when such a ward came down, its energy would come at anyone nearby, in a mad rush. Kiki was glad of the pentacle around her neck. It just might save her from the bombardment that would come at the moment of the ward's destruction. Maybe.

Either way, the ward had to come down or much worse would happen. Kiki shifted both hands, tied as they were, to her side and was just able to get one of her hands into her pocket, though it was incredibly awkward. Jack turned away to deal with the zombie horde that began harassing him again, while Carol worked on her potion. Thankfully, Carol was distracted enough that she didn't seem to notice what Kiki was doing.

Moving carefully and making as little motion as possible, Kiki maneuvered the sachet into her hand and then freed her hands from the pocket. Carol still didn't seem to notice anything, but Kiki strained around to keep an eye on the witch as best as she could, while also picking her spot and planning out how she was going to get the sachet onto the black line of goo that circled her and the altar.

She had one shot. Kiki breathed deep and shifted the sachet of herbs so that she held it in both hands. She'd never been much for sports, but desperate times called for desperate measures. Releasing her breath, she made her move on the exhale, praying hard that her aim would be true.

At the moment of release, Kiki saw Carol jerk her head up out of the corner of her eye. Too late, Kiki thought, even as

Carol screamed a single word.

"No!"

The vowel elongated as time slowed. The word turned into a scream of rage as the sachet landed squarely on the black line, and Kiki held her breath.

For one heartbeat, nothing happened. Then, she could see the black goo smoking as it ate away at the pure cotton of the little pouch. The moment the herbs were revealed, the black magic ward fell with a whoosh, and the bear's deep growl filled Kiki's ears as he sailed over her head to take Carol down to the ground behind her cursed altar.

Kiki didn't see what the bear did to Carol, but she felt the reaction as her magic drained away. The pentacle protected her from the swirling mass of dark energy. It came from the altar, from behind it where the bear and Carol were…and from the people.

Kiki could actually see swirls of darkness lifting off of every person in her immediate vicinity as they dropped to their knees. Some landed on their butts. All fell down in one way or another, to litter the concrete floor of the warehouse as they mostly fell unconscious.

The only one left standing was Ben Steel, who came out from behind a shelving rack, weapon in hand. He was on alert, checking over the bodies of those who had fallen. He took a few firearms off some of the men and women on the floor and dumped their ammo into a bag he wore over one shoulder, placing the empty guns into another bag worn over his other shoulder, the straps of both bags forming an X across his chest. He was wearing dress pants and a white shirt with the sleeves rolled up over muscular forearms, but he looked totally badass and very proficient with those weapons he was confiscating.

The bear came around from behind the altar, and Kiki could see blood on its fur and its muzzle, but she wasn't afraid.

"Jack?" she asked. "Can you understand me when you're like that?"

The beast's head nodded, even as magical sparks of golden brown engulfed the creature. The power of it tickled against her skin, a tangible sensation of the magic Jack could command. It was impressive…to say the least.

As she watched, the golden light intensified to a point where she could no longer see anything within the light. A moment later, it faded and Jack was left, in his human form. His very naked, very muscular human form.

He didn't seem to care that he was naked, but Kiki sure noticed. She'd made love to him just hours ago, but she doubted she would ever take Jack's naked body for granted. He was magnificent in every respect. Big, bold and built like a god. And he was hers.

She knew that deep within her heart. He'd been prepared to take a bullet for her. If that didn't signify a commitment on some deep, emotional level, she didn't know what would.

"Are you all right?" Jack asked her, his voice intense as he crouched at her feet to untie her ankles from the chair legs.

"I should be asking you that," she chided him. "That ward hurt you. I could tell."

He looked up at her and the amusement in his gorgeous brown eyes made the muscles of her abdomen clench. He really was just too handsome for his own good.

"It would take a lot more than that to hurt me, honey, though it did singe my fur a bit," he admitted.

"Jack. You were a bear." She felt stupid after the words came out of her mouth, but she couldn't recall them, and his eyes narrowed as her right foot came free, and he set to work on the left.

"I'm a shapeshifter. I hope you're okay with that," he said matter-of-factly, but he kept glancing up at her as if gauging her reaction.

"Okay with it…" She huffed. "Jack! I had no idea such things existed."

"But I bet you're glad we do, since a regular guy wouldn't have been able to stand up to Carol." He freed her right leg then urged her to scoot forward in the chair so he could work on her wrists.

He was bent over her as she sat. She felt enveloped by his warmth. Even naked, his body radiated pure, healing heat that felt like it touched her very soul.

"I'm glad you exist," she said softly as her hands came free.

"I'm glad you exist, too," he repeated the odd words, a twinkle in his eyes.

The blood was gone from his body. Had it disappeared when the magic turned him human again? "Did you kill Carol?" she asked, thinking about the blood.

He dropped his gaze. "I had to. Evil like that… It doesn't change with a defeat. The only way to free all these people and you, too, was to end her and release all her castings. I don't know what she was cooking up with your blood, but it couldn't have been anything good. The potion is gone now, with her demise."

"Thanks be to the Mother of All," she whispered, raising one hand to cup his cheek. His gaze sought hers.

"The Mother of All? I thought you were a Christian."

"Sorry. I thought you understood. My family follows the old ways, though I guess we sometimes dress it up in Christian garb so that we fit in with the neighbors. I figured since you just shared your secret with me, I could trust you with mine." She smiled shyly at him, wondering if this was going to be a problem for them.

"Thank you for trusting me. Just so we're clear… I serve the Light, and the Mother of All." His smile matched hers. "I think this is yet another sign that we were meant to be together."

"You think so?" she breathed, her heart in her throat at the implications of his words.

"Yes, Kiki. I really do." He bent his forehead to hers for a moment, then he repositioned so that he could kiss her deep and gentle, the way she'd been longing for.

Moments, or maybe hours, later, a throat clearing broke them apart. It was Ben, and he was grinning like a fool.

"I hate to break this up, but you're naked, Jack, and these people are starting to wake up," Ben observed. "Oh, and my backup has arrived."

Ben gestured toward the other side of the wide space where two men had appeared, seemingly out of nowhere. They prowled forward, holding snub-nosed assault weapons at rest, but ready should they be needed, barrels pointing downward. Both looked incredibly easy with their deadly weapons, and both were dressed, head to toe, in black military clothing that looked well-worn and comfortable.

"Hey kid," the elder of the two men addressed Jack as if he knew him. "Jimmy's got some spare kit you can use."

The older man pointed to his companion, who was right behind and to the side of him a bit. The man was younger and was rifling through a backpack he'd been carrying over one shoulder.

A moment later, a pair of black sweatpants flew through the air and straight into Jack's waiting hands. Jimmy—whoever he was—had thrown the balled up cloth over the wide distance with pinpoint accuracy. Kiki was impressed.

"When Ben calls in backup, I see he doesn't screw around," Jack muttered as he hastily donned the somewhat stretchy pants that weren't a great fit but would do under the circumstances. Both men laughed as they came closer. They'd clearly heard Jack's comments, even at that distance. Kiki began to get suspicious.

"Are they…um…like you?" she whispered, eliciting more laughter from the two who still approached at an easy walk.

"Not exactly the same, honey, but yeah," Jack admitted. "Let's save the rest, though, for a more private place, okay?"

Kiki nodded, standing gingerly as feeling returned to her feet. She leaned on Jack, and he quickly put a comforting, supportive arm around her waist.

They walked away from the circle where Carol had held Kiki captive, and she was just happy to be moving beyond what was left of that dark line on the floor. Ben was still clearing the area and speaking a few words with the groggy people on the ground when the two men met up with them. Jack reached out to shake their hands.

"Kiki, this is Arch and Jim. I've worked with them before," was all he said by way of introduction.

Both men nodded respectfully toward her. "Ma'am," the older one said as she nodded back.

"Thanks for coming to our rescue," Kiki said, meaning it, but they both chuckled.

"Feels like we got here a little late, but we're happy to do duty as the cleanup crew," Arch said, then redirected his attention to Jack. "I assume that's what you want us to do."

"By all means," Jack agreed. "I'm going to take Kiki home. Her place is the safest spot in town right now. Can you and Ben handle all this?" Jack asked, gesturing to the mess behind the altar, as well as the people recovering from their encounter with black magic, most of whom were still unconscious.

"You take care of your lady. We'll do what we do best. Ben's already concocting a cover story, if I'm any judge," Jim piped up, shooting an amused glance at the former Navy SEAL.

"Just how do you know Ben?" Jack asked, clearly curious at the connection.

"We served together," Jim answered promptly. "You know how we teams guys stick together. And Uncle Arch still teaches the odd class, now and again, for the units."

Jack whistled between his teeth as if impressed. "I'm glad you're here," was all he said, including both men in his heartfelt glance. "Meet us at Kiki's when you're done here. I think we'll need to debrief as a group." Jack gave them quick directions to the cottage.

"That's a roger," Arch said, already walking away, heading for the altar and the grisly scene behind it. Jack hadn't let her get a good look, but Kiki was certain whatever was left of Carol had been ripped apart by his bear teeth and claws.

"Come on, let's get out of here," Jack said quietly, his arm around her waist as they walked out of the warehouse through the closest exit.

The fresh air of the outdoors was a welcome relief as they exited into the early evening air. The sun was just starting its descent, and the air held a slight chill that felt good on her skin.

"Are you cold?" she asked Jack as they walked along at a brisk pace, heading for the front of the building and the parking lot where her car was parked. Jack was only wearing those borrowed sweatpants and no shoes.

"I'm not cold. It takes a lot to make me cold—in either of my forms," he admitted.

"What about your feet?" She glanced down at the sidewalk, littered with the occasional debris-filled cracks.

"Not a problem, though I hope Jim can salvage my boots," he mused. "I really liked those boots."

"I guess being...what you are...is hard on your wardrobe," she observed as they walked.

That sparked a laugh out of him, and he smiled down at her. "You could say that, but generally, I have time to strip before I change. What you saw was an emergency situation."

"Is it like the Hulk? Does it come out when you're angry or threatened?" she wanted to know.

He chuckled again. "No, honey. It's part of me that is fully integrated with my human half. I can be the bear or I can be the man, whenever I choose. I have total control over both halves of my nature."

"That is so cool," she mused aloud, earning her a questioning look.

"You're not afraid of me?" he asked, though the question was more of a statement.

She shook her head. "You stood in front of me when Bob would have shot me. How could I be afraid of a man willing to take a bullet for me?" Their steps slowed as their gazes met and held. Time stood still, then she breathed. "And by the way, don't ever do that again. What were you thinking?" she scolded him. "I couldn't bear watching you get hurt—or worse—because of me."

"Same goes for me, Kiki. I couldn't just stand by and let Bob shoot you. I'd rather die than have to watch that happen," he told her, and something in her heart broke free, winging its way to him, never to return.

They rounded the corner of the building, and the parking lot was blessedly near. "Keys," they both said at the same time.

Jack altered their trajectory, heading for the front door of the building and the office area just beyond the receptionist's desk. They detoured into Kiki's office, and she picked up her handbag, which had stayed put during the struggle, from the bottom drawer of her desk. She held it up triumphantly, and they headed back outside. Jack took only a moment to grab his own jacket from inside his office and then rejoined her.

"That's an interesting fashion statement you're making," she teased him, looking at the jacket and sweatpants, lacking shoes.

"Believe me, I've worn worse." He put his hand on her back as they walked side by side to her car.

CHAPTER 18

Ben was glad of the expert help when it came to cleaning up the mess left behind by the confrontation with the potion witch. Arch and Jimmy handled the corpse with professional ease. It was clear to Ben they'd disappeared a body before, but he wasn't going to ask questions. Right now, that was a useful skill, and he had his hands full with the dazed and confused workers who had woken up with no memory of how they'd gotten into the warehouse.

"May I have your attention please!" Ben shouted from the back of the warehouse, seeking and getting everyone's attention while Arch and Jim dealt with the carnage behind the altar. "There has been an unfortunate chemical reaction resulting in the release of what we believe to be chloroform gas," he told the easily led multitude. "Please walk slowly to this exit and go outside to sit on the grass while the safety inspectors evaluate the situation."

Somewhat to his surprise, they bought it and began shuffling toward him to get to the exit. Some moved faster than others, and a few stopped to ask him questions. Ben spun the same tale about a chemical leak and resulting reaction. Later, they could use that story to explain how Carol had died. They could say she had been killed trying to contain it. She would have died a hero, in that scenario, instead of the reason for so much misery.

Jim came back and joined Ben. "Arch is taking care of things," he told Ben quietly. They both knew he meant that the older shifter was dealing with Carol's corpse. "What do you want me to do?"

"I'm going to get all of these folks out onto the grass, and we can assess them one by one. We can use some of that medic training we all had to go through. There's a giant first-aid kit on the wall over there. See if there's anything useful in it," Ben instructed his former comrade-in-arms.

With Jim's help, Ben got everyone outside. They were sitting on the grass, recovering, while the supposed fumes cleared. Ben and Jim played at assessing everyone's conditions, using the blood pressure cuffs and penlights they found in the first-aid kit, among other props.

Mostly, everyone was okay, except for some scrapes and bruises on those who had come into contact with the bear. There was a broken wrist and three broken arms. A couple of broken toes and one broken leg along with a myriad of sprains and bruises. All in all, though, the bear had been remarkably kind to these people. Not one had a claw mark anywhere on their person.

Arch came back from around the back of the warehouse and declared the building off limits in a very loud voice that carried. He was playing the role of an emergency responder, and nobody questioned his right to make such a decree. The black fatigues lent him and Jim an air of credibility, since they looked somewhat official to the untrained—or, in this case, the very woozy and unfocused—eye.

Once the workers' heads started to clear, Ben and Jim herded everyone through the plant while they gathered their belongings and then ushered them all toward the parking lot. The plant was closed by order of Arch and wouldn't be reopening for the rest of the week, at the very least. They sent everyone home with orders not to return until next Monday.

A few were bundled into passenger seats of cars and sent to the local clinic where they could get patched up. Ben gave out business cards that had come in useful in similar situations, and told the injured that if anyone had any questions, they should call him directly. The business cards listed him as a representative of a federal emergency response team.

Ben had been given permission to use the cards, and the title, by an admiral who ran more than one black op. Ben had worked for the man in the past, and apparently, had earned his trust. Even though Ben was technically retired from the military, the admiral kept him on the covert books. Ben wasn't sure if he'd be called on to serve his country—and that well-connected admiral—ever again, but having friends in high places had come in very handy in situations like the one he found himself in right now.

"That ought to do it," Ben said as they watched the last of the employees drive away.

"Yeah, now we can do a more thorough job of cleanup without a potential audience," Arch concurred.

"Have I thanked you guys yet, for coming in such a timely manner?" Ben asked, one eyebrow raised as he turned to his fellow former SEALs.

"I'm just glad we were close enough," Arch said, his tone, as usual, low key.

"You can say that again," Ben agreed.

"Let's get to it," Arch urged them all. "You promised us dinner, and I'm getting hungry."

"Roger that." Ben couldn't help but grin as they headed back toward the scene of the crime. It was good to be around teammates again, even if they were shifters. Arch was a legend in SEAL circles, and Jim had been a good friend, even before Ben had found out about the unseen world.

Sometimes, he missed his old life in the military, but he'd come to accept that things changed. He'd thought his career was over when he'd left the teams, but in reality, a wider world had only just been beginning to reveal itself, and now, there was no going back to the naïve young soldier he'd once been.

*

Jack and Kiki arrived at her cottage just as the sun went down. Her fairy cottage was welcoming as ever and somehow, Jack felt like the spirit of the place cleansed him after the brush with evil he'd just been through.

"It feels so good to be home," Kiki said as she turned off the engine. "Today was…" She paused then tried, again. "It was insane."

"You can say that again," Jack agreed. "But we got through it in one piece, which is kind of a miracle. Kiki…" He turned to face her across the space of the front seat of her car. "Please forgive me. I made a really bad mistake in underestimating Carol. I knew black magic is a hidden art. I shouldn't have taken things at face value. Especially when my mistake in doing so almost got you killed. I'm so very sorry."

She reached across the space separating them and took his hand in both of hers. "You have nothing to apologize for, Jack. You saved me."

"Well, I seem to recall you did that yourself. Where in the world did you get that sachet? And how did you know it would work?" He was impressed, all over again, by her quick thinking and decisive action. She'd saved the day, way more than he had.

She let go of his hand and opened the car door, exiting the vehicle to stand in the middle of her fairy garden. She had a beatific smile on her face as Jack joined her, leaving the car behind.

"I made the sachet," she told him. "Just this morning, I cut the herbs and flowers from this garden, speaking the ritual words I'd been taught as a child, before they realized I had little power of my own."

"Just based on what I saw today, I wouldn't discount your magic, Kiki. You brought down a powerful black ward. Not everyone can do something like that. You saw me—with all my magic, I couldn't," he reminded her.

"It wasn't me. It was this garden. There's something special about it, you know?" She looked up at him, her gaze so full of innocence and wonder, he just had to take her into his arms.

"It's a fey garden," he whispered against her lips. "I felt it from the moment I saw it."

He kissed her, precluding any response, enjoying the moment in the twilight, the woman he loved in his arms. She was so supple against him, so compliant. He couldn't wait to make love with her again, but even more important right now, he wanted to see to her comfort and make certain she was all right after her ordeal.

Lifting her in his arms, Jack walked up the steps to the front door of the cottage. It opened, by magic, as if welcoming them home. Jack felt the magic of the house all over again, and wasn't startled when the door closed behind them, just as magically.

"This house really likes you, Kiki," he told her.

She smiled at him. "I know. I like it, too. Isn't it wonderful?"

"That's one word," he agreed, walking down the hall to the bathroom.

The first order of business was going to be a cleansing bath to remove any residue of Carol's evil from their skin. He would also take the opportunity to check Kiki over, to make sure she had no injuries she wasn't mentioning.

"What's it like?" she asked as he set her on her feet in the small bathroom while he turned the water on in the shower. "Turning into a bear?" she added.

Jack shrugged. "It's how I've always been. I was born this way, and I've never known anything different," he explained, then turned his head to catch her gaze. "You're really not afraid of me?"

Kiki shook her head. "I know your heart," she told him, making him catch his breath as she walked closer, moving straight into his arms. She reached up and put her hands behind his neck, drawing him downward. "I don't know how this is all going to work out, but I trust my instincts that say you would never hurt me."

"Bears are pretty big on instincts too," he warned her as their mouths drew closer. "Right now, my instincts are telling me to kiss you."

"Just kiss me?" Her eyes flashed up to meet his again, daring him.

"Kiss…and touch…and possess. Are you ready for that, honey?" He couldn't help himself. He knew he was rushing things, but the fire inside him demanded the closeness after such a harrowing ordeal.

"So ready," she said, closing the final inch between their mouths. She kissed him, and Jack didn't waste any time returning the favor.

The water in the shower was running, creating steam in the small room, but it was lukewarm in comparison to the heat they generated all by themselves. The room was tiny, but they'd make it work. Jack removed the borrowed sweatpants in one long slide, then he turned his attention to Kiki, touching, licking and exciting every inch of her skin as he revealed it. She was a gift he took his time unwrapping, kissing all the little bruises he found that were left over from her ordeal.

Her wrists had been badly abused, so he spent long moments touching the angry red lines on her delicate skin, using what little healing magic he possessed to try to make her more comfortable. Bears were intensely magical, among shifters, but they weren't mages. Still, he could do a little to at least take out the sting of her injuries.

"Is that you?" she asked, wonder in her voice as he kissed her wrist with a feather touch. "Are you numbing it?"

"Is it working?" he asked, looking up at her while still kissing her wrist. "It's not one of my specialties, but I do have a tiny bit of healing energy I can sometimes share with others."

"It's amazing," she breathed. "But you don't have to deplete yourself to take the sting out of my wrists. They'll heal on their own."

"Do I look like I'm depleted?" he challenged her, teasing. It was pretty clear he was raring to go for just about anything she might dream up, but it was cute of her to worry. Her blushing cheeks were charming, too.

"It's just that, whenever my sister uses her healing ability, it wipes her out," Kiki explained, her breath catching as he moved on to another raw spot on her poor abused wrists.

"So, your sister is a healer?" Jack didn't wait for an answer. "Human magic is a bit different from mine, and I'm not exactly sure how it all works, but if I had to come up with a theory, I'd say that my magic is of the earth, and I get it directly from the source. The earth is infinite, and as long as I'm in a place that is healthy and strong, so am I. Human mages tend to get their power from their own beings, I think. That might account for the drain, but I'm no scholar."

"I think you sell yourself short, Jack," Kiki whispered, eyeing him with a half-lidded gaze that was driving him wild all by itself. "That's probably the best explanation I've heard for something magical, like…ever. My family has a tendency to overcomplicate things."

"I can't wait to meet them," he said, chuckling. "Maybe I can help uncomplicated things for you."

Kiki couldn't wait for them to meet him, either. She wondered what they'd think of Jack and his amazing magic. She also felt a certain amount of pride in the idea that she could attract such a magnificent being—so intensely magical—when she'd always been discounted as the magical runt of the family. Wouldn't they be surprised?

Then again, they'd probably already seen it coming. After all, they'd seen enough to send that care package full of hex signs to her at the right time. She wasn't sure how she felt about them knowing she was having a steamy affair with a man who could turn into a bear. Some things, she would prefer to keep private, but that was a chore in her family.

Kiki forgot all about her family the moment Jack started

undressing her with his teeth. Never had a man done something so primal. He unfastened the hooks of her bra with his fingers then used his teeth to nudge down the fabric covering her breasts. Kiki gasped as his teeth grazed lightly over her sensitive skin.

The air in the room felt chilly against her bare skin, but not for long. Jack replaced the fabric of her bra with his hands, caressing her breasts with his thumbs, his gaze zeroing in on the pendant that hung between them.

"A pentacle?" He shot her an amused look. "You are a lady just full of surprises, aren't you?"

"I haven't worn it in a long time, but I dug it out this morning, and I'm glad I did. I could actually feel it protecting me at times, while Carol had me tied up," she told him.

"I have no doubt. Your family must be experts in all sorts of protective symbolism," he mused. "I'm going to enjoy learning more," he said, making her breath catch.

In order to *learn more*, as he'd put it, he'd have to stick around for a while, surely. She wanted that, like she wanted her next breath. She wanted Jack in her life for as long as she could possibly keep him.

Jack lowered his hands to the waistband of her skirt and made short work of removing both the skirt and the panties she wore beneath. She'd already removed the ruined pantyhose she'd worn to work that morning. They'd been shredded by the bindings around her ankles, and she'd quietly slipped them off the moment she'd gotten into the car back at the plant.

They were both naked, and he coaxed her with gentle hands toward the shower where the water was already flowing. He reached in and adjusted the temperature downward so there wasn't quite as much steam. That would be more comfortable for her, she was sure. He was so careful of her comfort it was really touching.

"Is that good for you?" he asked, waiting for her answer before letting go of the adjustment knob. She nodded and stepped over the rim of the tub, stepping into the water stream.

"That feels heavenly," she said, closing her eyes for a moment. She heard Jack moving around but she was enjoying the warm water too much to bother trying to figure out what he was doing.

When she opened her eyes again, sometime later, Jack was standing in front of her, blocking most of the water from hitting her, but she didn't mind. The fire in his eyes warmed her from within, which felt even better than the warm water on her skin.

He took her into his arms and kissed her. Kiki lost track of time and space. She felt motion and realized he was lifting her up, both of his hands supporting her butt. He turned her so that she was against the side wall of the shower, her back against the tile.

"Is it too cold?" he asked, his breath coming hard and fast.

"Nope," she replied, sparing only the single syllable before she moved in to kiss him again. She was fast becoming addicted to his kisses.

"I'm not gonna last long, Kiki," he told her in between kisses. "Are you ready for this?"

"More than ready," she replied, feeling a desperate urgency in the marrow of her bones. She wanted him, and she wanted him *now*. To heck with waiting. "Come into me now, Jack. I need you," she whispered, feeling greatly daring and utterly truthful.

He took her at her word and positioned himself for entry. She looked down, surprised to see that he'd apparently taken that time while she'd been basking in the warm water to go into her night stand and retrieve a condom. Thoughtful man.

After everything that had happened today, she needed him inside her. She needed the comfort and solidity of him, making love with her. She needed to feel the realness of them together. The joy and perfection after what had been a very ugly day.

Jack slid into her in one long push. Yes. There it was. This thing that defined them, as a couple. This unity. This purity.

This oneness. Kiki couldn't get enough of it.

Then, he started to move. Short digs and long strokes, he seemed somewhat uncoordinated at first, but then, she realized emotion was riding him hard. As it was her. She'd almost lost him today. He'd almost taken a bullet meant for her. She'd almost died at the hands of an evil woman who would have done who-knows-what with what little power Kiki had. Her very soul had been in peril with that kind of evil in control.

Relief made her sob as she joined in the desperate motion as best she could. Kiki was pinned to the wall and enjoying every delicious moment of it. This was real. This was good. This was all that mattered.

Everything that had come before was wiped out in the reality of their bodies straining together toward mutual bliss. Jack growled, and this time, she recognized it for what it was… The human expression of his beast half. The bear was part of him, but that didn't scare her. No, the bear was a treasure. A protector and a badass warrior that had taken out evil today. For her. And for all who wanted to live in the Light.

Good lord, how she loved this man!

He strained against her, his body hard and slick from the water that continued to pour over them from one side. This felt better than anything she'd felt before. This might just be nirvana, she decided, before Jack pushed her just that little bit higher.

Short, hard thrusts brought her to the very edge of madness. She cried out when he reached between them, touching her in just the right spot to send her crashing over the precipice, into the warm, welcoming void. She reached for the stars, and he came with her, roaring his release as they flew up toward heaven together. One.

CHAPTER 19

It was a long, long time before Kiki came back to herself. Jack let her down from the wall and stroked his powerful hands slowly over her body, washing her with the bath scrubby she kept in the shower, using her favorite foaming cleanser. He washed her with tender care, rinsing himself, as well, so that they were both clean of the dirt of the day.

Jack took such good care of her. He dried them both off and carried her into her bedroom, laying her on the soft sheets that she had changed this morning before going in to work. Had it only been that morning? It seemed like a lifetime ago after all that had happened.

Jack came down beside her in the small bed. The full size bed had felt large to her after a lifetime spent in a twin bed at her parents' home, but Jack was a big guy, and he made the formerly large space seem quite cozy. He leaned up on one elbow to meet her gaze. His expression was serious, but also warm and…caring.

"You know I love you, don't you?" he said, causing her breath to catch. The statement was as bold as the man himself, and she had to smile.

"I do now. Thanks for clearing that up," she teased him, knowing what he wanted to hear but holding out so she could enjoy the moment a bit more. Such profound moments came around rarely in life.

Jack chuckled. "You're going to make me work for this, eh?"

She reached up and cupped his stubbly cheek. "No, my love. I'll never hold out on you. Ever."

She saw the way his eyes flared when she called him her love. The same fire blossomed in her veins at the thought of having her feelings reciprocated.

"I figured it out when Carol told me she was only holding me as bait to get to you. She said you were the real prize…and she was right, but not in the way she meant." Kiki smiled at him. "I knew I loved you when I realized that I would rather die than have you walk into Carol's trap to save me." She took a deep breath. "And I knew you loved me when you stepped in front of me when Bob was going to shoot me. We're clearly willing to die for each other. Question is, how do we make it work so we both can live for each other?"

"Easy," Jack responded, moving closer and dropping a gentle kiss on her lips before drawing back again. "Defeating the bad guys was the first step, so we've done that. The next hurdle was going to be me breaking it to you that I'm a shifter."

"Carol used that word. Shifter. I've never heard that before," Kiki said, hoping he would elaborate more about his fascinating condition.

"It's short for shapeshifter," he explained, getting comfortable on his side, facing her, as if they had all the time in the world. "We're also called were. Like werewolves? Only, I'm a werebear. The two guys you met earlier—Arch and Jim—they're werewolves."

"They are?" Kiki wasn't surprised they were shifters, but she'd had no idea they were werewolves. She hadn't known such things were real until today. "What about Ben?"

"Ben? Nah. He's just a regular human as far as I know. Military trained. He was a Navy SEAL. That's how he knows Jim and Arch. They were both SEALs, too. Though Arch was in the teams way before his nephew, Jim. He's a lot older than he looks, and he's a legend in Special Forces circles. Even my brothers and I had heard of Arch, and we were Green Berets."

"You were in the military?" He just kept on surprising her.

"Yeah. I joined mostly because my brothers were in. Once the three of us were together, the Admiral who knew what we were, used us as a highly specialized team. Some wise guys started calling us the Three Little Bears. I thought it was funny, but my brothers took exception." Jack's eyes sparkled with humor. "A few broken noses later, and they stopped using that name when we were within earshot."

"So, when did you get out?" she asked, wanting to know everything there was to know about Jack. Her lover. Her love.

"Oh, over a decade ago. We were done fighting other people's wars, and we wanted to try to give ourselves a chance to find our way in the civilian world. I think, as the oldest, Ace was feeling it the worst, but we always followed where he led. He wanted to find his mate and settle down. King did too."

"I've been meaning to ask this. I hope you won't take it wrong. But your brothers are named Ace and King? Those aren't nicknames, are they?" She wanted to be clear.

"Nope. Ace, King and Jack. Those are our real names. Our parents were dealers in Tahoe for a long time." He shook his head, his smile turning into a chuckle. "I'll promise you right now, we can pick nice, normal names for our kids, if we have any."

Her breath caught. "You mean…" She couldn't put it into words. Her boldness had suddenly fled.

"I mean that, when a shifter finds his one true mate, it's for life. You're never getting rid of me, honey. Not in this lifetime or any possible future lifetimes. Our souls will always find each other, no matter what. That is…if you feel the same way." He looked uncertain for the first time. "If you were a shifter, you'd feel it, and I'd know, for sure, that we were on the same page. But you're human, and you need to tell me that you want this. I won't force it on you, not if you don't really want me, but you should know that there will never be another woman for me. Ever. I'm yours if you want me."

"If I want you?" she repeated, incredulous. "Are you kidding?"

"I've never been more serious in my life," he told her quietly. "What do you say? I can try to give you more time, if you need it, but my bear is set on you, as is my human side. I love you, Kiki."

She threw herself at him, taking him down to the mattress as she placed kisses all over his face. "I love you. I love you. I love you," she repeated over and over. She pulled back, a thought occurring to her. "But we have to get married the human way, for my family, okay?"

"Anything you want, Kiki. Absolutely anything," he promised, a joyful light in his sparkling brown eyes.

She thought about something else, through her happiness. "Can this really work? Can your kind… Can shifters marry regular people and make it work?"

"First of all, you are far from regular," he told her gallantly. "And second, shifters marry whoever the Mother of All picks out for us. You're the one She picked for me. I feel it in my soul."

"That's beautiful," Kiki said, feeling tears gather in her eyes at his candor and faith.

"It's the truth," he told her in a solemn, quiet voice, that she felt clear down to the depths of her soul.

They made love more gently this time, taking time to wallow in each other's presence and really learn what each of them craved. They got up to shower again, then dressed to have a late dinner that they both helped cook. Jack reminded Kiki that the others were expected at her cottage as soon as they finished with the cleanup at the plant, which he estimated to be within the next hour or so.

He raided her kitchen and headed outdoors with every last bit of meat she'd had on hand. Luckily, she'd had quite a bit, delivered a few weeks ago from the family farm. The meat delivery was meant to help her save money, but it had also served as an excuse to check up on her for her older brother. He'd wanted to see where she lived and if it was safe. He'd left satisfied with the cottage and had stocked her pantry, fridge, and freezer. It was one of the many ways her family showed they cared about her welfare, even if she wasn't the most magical of family members.

"I'll replace all this," Jack promised as he carried a small mountain of steak, chops, sausage and chicken out to the grill on the back patio. "It's just that, among shifters, it's good manners to provide a decent meal if someone goes out of their way to help you. Plus, Arch is...well...we're all a little in awe of Arch," he explained with a chagrinned expression. "He's legendary among shifters, as well. And his nephew, Jim, is a good guy."

"No problem, Jack," Kiki said, following him outside with the condiments and marinade she wanted to use on the chicken. "All that meat is from my family's farm. My brother stocked the kitchen for me a few weeks back when he came to see where I lived," she admitted to him.

Jack paused, meeting her gaze. He seemed impressed. "That's even better. I assume your family farm adheres to the old ways of farming, right?"

She grinned. "Better than that. We're one hundred percent certified organic."

A spark of pleasure lit his eyes. "That's fantastic. You should know that our senses are all sharper than yours. We are really picky about things like the drinking water in our homes. We don't like chemicals in anything we eat, and we're big time carnivores."

"Makes sense," she told him as she moved next to him at the small grill. "We're going to have to cook these a few at a time," she thought aloud. "I just want a chicken breast to go with my salad. You and your buddies can have the rest."

"I didn't see any salad in the fridge," Jack said, his entire expression dropping. She had to chuckle.

"That's because it's in the garden right now. I'm going to

pick myself a few greens while you man the grill." She smiled up at him, standing on tiptoe to kiss him gently on the lips.

The kiss was just starting to get interesting when there was noise at the garden gate. Jack heard it first, letting her go and placing her behind him a bit, the big teddy bear. He was protecting her again, and she loved every caveman-ish impulse of it.

He relaxed visibly when the three amigos walked around the side of the house and onto the patio area. Ben was leading, Jim in the center, carrying what looked like two cases of beer, with Arch bringing up the rear. He had a box in his hands that looked like it had come from the local bakery.

"We come bearing gifts," Ben said, setting his bottles of wine on the table.

"Perfect timing," Jack told him as he set the first pieces of meat on the small grill. "This is going to take a while to cook on this small setup, and the fridge is almost empty, so there's room for the excess beer and wine to stay cool."

"Ma'am," Jim said, addressing Kiki. "Is it all right with you if I put this in your fridge?"

"Sure thing," she replied, pleased with his formal manner. She liked that these big men hadn't just walked into her yard and taken over her home. "Please, make yourselves at home."

She smiled at Jim and headed out into the garden to find her salad patch. She heard Ben ask Jack in a stage whisper, "Where's she going? I hope we didn't scare her off."

"Nah," Jack answered back. "She just went to find some rabbit food to go with her chicken. The rest of this meat is for us." She grinned at the satisfied sound in Jack's voice. She finally understood why he ate so much. He was a *bear*!

It made perfect sense now. He probably used a lot of energy going from human to bear form. And bears were known to be big eaters at times.

"I like a good steak as much as the next guy, but are there, like, any potatoes to go with all that meat?" Ben asked, chuckling.

"I saw a sack of baking potatoes in one of the lower

cupboards," Jack told Ben. "Nuke one in the microwave if you want to. I'm sure Kiki won't mind. All this food comes from her family's organic farm."

Oh, she liked the pride in his voice when he said that. She thought that boded well for how he would get on with her brothers. Her siblings took great pride and worked hard on the farm. If Jack appreciated that effort—and it sure sounded like he did—he'd be golden with them. The thought made her happy.

Kiki thought about how and when they'd meet while she picked a bunch of the outer leaves off her lettuce plants. She had a nice mix when she went back toward the house. The three shifters were on the patio, and she heard the hum of the microwave inside the small kitchen. She went in, finding Ben staring at the machine while a lone potato went round and round inside. She had to stifle a giggle at the hungry look on his face.

"I'm glad I'm not the only one who'll eat a vegetable tonight," she said by way of greeting as she went to the sink to wash her lettuce leaves. "Do you want some salad to go with your meal? There's plenty."

Ben looked at her and smiled tentatively. "If you can spare a little, I wouldn't say no," he told her. "That's one thing you're going to have to get used to about shifters, they eat meat like it's going out of style and seldom think much about side dishes."

"We heard that," all three shifters chorused from outside.

Ben rolled his eyes. "That's another thing you'll have to get used to. They're big time eavesdroppers."

Sounds of protest came from outside, and Kiki laughed. She set up two salad plates and put them on the kitchen table. "I have balsamic vinaigrette that I made myself, or there's some ranch dressing in the fridge."

"The vinaigrette sounds great," Ben said with an easy grin as he pulled his baked potato from the microwave. "Just splash some on there. Thanks."

"Butter and sour cream are in the fridge. The sour cream

is in that glass jar in the door next to the taller one that has whipped cream in it. My family's farm is bordered on one side by an Amish dairy farm, so we get everything fresh from them. It's all organic, and it tastes better and lasts a lot longer than the stuff you buy in the store, but the packaging is very no frills," she explained.

"Bring that out here with you," Arch called from outside. "If the lady doesn't mind," he added.

"I don't mind at all. My brother brought way more than I could ever eat the last time he visited." She thought about that for a moment. "Huh. I think somebody was looking into their crystal ball again."

"You don't seem surprised," Ben observed. "And you seem to be taking everything that went on here in stride, if you don't mind my saying."

Jack opened the backdoor and stood in the opening, a looming presence. "Don't answer that, Kiki. Ben works for an ancient order of busybodies who take notes on every little thing that even hints of magic. You don't want to end up in an *Altor Custodis* file somewhere. Especially not since we're pretty sure they've been infiltrated at the highest levels, and those files are being used to target innocent people."

"Hey." Ben held up both hands, palms outward. "You know I don't file real reports anymore. Not since all that came to light. I'm on your side here."

"Cool it, Jack." Arch's voice came from behind Jack. His words were casual, but his tone rang with authority.

Kiki could see that Jack didn't like being contradicted, but she knew he thought very highly of Arch. She could read the conflict in his gaze as he looked at her. His need to protect her was making him touchy. Well, she could do something about that.

Kiki walked up to Jack and put her arms around him. He had no choice but to accept her hug as she snuggled her head against his chest.

"It's okay," she said, trying to soothe him. "Let's go outside. Ben, you bring the food, okay?"

"Sure thing," Ben answered promptly while Kiki pushed Jack out into the yard. She made him sit in one of the big patio chairs and followed him down to sit on his lap.

Arch just looked at her, one eyebrow raised, for a long moment, then picked up the spatula and turned to the grill. Jim was at his uncle's side, and they handled the grill while Ben brought out the salads and the other things.

Ben sat across from Jack and Kiki. "Look, Jack, I didn't mean anything by what I said earlier. I'm sorry. I won't be reporting on any of this to the *AC*, except the contact with the janitor. I suspect he'll keep filing reports, and he might mention me, so I have to say something about coming in contact with the guy as I was passing through." Ben sighed. "I have to keep up the *AC* contacts so I can help from the inside. I'm also looking to clean house there, if I ever figure out exactly where the trash is hiding that needs to be taken out."

"Personally, I've never seen the point of the *Altor Custodis* mission. Watching and reporting, but never getting involved? What for?" Jack scoffed. "It seems like the perfect recipe for disaster—and has proven to be such—when the wrong people get their hands on those supposedly secret files."

"Try to look at it from the human perspective," Ben said quietly. "I worked side by side with Jim for years and never knew he was a shifter. I didn't even know shifters existed. When I found out—rather rudely, for that matter, since they were trying to kill me in a South American jungle at the time—I embraced the idea of a human society dedicated to learning what we could about the Others who lived among us in secret, and keeping track of them so that, if strange things started to happen, we could at least try to protect the innocents in the area."

"I've heard that argument before, but I still don't buy it," Jack said.

"That's because you aren't powerless," Kiki piped up. "I've been the most powerless person in the room all my life. I knew about magic, but I could never do any," she went on, realizing she had everyone's attention. "I can see where I would've endorsed a group of watchers, had I known there were powerful beings like you guys in the world. What other defense do mere mortals have?" She looked down at her hands. "It's not easy being the weakling in a world full of magic."

Jack's hands covered hers gently, and she raised her gaze to meet his. "So, you're saying, you don't want me to kill Ben for being a nosy type who likes to watch?"

"Kill…? No!" Kiki couldn't believe what he was saying, but then the spark of laughter in his eyes caught her attention, and she swatted his shoulder. "Jack! Don't even joke about killing people. That could get you in serious trouble with the law, and I refuse to visit my fiancé in prison."

Ben practically choked on his beer before starting to laugh, but the two werewolves manning the grill perked up.

"So, you two?" Arch asked.

"Mates," Jack confirmed. "We haven't told anyone yet, so I guess you guys are the first to know."

CHAPTER 20

"That's fantastic!" Jim said, clearly happy for them.

Arch grinned. "Now we have even more reason to celebrate. Congratulations!"

The dinner turned into a bit of a party. Either Arch or Jim was at the grill for most of the meal, taking turns, serving up fresh cuts of meat. They refused to let Jack or Kiki do any work, instead, waiting on them. Everyone universally praised the food from Kiki's family's farm, and she even got Jack to try some of her salad.

Ben ran back and forth into the house to fetch the drinks, as needed. They all toasted the happy couple with wine—a fine vintage from the Maxwell Vineyards, Jack pointed out, thanking his friends for the thoughtful gifts they'd brought. Kiki sipped at her wine, having learned her lesson at that first dinner with Jack. The men switched to beer after a while, and Kiki went out into the garden once she realized they didn't have enough for dessert. The bakery box the men had brought wouldn't go far with three shifters who ate more than any beings she'd ever encountered.

Thankfully, she'd noticed, while she'd been picking herbs in the morning, that the berry patch starting to show some fruit. She went to it now, only to find the vines almost overflowing with juicy ripe fruit. Blackberries, raspberries, blueberries and even a few strawberries were ready for picking. Kiki had brought a bowl with her, and when she returned to the patio, the bowl was chock full. The men stared at it, each with varying degrees of surprise on their faces.

"I don't think all of those should be ripe at the same time. Especially this early in the season." Jim was the first to speak.

"They're not," Arch seconded.

"It's this garden," Jack said, his voice holding a tone of reverence in it. "I suspected it was a little fey the moment I saw it."

He swallowed and looked around the patio, out into the dark garden. They were using only the little lights over the patio to illuminate their impromptu party, but to Kiki's vision, the garden glowed with an ethereal life.

"Kiki picked the herbs that broke the black ward in this garden," Jack went on.

"I was wondering where she got something so powerful," Jim whispered.

"When I was out in the garden this morning, I noticed the berries starting to show," Kiki told them. "But I was surprised when I went to the berry patch just now, at how much was ready for picking."

"I said it before, honey," Jack said, smiling at her. "This house likes you. A lot."

"It's got to be fey," Jim said. "Or some kind of powerful human magic woven over centuries."

"Fey, I think," Arch put in, his head tilted to one side as he considered the grounds. "It glows with life, even in the dark."

"You can see that, too?" Kiki asked. All the men looked at her in surprise.

"I don't see anything," Ben told her. "But I feel it. I'm fully human, but I'm what they call a Sensitive. I can feel powerful magic, though I never knew what it was before I learned about all the Others in the world. What do you see, exactly?"

"What Arch said," Kiki answered hesitantly, trying to put it into words. "There's a glow around the garden. It's how I could see where I was going to pick stuff.

"Well, whatever it is, it seems benevolent," Jim said, reaching forward to grab a strawberry out of the bowl and toss it into his mouth. He chewed a bit then grinned as he swallowed. "And tasty."

Arch rolled his eyes at his nephew. "Boy, if there was a grenade made out of chocolate, you'd eat it." The older man shook his head.

"Well, I'm the youngest one here. I figured I'd be the official guinea pig," Jim claimed.

"Dumbass," Arch said, though with little heat. "Kiki and Ben have already eaten salad out of this garden."

Jim grinned. "Well, they're okay. So, it's cool." He looked at Ben expectantly. "How was the rabbit food?"

Ben wiped his mouth with his napkin in a show of good manners and smiled. "Delicious."

"And let's not forget, it was the herbs from this garden, picked by Kiki this morning, that nullified one of the strongest dark wards I've ever seen," Jack reminded them all.

"There is that," Arch allowed.

"Nothing bad comes out of this garden," Kiki affirmed, doing what Jim had done and stealing a strawberry from the bowl.

She didn't mention she'd already eaten a few of the berries as she'd been picking them. She nibbled at the large berry and closed her eyes in bliss as the strong flavor burst over her tongue. Her eyes shot open when Jack covered her lips with his in a sweet kiss.

He drew back and gazed into her eyes. "I can see I'm going to have to watch you. You've got a daredevil streak under that innocent exterior."

The backdoor banged, breaking them apart. Ben returned to the table, the tall jar of whipped cream in his hands. Kiki hadn't even realized he'd left the table. Ben had apparently already taken a portion of the berries onto his plate and went on to scoop a generous dollop of cream on top before passing the bowl to Jim.

"This is really good," Ben commented after his first bite.

"You're renting this place, right?" Arch asked, his gaze quizzical.

Kiki nodded. "I moved in the day before I started my new job at the plant, so I've only been here a few weeks."

"Where did you hear about this rental? Did you find it in the newspaper?" Arch persisted with his questions.

"Oh, no. When I got the job and knew I'd need to find a place to live near the plant, my mother asked around through the extended family grapevine. This cottage belongs to a distant cousin."

All three men stopped eating and just looked at her. Kiki felt a bit conspicuous at the way they were staring.

"What?" she asked, when the silence dragged on a bit too long.

"You have any fey blood, Kiki?" Arch asked in the silence.

"Fey? Like fairies?" She shook her head. "Not that I know of."

"What's your mother's maiden name?" Ben posed the question, drawing her attention.

"I don't see why that's important," Kiki replied, feeling a bit uncomfortable with all the scrutiny.

Jack took her hand in his. "What is it, Kiki?" he asked.

"Llewelyn. But I don't see—"

Her words were interrupted by Ben's laughter. "Well, that solves that mystery," he said after a long guffaw.

"How are Llewelyns connected with the fey?" Arch looked at Ben expectantly.

"Well, you probably all know that the Llewelyn family is famous for its mages going back more than a few centuries. What you may not know is that, according to recent reports that I intercepted and deleted from the *AC* files, one of their number married into a half-fey bloodline. I believe some of their offspring live just over the state border. I'm guessing that's the extended family that owns this little oasis of fey magic."

"Why were there recent reports?" Jack wanted to know.

"There was activity when one of the half-fey children mated with a wolf of Canadian origin. Lots of those wolves traveled south for the festivities, and that drew the attention of at least two *AC* agents in the areas they left and the place they congregated," Ben explained.

"Our Pack gave the wolves safe passage across our lands," Arch added, nodding. "We knew they were traveling for a mating celebration, but we didn't know all the details. That Pack has always been on good terms with ours." Jim nodded, agreeing with his uncle's assessment.

"A couple of my distant cousins have gotten married recently," Kiki admitted.

Ben gestured with his hand. "There you go, then. As I said, mystery solved."

They ate their berries in peace for a few minutes before Ben spoke again, this time on a different subject. He explained what he and the two werewolves had done at the plant, shutting it down until Monday.

"That's great," Jack praised Ben's solution. "That'll give us time to do a full investigation and sweep the entire place clean in case Carol left any nasty surprises."

"You might want to consider getting in some magical help to set up wards against this sort of thing happening again," Arch suggested. "Could be Kiki's people might be willing to lend a hand." He eyed her speculatively.

"I rescued Jeff the janitor from the closet where we'd stashed him," Ben went on, drawing the attention off Kiki, for which she was grateful. She couldn't promise anything on behalf of her family. She wasn't magical, and she couldn't commit them to doing any kind of magical work for anyone.

"Do we need to do anything with him?" Jack asked, referring to the janitor.

"Actually, he seems to have no memory starting a few weeks ago. Very similar to the rest of the people we talked to after they woke up. One interesting thing is that Jeff doesn't want to be in the *Altor Custodis* anymore. He said he didn't realize his reporting job could actually be dangerous, and he's *upset*, to put it mildly." Ben rolled his eyes. "I'm going to talk to him tomorrow. Maybe we can utilize his talents on the right side of things."

"You know, Arch," Jack said contemplatively, "I like your idea about enlisting some magical help in clearing the plant. Kiki…" Jack turned to her, "…if you're uncomfortable asking your family, I may know some people we can call."

"Well, I can't commit to anything for them, but I wouldn't be surprised if someone from my family is already on their way here. They have this way of knowing things…" She shrugged, knowing she was blushing a bit. She always got a little uncomfortable talking about her family's magic when she had none.

At that moment, Kiki heard a knock on the cottage's front door. Everyone stilled as she rose to her feet. "And there they are, I have little doubt," she muttered.

Jack rose and walked with her into the house, heading for the front door. "You think this is one of your family?" he asked in a low, urgent tone.

"Who else could come up to my door, through all the wards?" she asked. "It's got to be one of them."

Jack stepped in front of her when Kiki would have thrown open the front door. "Please," he said quietly. "Allow me."

Kiki stood back and let him do what he wanted. It was sweet that he was so protective of her, but he'd learn soon enough that her family was a force to be reckoned with. She felt a little wave of apprehension, hoping he would like them and, especially, that they would like him. They could make her life very difficult if they didn't, but there was no way she was giving Jack up. Not for her family. Not for anyone.

Jack opened the door, and Kiki breathed a sigh of relief. Of all the emissaries they could have sent, her sister, Helen, was the perfect candidate. Calm and capable. Powerful in a non-threatening way. Her healer sister was one of her favorite people in the universe.

"Patches!" Helen cried out, seeing Kiki's face.

Kiki stepped forward and was enveloped in a hug. Other than that, Helen didn't seem able to say anything. She just kept staring up at Jack. Kiki couldn't help the amusement that bubbled up inside her at the expression on her sister's face. Usually unflappable, Helen looked both shocked and impressed.

"Jack, this is my sister, Helen," Kiki made the introductions. "Helen, this is…um…Jack."

"Pleased to meet you," Jack said politely, opening the door wider.

"Likewise," Helen just about stammered as she stepped over the threshold, looking all around the cottage. "Patches, this house is…"

"Yeah, I know. We've just arrived at the startling idea that some of our extended family is fey, or half-fey. It wasn't exactly clear." Kiki shook her head, smiling. "Whatever the case, this whole place is a little fey. Come out and see the rest of the garden and meet my guests."

"There are more of them?" Helen blurted out, clearly caught off-guard. Kiki had to laugh.

"Friends and colleagues of Jack's who helped us with a tricky problem earlier today," Kiki explained without really saying much of anything. "We were just finishing up dessert." She led the way into the little kitchen, surprised to find Ben brewing a pot of coffee.

"Oh, Ben, this is my sister, Helen. Helen, this is Ben Steel."

"Would you like some coffee, Helen?" Ben asked politely. "Or I could put water on for tea, I suppose."

Kiki shook her head at how Ben had just made himself at home in her kitchen, but she really didn't mind. Playing hostess tonight wasn't her first priority. Not after the crazy day she'd had—that seemed to be still ongoing, though things had definitely taken a sharp turn for the better. She loved her sister and was glad to see her. She just hadn't planned to host a party in her backyard after the scary adventure of the earlier part of the day.

"Coffee is fine, thanks," Helen replied, her gaze sparking as she looked from Ben to the sound of male voices on the patio. "Are you having a party, Patches?"

"More of a debrief that turned into a celebration," Jack replied while Ben got down an extra coffee mug from the cabinet. He shooed Kiki away when she offered to help, and she ended up leading the way out into the backyard.

"Debrief? You sound like a military man, Jack," Helen observed with an intrigued smile as Kiki rolled her eyes.

She could just see it now. Helen was going to grill Jack and all his friends until she learned every last thing about them. She'd seen Helen in action before, and it always made Kiki uncomfortable.

"Hel, leave Jack and his friends alone. Yes, they were all in the military. Yes, they came to my rescue today at work. Yes, we defeated a potion witch who had the entire plant under her control, and no, you do not get to give all my guests the third degree." That last bit came out a bit angrier than Kiki wanted it to, and Helen was brought up short, her steps faltering as she exited the house.

"Oh, sweetie, are you okay?" Helen was instantly mother-henning Kiki, as she had done all their lives when Kiki got in trouble or lamented the fact that she was the ugly duckling of the family with no real magic of her own.

"Everything's fine now," Jack said, coming up beside Kiki and putting his arm around her shoulders.

Now, he'd done it. There was no way Helen had missed the implications of that protective move.

"Let's start over," Jack suggested. "I'm Jack Bishop," he said, obviously trying to lighten the mood. "Your sister saved my skin today with some herbs she picked this morning out of her fey garden." Kiki liked the way Helen's eyes widened at Jack's claim that it had been Kiki that had saved the day— using magical herbs, at that. "Oh, yeah, and I'm a werebear. Do you know more about shifters than your sister did?" he asked, his tone polite, his head tilted to one side in inquiry.

Kiki wanted to laugh, but she held it in as Helen just looked at him, blinking her eyes like an owl.

"I'm sorry. Did you say you were a bear?" Helen asked for clarification.

Jack nodded solemnly. "Yes, ma'am. Are you acquainted with any other shifters?"

Slowly, Helen nodded, shocking Kiki. "Our cousins married into a wolf Pack recently," she said, stunning Kiki further. "We're all just learning a bit more about it. All we had before were rumors and really old stories in the family archive."

"The Llewelyn Archive?" Arch asked, speaking from the other side of the table, drawing Helen's attention for the first time. Helen nodded, clearly nonplussed at the stranger's knowledge.

"We were just piecing that all together when you arrived," Jack clarified. "Kiki told us your mother's maiden name, and Ben was connecting the dots for us."

"I know your cousins' new Pack," Arch said, respect in his voice. "Good group of wolves. Very tight knit. Had some trouble a few years back, but they seem to have it sorted, now."

"Helen, this is Arch and his nephew, Jim," Kiki made the introductions belatedly.

When Kiki looked at Jim as she spoke his name, she realized the younger man seemed a bit dazed as he stared at Helen. A shaft of moonlight cut through the night sky at that moment, pouring down on Jim and Helen, though neither seemed to notice. Kiki saw it, though, and she realized there might just be a connection there.

Time would tell, of course, but Kiki thought she might just have seen a little glimpse of a possible future. Wouldn't that be something? Her mother would be proud.

Though, suddenly, she realized she didn't really care if she ever developed a strong magical ability. She'd wanted it so badly all her life, but when it came down to it, she realized it didn't really matter. She had all the magic she wanted, knowing that Jack was in her life and not likely to ever leave her. How had she been so blessed?

The family runt had won the prize, after all. Somehow, she'd won the everlasting love of a wonderful man who was more magical than the rest of her family put together. She finally knew a secret the rest of them didn't even suspect... That the real magic was love.

CHAPTER 21

Helen sat at Jim's side, seemingly fascinated by the younger werewolf as they recounted the events of the day for her. Helen was both appalled at the dire situation Kiki had been in and proud of her little sister for having saved the day with her knowledge and bravery. Helen admitted that she'd been sent to get Patches, as she called her, out of trouble but was very happy to see that it was unnecessary. Then, Helen volunteered to go to the plant tomorrow with the rest of them to help clear the place of possible magical traps and begin cleansing the area.

Ben, Arch and Jim left with Helen, taking her to the hotel where she had already reserved a room, knowing the cottage was way too small and not wanting to impose. Helen's eyebrows rose when Jack stayed behind with Kiki, but then she just smiled and left with the others. Kiki was going to have to have a long, private conversation with her sister about shifter mating, but that could wait until tomorrow.

Tonight, she was going to enjoy being alone with her shifter mate…

*

Kiki was doing her best to catch her breath after some of the most intense lovemaking of her life. She'd never known there could be such pleasure, such joy…such love. Jack was showing her things she never imagined she'd ever find. He'd arranged them in her bed so that she rested her head on his shoulder.

"We've got to get a bigger bed," Jack said, his voice pitched low, his tone teasing.

"You think?" she replied, content and amused but too wrung out to expend much energy on talking.

"Where do you want to live?" he asked, his arm tightening around her waist. "I mean, if you want to go on working at the plant after all this, I guess we could stay here, but much as I love this cottage for protecting you, it's not really big enough for me."

"Where do you live? The headquarters for SeaLife is near Seattle, right?" she asked, frowning a bit. Where they'd live hadn't really occurred to her until he'd brought it up.

"Grizzly Cove. It's below Seattle, on the coast. The town is new and sort of off the beaten track, but I don't really live there. My brothers just moved there to be with their mates. Before that, we moved around a lot. The last place we spent any real time was Phoenix," he said, a contemplative tone in his voice.

"But you'd probably like to be near your brothers, right?"

"Yeah, but don't you want to live near *your* family?" He shifted them around so he could lean up to meet her gaze.

Kiki shook her head. "I love them, but I've never really fit in with them," she explained, finding it difficult to put a lifetime of disappointment in herself into words. "I was happy to leave so I could go to college and content to work away from the family farm, so I could try to be a success on my own, in the non-magical world." She tried not to let the hurt show, but she had to be truthful with Jack, of all people. "They love me, but I was always a bit of a disappointment to them."

"You could never disappoint me. In any way," Jack

whispered, then leaned down and kissed her.

From him, she had the love and acceptance she'd always craved. He was her magic. He was the thing she'd searched for all her life without even knowing it. Love. Laughter. Acceptance… Jack.

He drew back and gazed solemnly down at her. "Do you want to keep working at the plant? If not, I think Ezra would probably hire us both on a more permanent basis if we wanted to troubleshoot for SeaLife. This plant wasn't the only business in their portfolio that has problems, and since the new ownership took over, they've been working overtime to straighten things out. Or we could find something a little less dangerous."

"Where's the fun in that?" she quipped, though she wasn't really sure she wanted to be involved in anything like what had happened the previous afternoon, ever again.

"Well, we can visit Grizzly Cove for a bit, if you want. I'd like you to meet my family. We can take a look around and see if it's for us. If not, then we'll find another place." Jack shrugged. "As long as I'm with you, I'm happy."

Kiki rose and rolled so that she was on top of him. "I feel the same," she told him, reaching between their bodies to see if he might be interested in a little more…uh…vigorous demonstrations of their commitment to each other. Surprise, surprise. He was.

Their lovemaking, this time, was eager and playful. Kiki stayed on top and took him at her pace as he gazed at her with what she could only describe as eyes full of love. She was never in doubt when she was with him. She knew he loved her, now, and she had the delicious feeling that this mutual lovefest would last for the rest of their days.

She rode him gently at first, then with more focus, as she drove them both higher and higher. When her hunger came to the apex, she cried out his name, and he held her, helping her through the climax that stole her breath. After she'd had a moment to regain her sanity, he sat up and reversed their positions. Then, he started all over again, raising her passion thrust by delicious thrust, until finally, they exploded toward the stars, together.

*

Jack and Kiki were just getting ready to leave the cottage so they could meet up with Helen, Ben, and the two werewolves when there was a knock on the front door. Jack went immediately on alert. That knock hadn't sounded like any of the four they were supposed to meet, and there was a scent—very faint, but very familiar.

Jack went to the door. The fey garden and Kiki's rudimentary wards wouldn't let anything dangerous through, and if he was right, he'd be very happy to see the new guests. He opened the door and sure enough, there were his brothers and their new mates, grinning at him on the other side of the threshold.

"Sorry to barge in unannounced," Sabrina said, standing next to Ace.

"A few of the magic circle folks in Grizzly Cove sort of insisted we make the trip," Ace added, grinning at Jack. "Apparently, you've stumbled onto something important here, and we're supposed to make connections that will help everybody in the future."

Kiki picked that moment to join Jack at the door. She had been finishing dressing in the bedroom and was just putting in her second earring as she walked up behind him.

"Who's at the…?" Her voice trailed off as she caught sight of the crowd outside. Four people. Two big men who looked a lot like Jack and two women. Jack's brothers and their wives?

Jack turned to her, his expression tight. "I'm sorry, honey. I didn't know they were coming, or I'd have said something." He turned back to the group outside. "You really should've called, Ace."

"It's okay," Kiki insisted. "Don't leave them standing on

the doorstep. Invite them in," she told Jack, patting his shoulder.

He stepped back and opened the door wide, making room for the others to enter. "You heard the lady. Welcome to Kiki's cottage." He was shaking his head, but he had the hint of a smile on his lips.

The big men filled the cottage's small living room, one couple taking the couch, the other fellow taking the overstuffed chair and tugging his wife down onto his lap. Cozy. Kiki was nervous. This was Jack's family. Would they like her? Had they come to pass judgment on her or something? She didn't know what to do or say, so she fell back on the manners her mother had taught all her children.

"Can I get you some coffee?" she asked her guests, but they all declined.

"Sorry for barging in on you like this," the woman sitting on her husband's lap said, a slight flush of pink on her cheeks. "Your address was in your file and Ezra gave it to us."

"We got here as fast as we could, but it's a long trip from the coast, and we realized too late that we'd probably miss the main event." The brother sitting on the chair added. "Sorry, Jack."

"That's okay," Jack said with a big grin as he put his arm around Kiki's shoulder. "As it turned out, Kiki saved the day."

"But you said she had no magic," the man on the couch stated rather bluntly, making Kiki cringe. The woman next to him put her hand on his shoulder and smiled at Kiki.

"I wouldn't be so sure about that," she said, giving Kiki a conspiratorial wink. "I'm Sabrina, by the way."

"Oh, sorry," Jack muttered. "Kiki, that's my brother, Ace, on the couch with his mate, Sabrina, and the two on the chair are King and Marilee."

"Nice to meet you all," Kiki murmured.

Jack tightened his grip on her shoulders. "Kiki is my mate," he proclaimed, seeming to take his brothers by surprise, though the women just smiled as if they'd guessed.

"That's fantastic news, little bro," King said, smiling broadly as he and Marilee stood and came over to Jack and Kiki, who were still standing. "Welcome to the family, Kiki."

Hugs were exchanged, and Kiki started to feel as if maybe these people would accept her as she was, no magic and all. Ace and Sabrina hugged her too, uttering welcoming phrases that touched her heart. They all seemed like such nice people. Kiki shouldn't have been surprised. Jack was a keeper. His family was bound to be just as nice as he was.

When they'd all settled down again, Ace demanded an explanation of everything that had taken place the day before. Jack gave him a precise play-by-play, and when he got to the end of the story, they were all very complimentary about the way Kiki had thought to use the herbs to break the dark ward. They were also surprised by the appearance of the two werewolves.

"Arch and Jim are here?" King demanded.

"Yeah, we were just about to head out to meet them at the hotel and then go over to the mill and begin investigating and cleanup. I think they took turns watching the place overnight, just to make sure nobody messed with anything," Jack explained. "Oh, and Kiki's sister, Helen, also showed up last night. She's at the hotel, too."

"Great," Sabrina exclaimed. "I think she's the one I need to speak to. At least, according to Gus." Sabrina grinned at Kiki. "Gus is the resident shaman in Grizzly Cove. He has his mysterious ways." She waggled her fingers in the air while making a ghostly *woo* sound, which made Kiki laugh. "I'm a weather witch, in case Jack didn't tell you," Sabrina went on. "Need more rain on your crops? I'm your girl."

"I don't have any crops, per se, but be careful around my brothers. They might just put you to work," Kiki warned, liking Sabrina instantly.

"Well, we're here now, and we're happy to help with the investigation and cleanup at the mill. Beth and Trevor are footing the bill for this entire excursion, so we might as well do some work for them," Ace said. It took Kiki a moment to realize the Beth and Trevor he was talking about so casually were the new owners of SeaLife Enterprises.

"We've got a rental car, so we'll follow you," King said, already dangling the keys from his hand. Apparently, when the brothers decided to take action, they didn't let any grass grow under their feet.

Marilee touched Kiki's arm as she passed, following her mate toward the door. "Don't worry. You'll get used to them," Marilee offered quietly, grinning. Kiki wasn't so sure.

Jack and Kiki rode to the paper mill on his bike. She'd dressed casually today, knowing it wasn't going to be a regular work day. Nobody else would be at the mill, just the team of shifters and magical folk who had come to assess the site and figure out what to do next.

They led the way to the hotel, where they met up with Helen, Ben and Arch. Jim, they explained, was already on duty guarding the factory. Arch had a motorcycle, but Ben had a rental car, and he drove Helen in the little parade that eventually ended up at the plant. They'd waited to make introductions to Jack's family until they were at the plant and away from possible prying eyes.

They parked right by the front door, finding Jim there, waiting. Kiki heard Arch ask Jim if there'd been any problems, but she couldn't hear Jim's reply. It was lengthy, which led her to believe there had been something going on here while the rest of them had been resting.

They all headed into the main lobby, and Kiki introduced everybody to her sister. Arch and Jim exchanged friendly greetings with Jack's brothers, and everybody was made aware of everybody else and where they fit into this odd little troupe.

"A few of the employees tried to get in earlier," Jim reported once introductions had been made. "I took names and license plate numbers and told them to go home until next week. A few were more insistent, and I had to threaten to call the police."

Jack took the clipboard Jim held out that had the names and notations. He shared it with Kiki, which she appreciated.

"Bob is the manager, so it makes sense he thought he should at least check on things," she mused as they read over the list. "But Buford Somersby? He's a warehouse employee. He's a forklift operator, if I remember correctly. He doesn't have any real responsibility for the operation. He's just an entry-level employee. I would've thought he'd be happy for the paid time off."

"And he made a big stink about needing to check his area," Jim put in.

"Which makes me think we'd better check his area very closely," Jack observed.

"I'll work security with Jim, if you don't need me back there," Ben said. "That way, one of us can stay up here while the other does a perimeter sweep."

"Good thinking." Jack nodded in agreement. "If we need your input, we'll call you, but I really don't expect anything urgent will turn up."

Jack led everyone except Ben and Jim to the back of the building where it went from office to lab, taking time to explain the basic layout of the place and, specifically, where Carol had worked. They decided to look at her lab first, then the ritual site in the warehouse where everything had happened, and then check the cafeteria kitchen. After those locations, they'd fan out and check every inch of the place in more detail.

When they entered the lab, Jack took point. "I can't sense anything overt," he said after a moment. "Sabrina? Helen? Do either of you sense anything?"

"Not here," Sabrina said quietly. "This area is clear, but that office…" She pointed to the opening that led to Carol's private office.

"Yeah, that makes sense. That's Carol's desk and her private papers," Kiki said, moving to stand next to Jack.

"Do you have any of those herbs, honey?" Jack asked

gently. He'd suggested that Kiki bring whatever she had with her this morning, and she'd even taken a few minutes to pick some fresh springs on her way out of the cottage.

Kiki smiled at him and opened the little bag she'd brought with her. It was chock full of magical herbs from the fey garden.

"That little willow wand might be useful—" Helen began, but Kiki cut her off.

"Hel, please. I know what I'm doing." Kiki grabbed the willow wand and a sprig of lavender, twining them together before she made a counter-clockwise, spiral motion, with just the tip of the wand, starting in the center of the opening to the office.

Kiki recited the words she had been taught to unwind a spell. Not that she'd ever been able to do much with those words before. The magic of the ingredients from the fey garden at the cottage had to be making all the difference.

Or, maybe it was Jack. He was at her side. Her good luck charm. Her very own magic in a tall, sexy package.

Whatever the reason, Kiki was able to cut through Carol's residual magic like a hot knife through butter. She gathered the threads of the sturdy wards that had survived Carol's demise on the tip of her willow wand, the lavender acting as a block to protect Kiki. When she had it all, she redirected the energy to the earth, where it could dissipate harmlessly.

"Nicely done," Sabrina paused to comment.

Kiki felt the compliment down to her toes. She stepped back when Jack indicated he wanted to go into the office first.

"Is that safe?" Helen asked, moving to stand at Kiki's side while they watched Jack check out Carol's office.

"He's a bear, Hel." Kiki said, sounding like more of an authority than she really was on the matter. Although, she had seen him take a pounding from Carol's ward in the warehouse and just shrug it off. "Jack is very sturdy," she added. "I've seen magic just roll off his fur."

"But he's not furry now," Helen said, watching Jack with a concerned expression.

"Don't worry," King said, coming up beside Helen. "We bears are among the most magical of shifters, and we're pretty impervious to a wide variety of things. Jack will be fine."

"He's also the biggest of the three of us," Ace put in, standing beside Kiki.

"As he constantly reminds us," King added.

"He's built pretty much like a tank," Ace assured them as something sparked, and Jack muttered under his breath.

CHAPTER 22

"You okay, Jack?" Kiki couldn't help but ask.

"Fine. Just a little singed. Carol had a nasty trap on her personal space, but it's been sprung now, and it's dissipated. I think the office is clear," he reported, coming back to the doorway.

"If you've got the office covered, we'll look at the lab areas," Ace told his brother. Jack nodded, and the other two men left to check out the other parts of the lab. Their mates stuck with them, leaving Helen with Kiki and Jack.

"Would you ladies like to help me examine Carol's filing cabinets?" Jack asked.

Helen stepped right up. "Sure. What are we looking for?"

"Any evidence that might help us figure out who else she was working with or allied with. Why she chose this plant for her efforts. Any magical texts that need to be handled with care and removed to a safer location. That sort of thing," Jack told her as he sat down behind Carol's desk and started rifling through the drawers.

Kiki took one of the tall filing cabinets against the far wall of the office, where there was an entire row of the things. Helen started at the opposite end of the row from Kiki, and they worked toward the center while Jack checked out the desk and the smaller cabinets behind it.

"Oh, man. Ben isn't going to like this," Jack muttered after a few minutes. Kiki looked up to see him holding a leather-bound book.

"What have you got?" Kiki wanted to know.

Jack held up the book. "If I'm reading this correctly, it's a list of all the *Altor Custodis* agents in North America."

"Holy cow. Someone's watching the watchers?" Kiki thought aloud.

"More like somebody got the list of watchers from the watchers themselves. I think this is from one of the *AC* archives," Jack said. He whistled between his teeth. "Wherever this came from, it's just possible Ben might be able to trace it back. Then, we might be able to track down some of the real problems in the *Altor Custodis*. This is a good find."

"What is the *Altor* whatsit?" Helen asked. Kiki took pleasure in finally knowing something her talented sister didn't. She explained what Jack had told her about the group while he kept searching.

"This looks interesting," Helen said sometime later, after going through a couple of drawers. She pulled out a file, and inside the file was a sheaf of parchment papers that looked as if they'd been ripped out of a book. A very old book.

"What is it?" Kiki asked.

"Recipes," Helen replied, still reading. "Not my field, but these look like they were torn from a potion grimoire."

"Good or evil?" Jack asked, his mouth firming in a grim line as if he expected bad news.

"Neither," Helen said, turning toward him. "In general, a spell is neither good nor evil until someone puts their intent behind it." Kiki had heard that before. It was word for word from their mother's teachings.

"Hey, Jack?" Ace's raised voice came from the other room. "You might want to come in here."

The note of dismay and anger was clear in the other man's tone, and Kiki followed right behind Jack as he left the office behind and headed for the inner laboratory. There was a small dark room attached to that lab. The door was open, and Kiki peered around Jack's shoulders to get a look inside.

"Oh, Sweet Mother of All," she whispered, seeing the little brown ball of fur curled up on the floor of the tiny room. The creature had a collar around its neck, and its bones were protruding from starvation and maltreatment.

"Is that…?" Helen whispered at Kiki's side.

"It's a bear cub," Kiki replied.

"It's a shifter cub," Jack growled as he regarded the poor, abused bundle of skin, fur and bones. It blinked up at them, clearly scared out of its wits, trembling in fear.

"Everybody back off," Kiki said, surprising herself with the authority in her tone. "You're overwhelming her."

"She's right," Jack said, getting a handle on his temper. "Let me handle this." He moved closer while everyone else backed off a few feet. Everyone except Kiki and Helen, that is. "Hey, little lady," Jack coaxed the small cub, crouching down and holding out one hand toward the bear cub. The cub snarled and tried to bite him, but Jack just stayed calm and tried again. "I know you can understand me, sweetheart. I'm like you. I'm a bear shifter, too. Can't you scent the bear in me?"

The cub just looked confused. Kiki leaned in over Jack's shoulder. "Carol's dead," she told the cub bluntly. "She can't hurt you anymore. We want to help. My sister is a healer. Will you let her take a look at you?"

Golden sparks filled the small space, and where there had been a bear cub, there now sat a little girl of about six or seven years of age, completely naked. "Is she really dead?" The words were hard, but the girl's eyes were starting to come alive with hope.

"I killed her myself," Jack admitted.

The little girl broke into tears. "Thank you," she sobbed.

Helen found a clean lab coat and handed it to Kiki. Kiki gave it to Jack, and he helped the little girl put it on like a dress. Then, he picked her up in his strong arms and hugged her close.

"Kiki?" He spoke quietly, over the girl's head, as he continued to hold her while she wept. "Can you get the chain off her?"

Sabrina stepped closer to help when Kiki began looking for a way to get the chain off the child. Helen helped too, but Kiki noticed all the other shifters stood clear. On closer inspection, Kiki realized the chain was made of silver. Poison to shifters, she had learned. The chain had burned the girl's skin where it touched, leaving angry red marks. Kiki was disgusted but determined to get that filthy chain off the little girl's neck.

"Keys are in the drawer," the child rasped out, rubbing her eyes as the storm of her emotions let up a little.

Everybody searched the drawers, and it was Marilee who found a set of keys in the drawer farthest from the room where the girl had been held. The length of the chain would let her go only so far. The keys were there, just out of reach. She could only imagine how that taunt had hurt the girl, knowing freedom was so close, but unable to reach it.

"What kind of monsters...?" Kiki heard Helen mutter as the keys were passed forward.

Kiki got them and quickly removed the chain. Helen took charge of the girl, using her healing talent to help her while Kiki unwound the dirty black magic from the chain and the small room where the girl had been kept. She took great pleasure in returning that energy to the earth, where it would disperse to harm none.

Helen took the child into the outer room, settling into a chair with the girl on her lap. Jack followed with Kiki, his expression grim.

"What's your name, sweetheart?" Helen asked the girl.

"Melissa Ebersole," she replied promptly.

"Do you live around here?" Helen continued, her healing energy working even as she spoke to the girl.

"I don't know where I am," Melissa said finally, shaking her head a bit. "The bad lady took me from the playground when I was at school."

"How long ago was that?" Jack asked gently. "Do you know?"

"Days and days. The mean people fed me ten times. I counted. But they only fed me once in a long while, and the food tasted really funny. I ate a little anyway, because I was *so* hungry," Melissa told them, just as her tummy growled.

"That was a bear-sized growl if I've ever heard one." Jack chuckled, making the little girl smile. "Tell you what. There's a cafeteria down the hall. Let's go raid the snack machines and feed the bear, then we'll figure out where you come from and how to get you home."

"You mean I can see Mommy and Daddy again?" Melissa's eyes brightened even more.

"Absolutely," Jack promised. "We're going to do everything in our power to get you home."

The search continued in the lab, but Kiki and her sister focused on Melissa once Jack had set the little girl up with a mountain of food out of the snack machines in the cafeteria. She ate and ate, but she also answered questions, and Kiki was able to get a laptop and use the WiFi connection to try to track down Melissa's parents based on what the girl could tell them.

The real breakthrough didn't come, though, until Jack put in an urgent call to the Alpha in Grizzly Cove. The fellow, who Jack called Big John, had already known a girl had been snatched from her schoolyard in Pennsylvania. The Alpha called the Lords, which Jack explained were the recognized authority over all shifters in North America, and within ten minutes, a man named Rocky called Jack.

They had a quick conversation, and Jack began grinning and nodding. He sent Kiki a thumbs up, which she took to mean they'd found the girl's parents. Jack ended the call and came back to the table, where Melissa was only about halfway through the pile of sandwiches and snacks Jack had procured from the machines.

"Your parents are coming here, Melissa. They've been

looking for you all over since you were taken, and they're very close. They'll be here in an hour or two," Jack told the little girl.

"I knew they would look for me," Melissa said, sure in the knowledge of her parents' love. Kiki wanted to meet these people—these shifters—that had searched high and low for their lost little one.

"They followed your trail really well," Jack praised the couple. "I'm sure it was hard because the people who took you were using black magic. Do you know what that is?"

Melissa nodded, her little head bobbing up and down. "Daddy says it's hidden evil. He's teaching me about the different kinds of magic because he says I have a powerful gift and will be good at fighting bad people when I'm grown." She put down her sandwich and looked sad. "But I wasn't very good at it when the bad lady took me." She looked about ready to cry again, and Jack reached out for the girl, touching her hair.

"You're alive. You lived to fight another day. You did very well, Melissa."

The little girl looked up at Jack, her gaze watery. "It didn't feel that way. The bad lady sucked my energy, and I couldn't stop her," she admitted in a small voice.

"Aw, honey, I'm a full grown grizzly bear, and I couldn't break through her wards. She was very powerful. Don't beat yourself up. You did the best thing you could—you stayed alive so we could rescue you. When you're a grown bear, you'll do the same for others, if the opportunity arises, and you'll remember this day. I hope you'll remember that you were strong enough to stop the bad lady from taking all of your energy." Jack's voice lowered, but Kiki could still hear him. "She tried, didn't she? She tried to drain you dead." It wasn't a question, but Melissa slowly nodded.

"I held a piece of me back, like Daddy told me to," she whispered. "It was hard," Melissa admitted. "And it really hurt."

Jack stroked the little girl's hair. "But you were stronger

than the pain. You did really well, Melissa. Remember that. You saved yourself."

The girl's eyes brightened but then turned curious. "So, how did you stop the bad lady if you couldn't break through her ward?"

"Oh, that wasn't me. Kiki here did it, with human magic," Jack said, sitting back in the cafeteria chair and sending Kiki a heated gaze that warmed her blood.

"Human magic?" Melissa blinked with wide eyes. "Are you a mage?"

"Me?" Kiki was startled into laughing. "No, I'm not, actually, though my sister is a healer. The rest of my family is magical, but not me."

"Then, how did you stop the bad lady?" Melissa's face tilted as she scrutinized Kiki.

"I have a special garden," Kiki said, as if sharing a great secret. "See this?" Kiki took a few fresh sprigs of lavender from her bag and handed them to the girl. "Smell the purity? Just like soap, they cleaned away the black magic and broke the protections the bad lady had around herself."

The girl sniffed the lavender then promptly sneezed, making everyone chuckle. "Tickles," was Melissa's observation.

"Herbal magic is a still a form of magic, Patches," Helen reminded Kiki. "You were always better at the herb lessons than the rest of us."

"You know Mom only taught us that stuff because she wanted to include me and show us something that even I could manage," Kiki said, the old hurt coming out, despite her intentions to keep silent on the matter.

"Oh, sweetie, I don't think that's true. Mom wanted us all to have a well-rounded magical education. Just because you couldn't do the other kinds of magic never made any of us think you were somehow lacking. Look, nobody else in the family can heal like me. And nobody can see the future like Mom. We each have our own special gifts."

"That's just it. You all had gifts, and I didn't."

The silence was deafening. It was Melissa, oddly enough, who broke it. "But you stopped the bad lady," the girl reminded Kiki.

Kiki looked at Melissa and smiled. "Yeah. I did, didn't I?"

Suddenly, it didn't matter anymore, who had what gift or that Kiki had none. She had done what others couldn't. She'd been at the right place, at the right time, with the right knowledge, and she'd done her best.

What Jack had said to Melissa made a lot more sense. Kiki had also saved herself from Carol. She'd used what little knowledge she had to do the one thing that would allow others to help her. As had Melissa.

"We're a lot alike, you and me, Melissa," Kiki told the little one. "You did what you'd been taught to keep yourself alive. I did the same. We both did well, when the going got tough, and we both need to cut ourselves some slack for not being perfect. We did our best, and it was enough to live to fight—and learn—another day."

Kiki met Jack's gaze. She knew Melissa probably didn't understand everything she'd said, but it didn't matter. What mattered most was that she finally believed, in her heart, that she had done the best she could. She'd done enough. Learned enough. *Was* enough.

Melissa's parents arrived about an hour later, frantic to see their child. Jack and Kiki had brought her up to the lobby to wait after she ate her fill. Helen had examined her briefly and told them that Melissa would be fine once she regained the weight she'd lost and had a chance to rest and recuperate. Helen had left the little girl with a benevolent kiss on the forehead, letting Kiki and Jack handle the reunion.

Jack had said that was probably for the best because the parents were likely to see everything and everyone as a threat for a while. Bear parents were notoriously protective of their cubs.

What Kiki hadn't expected was that Melissa's parents would be a mixed couple. Mixed, in the sense that her father was clearly a bear shifter—he was built like the Bishop brothers in that he was tall, heavily muscled and moved as fluidly as all the shifters she'd met so far. But Melissa's mother was clearly not a shifter.

Human, Kiki thought. Non-magical. One hundred percent human.

When their pickup truck stopped in front of the entrance, the woman threw open the passenger door and dropped to a crouch. Melissa ran into the woman's arms, both of them crying tears of joy and relief.

The big man who was Melissa's father came around the truck and enfolded them both in his arms, showing his deep care and relief as he held them both close. Kiki's heart ached for them. The terror these parents must have experienced when their baby was kidnapped. She could hardly imagine how awful that must have been.

After a long moment, the man stood, putting himself between the two females and everyone else. Jack had told Ben and Jim to stay inside. Only he and Kiki had stood out by the entrance, waiting for Melissa's parents to arrive. Kiki realized that had been for the other men's safety. It was clear, this bear shifter would have ripped apart anyone he saw as a threat to his family.

"I'm Martin Ebersole," the man announced, looking from Jack to Kiki and back.

Jack stepped forward. "Jack Bishop," he said, offering the man his hand. They shook, seeming to come to some sort of male understanding. Kiki breathed a sigh of relief. The father was calming and didn't seem like he felt threatened by Jack.

"Did you find my daughter?" he asked.

Jack shook his head. "My brothers found her when we were searching the building. I killed the woman who kidnapped her yesterday evening after a bit of a struggle." Jack filled the man in quickly about how Carol had the entire plant under her spell and had baited a trap for him, using Kiki as a hostage. He ended his story by stating simply that Kiki was his mate, and Martin nodded.

"Thank you, ma'am, for what you did. We've had a hell of a time following the witch's trail," Martin explained.

"I'm amazed you could follow it at all," Jack told the man. "Carol had a lot of power, and I underestimated her. Almost fatally."

"I'm a tracker," Martin told them. "I was a Recon Marine in 'Nam. Tracking's my specialty. Always has been. But this…" Martin shook his head. "This was like no trail I've ever followed before. That witch fouled the scent, and I had to go on gut instinct more than not."

"Your instincts were spot on," Jack complimented the other man. "In a day or two, you'd have been here, yourself."

"Maybe," Martin allowed. "But I'm grateful that you took care of the problem and found my cub."

"I'm only sorry we didn't realize she was here sooner." Jack lowered his voice. "They were keeping her in a small room, and she was sleeping when we found her. If I'd known she was here, I would've had her out of there last night."

Martin looked back at his little girl, now chatting happily with her mother. "No harm done, I think, but I appreciate your candor. We'll probably go bear for a while and just stay outside, under the stars. No more small rooms for my cub. Not for a good long while."

CHAPTER 23

"She was really brave," Kiki put in. "She even told us where to find the key."

"Key?" Martin's brows lowered, and Jack shifted uncomfortably.

"Yeah, that's the other thing. They had a silver chain around her neck," Jack admitted. "The key was in a drawer within her sight, but too far for her to reach."

Martin cursed under his breath. "She's not burned," he said, when he could talk again. "Are you sure it was silver?"

"My sister is a healer, and she took away the damage," Kiki told the man. "I took the spells off the chain with a willow wand and some lavender," she added as his eyes narrowed.

"Are you a witch?" he asked, almost angrily.

"Me? No. But I know some herbal cures. My family is magical, but I'm not." For the first time, saying that didn't hurt at all.

Kiki had to wonder at the change in herself. All her life, she'd felt inferior. Now, she felt just fine. There was no sadness for what might have been. No envy for her siblings who had so much power. Kiki was content within herself.

"The silver chain is worth a small fortune," Jack said quietly to Martin. "Our shaman in Grizzly Cove has connections to craftsmen in the Native American community who would probably be glad to buy the silver and melt it down for use in their jewelry designs. Even just at the spot price on silver, the weight would add up to a pretty penny. I'd like to give that money to you, for Melissa. It's only fitting that what was used to harm her be turned into something that will help her in the future."

"Are you sure you can do that?" Martin asked. "I mean, isn't this place owned by some big conglomerate?" He looked up at the sign above the door.

Jack nodded. "SeaLife Enterprises," he affirmed. "Now owned by the mate of a friend of mine who lives in Grizzly Cove. He's like us, and she's a mer, believe it or not. I'm sure they'll have no objection to my plan for the chain, and they may go a bit farther, once they learn about everything that happened here. They knew something was wrong with this operation. That's why they sent me to check it out. But none of us had any idea about Melissa being kept here. We'll probably be piecing together everything that potion witch was involved in for a while. There's a lot of evidence to sift through, but what we've already discovered is damning enough."

"Grizzly Cove," Martin mused. "That's Big John Marshall's group, isn't it?"

"You know Big John?" Jack asked.

"In passing. I got out of the service before he came up the ranks, but I keep my hand in, and I've heard good things about him and his men. Are you part of that group?" Martin asked outright.

"On the periphery," Jack explained. "My brothers and I were a specialist team working directly for Admiral Holland, but we got out a few years ago and have been on walkabout ever since. My older brothers have recently found mates and are settling down in Grizzly Cove. I may do the same, but Kiki and I haven't figured all that out yet. We only just found each other." Jack's arm came around Kiki's shoulders, and she grinned as he drew her to his side. She loved belonging to him, and she loved that he belonged to her, as well.

"Bishop, you said? Jack Bishop…" Martin seemed to be thinking out loud. "You wouldn't have an older brother named Ace, would you?"

Jack nodded. "You know Ace?"

"A little," Martin said. "I did a stint as a trainer for Spec Ops. Ace was in one of my last classes."

"Are you going to stay in town, or are you heading straight back home?" Kiki asked.

"Well…" Martin looked back at his mate, and she stepped forward, holding Melissa in her arms.

"We should probably stop here for the night," she said. "Give Melissa a chance to catch her breath and sleep a bit."

"My mate, Lisa," Martin introduced his wife.

"I think you should use my cottage," Kiki declared, feeling it was the right thing to do. "We're going to be here all day, and you three need to rest and regroup. My cottage is secure and, if my new bear friends are to be believed, protected by fey magic. It's the safest place for you until you're ready to travel on."

"Fey, you say?" Martin looked skeptical.

"Kiki's family line is pretty complicated, and there's fey blood mixed in on the other branches. One of those cousins rented her the cottage," Jack explained. "It's a good, safe place. You have my word on it."

"Well, if you're sure it's not too much trouble," Lisa said.

"No trouble at all. I hope you're able to catch your breath and relax a bit," Kiki said, fishing her keys out of her pocket. She handed them over to Lisa while Jack gave Martin directions.

When the family pulled away in the big pickup truck, Jack put his arm around Kiki's shoulders. "That was nice of you," he said, his tone warm and approving.

"It was the right thing to do. Plus, this way, we can have a little get together tonight, and your brother can catch up with his old instructor. I'd like to be certain Melissa is okay, too," she added. "Helen can look at her again, and make sure."

Jack leaned down and kissed her. "You have a beautiful soul, Kiki," he whispered when he finally pulled back. She felt a bit dazed. As she always did when Jack kissed her.

As predicted, they spent the rest of the day at the plant, discovering many things. They used the teleconferencing abilities in the boardroom to communicate with Grizzly Cove, and Kiki got to meet—electronically, at least—the folks who ultimately owned the plant. They were cordial and welcoming, and very thankful for what Kiki had done to stand against Carol. Kiki liked them both—Trevor and Beth—instantly.

She also got a look at the man they'd all been referring to as Big John. He impressed her, as well. He thanked her and congratulated Kiki and Jack on their mating, promising a big celebration whenever Jack and Kiki came back to Grizzly Cove. The fact that they were expected to go to the town in Washington State she had never seen still amazed her, but the welcome message John gave was unmistakable. Kiki was moved by the big hearts of these bears and all the people associated with them.

One of the more gruesome discoveries came when they were examining the area of the warehouse that man, Buford Somersby, had been so hot to check on. There were freezer units. Big chest freezers and a large walk in unit that had to have been installed very recently based on the factory stickers, and shine still on the parts. When they opened those freezers, they found bodies.

Several bodies. One turned out to be Kiki's predecessor in her job, Josh Moll. There were others, that looked as if they'd been killed earlier, mutilated in various ways, then frozen. Kiki couldn't bear to look, but the men dealt with the horror and reported back on the carnage to Trevor and Beth, who took the news with stony expressions.

"It looks as if Carol was feeding off the employees as early as a year ago. Maybe more. She started slow, based on what we've been able to piece together from the personnel files and matching up I.D. photos, but in recent months, she's been killing more often and using various body parts for...something," King disclosed as they all sat around the teleconference set-up.

"Her potions, I'd bet," Beth said in a weak voice, her face pale. "Our resident potion witch has been giving us a crash course on the kinds of things the evil side of her craft get up to. Using blood and body parts in potions isn't uncommon, apparently."

Kiki felt nauseated by the idea. Beth's face, over the screen, looked like she felt the same.

"You'd better pick up that Buford Somersby fellow," Trevor intoned, getting them back on track. "He had to have been in on it, somehow, if he was so fired up to check his area earlier today."

"We're working on it, but it looks like he might've already skipped town," Ace reported. "I suspect that when he couldn't get in this morning, he realized the jig was up and took off."

"We'll have to track him," Beth put in, touching her mate's arm where it rested on the table.

"We will, honey," Trevor assured his mate, then turned back to the camera. "You have until Monday to complete your investigation at the plant. I might be able to extend it after that, if necessary, but ideally, if we could clear this up over the weekend, it would draw a lot less attention from the human world."

"Understood," Jack replied. "I think we can make that deadline. We made good progress already, today. And, that little girl's father is a tracker. I'll ask him to take a look at Somersby's trail and see if he can give us any leads before he heads home with his family."

"Good idea. I want you all to stabilize the situation at the plant so we can save the place and everyone's jobs," Trevor added. "We don't want to draw unnecessary attention, so having you all on-site to fix things is essential for right now. We'll find someone to send after Somersby. Just gather what you can to make the hunt as easy as possible."

"If he's really involved, then he probably knows some tricks to make it difficult to find him," King said, his tone grim.

"Understood," Trevor replied. "But if that's the case, a delay of a day or two before following his trail, isn't going to change things much."

The men were nodding their agreement and the meeting went on. They talked about accounting discrepancies and the plans to tear the warehouse apart piece by piece the next day. Kiki was impressed by how thorough they all were and the new owners of SeaLife impressed her particularly, with their dedication to doing what was right.

That night, there was another impromptu party in the backyard of the cottage. Ace was glad to see his old instructor again, and they spent some time catching up. Helen had another a chance to look at Melissa and assured both Kiki and Melissa's mother that she was well and would only improve from here. The garden glowed with fey light, and Kiki could almost swear she heard the tinkling laughter of fairies and garden gnomes, but that might just be her overactive imagination.

Still, she felt certain that the house was happy. Kiki knew she was certainly happy. In fact, everybody in the gathering seemed happy to be here. To be alive and safe, and blessed.

Kiki bowed her head in thanks for a moment as she contemplated the scene from out in the berry patch, where she'd gone to collect some sweets for Melissa. She wasn't surprised to feel Jack's arm come around her from the side, though she hadn't heard him approach.

"What are you doing out here?" he asked gently, kissing the shell of her ear with a gentle nibble.

"Just thanking the Mother of All for the happiness here tonight," she told him honestly, turning to put her arms around him. "I never knew I could be this content, and it's all thanks to you, Jack."

"Same goes," he replied, tightening their embrace. "You complete me, Kiki."

"I love you, Jack," she whispered in the peace of the berry patch with fey Light glowing all around. It felt like a solemn vow.

"I love you too, Kiki. Now and forever," Jack whispered back, sealing his words with a deep, meaningful kiss. Yes, that really did feel like a vow, spoken in a magic glen, with the fey magic as witness.

When he let her up for air, she was smiling. "Jack. Look…" she said, wonder filling her voice.

All around them, every single berry plant offered up ripe, succulent fruit that definitely hadn't been there before. A gift from the garden itself.

"I think the garden approves," she whispered.

"And I approve, wholeheartedly, of this magnificent garden." Jack reached out for a handful of raspberries, shoveling them into his mouth and closing his eyes in bliss as the flavor hit his tongue.

Kiki laughed and retrieved the mixing bowl she'd brought out with her, from where it had fallen to the ground. She sent up a prayer of thanks and then began picking the bounteous berries.

"I was hoping to pick enough to give Melissa a treat, but now, we have enough for everybody," she enthused while dropping berries gently into the bowl.

Jack grabbed another handful and put them in his mouth. "Speak for yourself," he teased, but he was also helping her pick the berries.

If he ate a few on the way to the bowl, she didn't mind. Apparently, her big bear of a mate had a bit of a sweet tooth. She was sure she'd learn a lot more about his likes and dislikes in the years to come, and she was looking forward to every minute spent with him. Kiki had never expected to find a magical mate, but Fate had apparently had other plans for her.

Boy, was she glad things had worked out the way they did.

Even with all the danger and peril, she wouldn't change a thing about meeting Jack. He was her future. Her life. Her everything. And she had the very real sense that she was the same to him.

He didn't care that she had no real magic of her own. To him, she was just fine the way she was.

And that…was a real gift.

# # #

ABOUT THE AUTHOR

Bianca D'Arc has run a laboratory, climbed the corporate ladder in the shark-infested streets of lower Manhattan, studied and taught martial arts, and earned the right to put a whole bunch of letters after her name, but she's always enjoyed writing more than any of her other pursuits. She grew up and still lives on Long Island, where she keeps busy with an extensive garden, several aquariums full of very demanding fish, and writing her favorite genres of paranormal, fantasy and sci-fi romance.

Bianca loves to hear from readers and can be reached through Twitter (@BiancaDArc), Facebook (BiancaDArcAuthor) or through the various links on her website.

WELCOME TO THE D'ARC SIDE…
WWW.BIANCADARC.COM

OTHER BOOKS BY BIANCA D'ARC

Guardians of the Dark
Half Past Dead
Once Bitten, Twice Dead
A Darker Shade of Dead
The Beast Within
Dead Alert

Gifts of the Ancients
Warrior's Heart
Future Past
A Friend in Need

Dragon Knights
Daughters of the Dragon
Maiden Flight*
Border Lair
The Ice Dragon**
Prince of Spies***

Novellas
The Dragon Healer
Master at Arms
Wings of Change

Sons of Draconia
FireDrake
Dragon Storm
Keeper of the Flame
Hidden Dragons

The Sea Captain's Daughter
Book 1: Sea Dragon
Book 2: Dragon Fire
Book 3: Dragon Mates

The Captain's Dragon

Resonance Mates
Hara's Legacy**
Davin's Quest
Jaci's Experiment
Grady's Awakening
Harry's Sacrifice

StarLords
Hidden Talent
Talent For Trouble
Shy Talent

Jit'Suku Chronicles
Arcana
King of Swords
King of Cups
King of Clubs
King of Stars
End of the Line
Diva

Sons of Amber
Angel in the Badlands
Master of Her Heart
Starcrossed

In the Stars
The Cyborg Next Door
Heart of the Machine

StarLords
Hidden Talent
Talent For Trouble
Shy Talent

* RT Book Reviews Awards Nominee
** EPPIE Award Winner
*** CAPA Award Winner

Welcome to Grizzly Cove, where bear shifters can be who they are - if the creatures of the deep will just leave them be. Wild magic, unexpected allies, a conflagration of sorcery and shifter magic the likes of which has not been seen in centuries... That's what awaits the peaceful town of Grizzly Cove. That, and love. Lots and lots of love.

This series begins with...

All About the Bear
Welcome to Grizzly Cove, where the sheriff has more than the peace to protect. The proprietor of the new bakery in town is clueless about the dual nature of her nearest neighbors, but not for long. It'll be up to Sheriff Brody to clue her in and convince her to stay calm—and in his bed—for the next fifty years or so.

Mating Dance
Tom, Grizzly Cove's only lawyer, is also a badass grizzly bear, but he's met his match in Ashley, the woman he just can't get out of his mind. She's got a dark secret, that only he knows. When ugliness from her past tracks her to her new home, can Tom protect the woman he is fast coming to believe is his mate?

Night Shift
Sheriff's Deputy Zak is one of the few black bear shifters in a colony of grizzlies. When his job takes him into closer proximity to the lovely Tina, though, he finds he can't resist her. Could it be he's finally found his mate? And when adversity strikes, will she turn to him, or run into the night? Zak will do all he can to make sure she chooses him.

Phoenix Rising

Lance is inexplicably drawn to the sun and doesn't understand why. Tina is a witch who remembers him from their high school days. She'd had a crush on the quiet boy who had an air of magic about him. Reunited by Fate, she wonders if she could be the one to ground him and make him want to stay even after the fire within him claims his soul...if only their love can be strong enough.

Phoenix and the Wolf

Diana is drawn to the sun and dreams of flying, but her elderly grandmother needs her feet firmly on the ground. When Diana's old clunker breaks down in front of a high-end car lot, she seeks help and finds herself ensnared by the sexy werewolf mechanic who runs the repair shop. Stone makes her want to forget all her responsibilities and take a walk on the wild side...with him.

Phoenix and the Dragon

He's a dragon shapeshifter in search of others like himself. She's a newly transformed phoenix shifter with a lot to learn and bad guys on her trail. Together, they will go on a dazzling adventure into the unknown, and fight against evil folk intent on subduing her immense power and using it for their own ends. They will face untold danger and find love that will last a lifetime.

Lone Wolf

Josh is a werewolf who suddenly has extra, unexpected and totally untrained powers. He's not happy about it - or about the evil jackasses who keep attacking him, trying to steal his magic. Forced to seek help, Josh is sent to an unexpected ally for training.

Deena is a priestess with more than her share of magical power and a unique ability that has made her a target. She welcomes Josh, seeing a kindred soul in the lone werewolf. She knows she can help him... if they can survive their enemies long enough.

Snow Magic

Evie has been a lone wolf since the disappearance of her mate, Sir Rayburne, a fey knight from another realm. Left all alone with a young son to raise, Evie has become stronger than she ever was. But now her son is grown and suddenly Ray is back.

Ray never meant to leave Evie all those years ago but he's been caught in a magical trap, slowly being drained of magic all this time. Freed at last, he whisks Evie to the only place he knows in the mortal realm where they were happy and safe—the rustic cabin in the midst of a North Dakota winter where they had been newlyweds. He's used the last of his magic to get there and until he recovers a bit, they're stuck in the middle of nowhere with a blizzard coming and bad guys on their trail.

Can they pick up where they left off and rekindle the magic between them, or has it been extinguished forever?

Midnight Kiss

Margo is a werewolf on a mission...with a disruptively handsome mage named Gabe. She can't figure out where Gabe fits in the pecking order, but it doesn't seem to matter to the attraction driving her wild. Gabe knows he's going to have to prove himself in order to win Margo's heart. He wants her for his mate, but can she give her heart to a mage? And will their dangerous quest get in the way?

The Jaguar Tycoon

Mark may be the larger-than-life billionaire Alpha of the secretive Jaguar Clan, but he's a pussycat when it comes to the one women destined to be his mate. Shelly is an up-and-coming architect trying to drum up business at an elite dinner party at which Mark is the guest of honor. When shots ring out, the hunt for the gunman brings Mark into Shelly's path and their lives will never be the same.

The Jaguar Bodyguard

Sworn to protect his Clan, Nick heads to Hollywood to keep an eye on a rising star who has seen a little too much for her own good. Unexpectedly fame has made a circus of Sal's life, but when decapitated squirrels show up on her doorstep, she knows she needs professional help. Nick embeds himself in her security squad to keep an eye on her as sparks fly and passions rise between them. Can he keep her safe and prevent her from revealing what she knows?

The Jaguar's Secret Baby

Hank has never forgotten the wild woman with whom he spent one memorable night. He's dreamed of her for years now, but has never been back to the small airport in Texas owned and run by her werewolf Pack. Tracy was left with a delicious memory of her night in Hank's arms, and a beautiful baby girl who is the light of her life. She chose not to tell Hank about his daughter, but when he finally returns and he discovers the daughter he's never known, he'll do all he can to set things right.

Dragon Knights

Two dragons, two knights, and one woman to complete their circle. That's the recipe for happiness in the land of fighting dragons. But there are a few special dragons that are more. They are the ruling family and they are half-dragon and half-human, able to change at will from one form to another.

Books in this series have won the EPPIE Award for Best Erotic Romance in the Fantasy/Paranormal category, and have been nominated for *RT Book Reviews Magazine* Reviewers Choice Awards among other honors.

WWW.BIANCADARC.COM

Manufactured by Amazon.ca
Bolton, ON